BIG GUNS

Steve Israel served in the US House of
Representatives from 2001 to 2017, representing
the 3rd Congressional District of New York. He
is the author of two novels, *The Global War on
Morris* and *Big Guns*.

BIG GUNS

STEVE ISRAEL

HEAD OF ZEUS

An Apollo Book

This is an Apollo book. First published in the UK in 2018 by Head of Zeus Ltd
This paperback edition published in 2018 by Head of Zeus Ltd

9 7 5 3 1 2 4 6 8

A catalogue record for this book is available from the British Library.

ISBN (PB): 9781788544306
ISBN (E): 9781788544276

Interior design by Lewelin Polanco

Printed and bound by CPI Group (UK) Ltd, Croydon, CR0 4YY

Head of Zeus Ltd
First Floor East
5–8 Hardwick Street
London EC1R 4RG

WWW.HEADOFZEUS.COM

Dedicated to Colonel William C. Church & General George Wingate, who founded the National Rifle Association in 1871. If they only knew then . . .

PROLOGUE

Chicago mayor Michael Rodriguez sat at a long, wide table in the darkened Crime Command Center, surrounded by city officials in suits, police brass in uniform, and aides in fear. They all stared, wide-eyed and open-mouthed, at a massive digital map of Chicago that was projected onto an entire wall of the room. Thanks to a generous grant from the federal government, ShotWatch Technology had been installed all throughout the Windy City and now, when a bullet was fired anywhere south of Devon Avenue, north of 138th, east of Harlem Avenue, and west of Lake Michigan, the sound was instantly tracked, transmitted, and indicated on the map by a flashing pinpoint of light.

At the moment the map showed Chicago as a single gigantic pulsating orb.

To make matters worse, the Cubs had just announced a postponement of that night's game against the LA Dodgers, whose owner had cited "prohibitive local conditions" in a news interview. He meant gunfire.

The only sound in the room was a persistent thumping. The mayor was an incessant leg thumper. When he was calm, he thumped gently, rocking his right foot on its heel, just barely lifting his toes and then lowering them softly. When he was excited, the thumping accelerated, his knee jumping up and down at a steady clip. And when he was angry, like he was most of the time, his leg became a jackhammer, pistoning up and down with a force that shook his entire short, lean body. The jackhammer stage was often accompanied by an eruption of curses in Spanish, and those present in the command center braced themselves for the torrent.

The police commissioner rubbed his craggy face with his hands, looking defeated. His eyes were bloodshot and his cheeks were drawn. "We're getting our asses kicked," he said. "I got thousands of cops flooding high-crime areas, and we're literally outgunned." He sighed.

Rodriguez thumped and opened his mouth to speak. An aide winced. "Commissioner, what can I do to help?" he asked, in a surprisingly calm voice. "Would you like me to call the Pentagon and have them send in a squadron of F-16s? Would that make your job easier?"

The commissioner knew better than to answer this, but the city counsel, a man who liked to demonstrate that he operated above the rough-and-tumble of Chicago street politics by wearing bow ties and smoking a pipe, and who had apparently taken the mayor at his word, said, "Your Honor, posse comitatus would prohibit the president from—"

It was as if the pin had finally been plucked from a grenade. The mayor, still thumping, exploded. "Counselor," he bellowed, "you can take your posse comitatus and shove it up your ass!" When no one responded, he shouted for good measure, *"Maldito idiota!"* Fucking idiot. One of the mayor's signature insults.

More flashes on the map.

The mayor's executive assistant cleared her throat and reminded him it was time for his daily crime scene press conference.

Rodriguez ceased his thumping, finally, and stood. *"Púdranse todos!"* he shouted over his shoulder as he left the room. Fuck you all! Another favorite.

1

On the glittering East End of Long Island, hidden between the jewels of Southampton and East Hampton, sat the little village of Asabogue.

You could easily drive through Asabogue and not even know you'd been there. The only indications of the village was Main Street, narrow and tree-lined, with flower boxes, an ice cream shop, a bakery, a café, and a few tiny boutiques that sold beach house paraphernalia and trinkets. There was also a triangular plot of grass on which sat Village Hall, a white clapboard house, constructed in the early eighteenth century, that creaked and groaned and drooped from age.

Even if you knew you were in Asabogue, you wouldn't know who else was there, and that was the point of the place. When East Hampton became passé, when Southampton became too common, the next and final step had been to head for the hills, and in this case, the hills were Billionaires Bluff. Here, several dozen summer residents of Asabogue could look down their noses at the rest of the Hamptons and, for that matter, at the entire Atlantic, which rolled placidly against their beaches, the only intrusion of the outside world on their lives by the rest of the planet. Whenever someone accidentally wandered onto the beach, it would only be a minute before a goon from a private security firm swooped down and redirected the interloper back to where he belonged—which was anyplace but Asabogue.

The joke was that Asabogue was an Indian phrase meaning "place of many assholes." The people of Asabogue weren't big fans of that translation.

On a glorious June morning on Billionaires Bluff, Otis Cogsworth, chairman and CEO of Cogsworth International Arms, awoke to what he thought would be another fine day.

His eyes opened upon the immense master bedroom of Trigger Happy, his summer encampment in Asabogue. He could feel a salty ocean breeze drifting through an open window, and hear seagulls squawking over the sound of softly rolling waves. He sucked in a breath and held it. Sometimes—rarely, but sometimes—Otis experienced flickering acknowledgments of what a good and enviable life he had. He was an immeasurably successful businessman. His work was something he believed in. He had a steady marriage with a loyal and loving, if boring, wife, and he had, among others, this beautiful home on the most expensive street in the greatest country on earth. This was one of those mornings when, for a few waking seconds, he took stock of his triumphs and said to himself, *It is good*.

Then he fumbled for the remote control on the bedside table, pressed a button, and proceeded to ruin his day before it began. From the large television above the marble fireplace, Otis heard scraps of a news broadcast: ". . . epidemic of violence . . . Chicago overnight ... six separate gunfights ... seventeen fatalities ... death toll here to over three thousand ... Rodriguez demanding a federal ban on handguns."

On the screen, in what must have been a press conference from the previous night, the pugilistic mayor of Chicago was barking, as if, Otis thought, he were about to take a bite out of someone's thigh. He was standing in front of a children's playground, now festooned with yellow crime scene tape, which some journalists had grimly taken to calling the new flag of Chicago. A kaleidoscope of police lights swirled behind him, and uniformed cops stood at his side.

"Look," Rodriguez said to a bouquet of microphones, "our city has the strictest gun laws in America, but without federal laws, it doesn't mean shi—squat!" He held up a black semiautomatic pistol. "The police found this on the playground behind me after last night's shooting. It was manufactured by Cogsworth International Arms and sold by one of their distributors. My city has banned this weapon. But it came in from another city that doesn't give a fu—a damn. Enough! I've had it with the gun lobby. I've had it with death merchants like Cogsworth International Arms. I've had it with fuh—freaking guns! It's time to ban them! Ban them all!"

Behind him a crowd started cheering: "Ban! Them! All! Ban! Them! All!"

Otis mumbled at the television in a low, gravelly slur.

"Otis?" his wife murmured, next to him.

"Go back to sleep, Lucille. I'm taking breakfast in the solarium."

"Okay," she murmured. "Remember we have brunch at the Steeles' later."

Of course we do, thought Otis. *As if today won't be bad enough.* He needed to deal with the crisis in Chicago, not schmooze his way through another Asabogue charity affair. Especially with Jack Steele, that awful B-list actor from those hideous movies. Jack Steele. Living just down the street. ("Down the street" on Billionaires Bluff meant several beaches away.)

Otis wrapped himself in a cotton bathrobe and shuffled out into the hallway and down the dark main stairway, passing under family portraits mounted on the mahogany walls. Every painting, across generations, captured the Cogsworth genes: heavy jowls that dropped over shirt collars, thin lips that seemed to sneer even though their intent was clearly to smile, and black, skeptical eyes set deep in ruddy faces, as if some strain of Cogsworth evolution had slowly buried the eyes deep enough for them to watch you without you watching them. All these traits had been passed on to Otis, and yet the portraits made him uncomfortable. They passed judgment on him with every step. They haunted him.

There had been great worry about Otis as a child. He was the only son of Charles and Eleanor Cogsworth, and, in his earliest years, he seemed uninterested in firearms manufacturing, which had been the family business since before the Civil War (when the family had made an acceptable profit by managing to sell to both sides). Young Otis had stared blankly at the guns he unwrapped on Christmas and birthdays. He'd seemed ambivalent when Charles would take him shooting on the estate in Connecticut. He'd spend an inordinate amount of time in his room, reading books and painting the view of the Long Island Sound from his third-floor window. But there eventually had come a day when Charles summoned Otis to the family library. He was going to have a heart-to-heart minus one heart.

Animal trophies peered sadly at Otis as he entered. Floor-to-ceiling shelves were crammed with books on hunting and hiking and sportsmanship and nature and many other subjects that bored him. A heavy cloud of cigar smoke had fouled the air, stinging his eyes.

Charles directed Otis to sit opposite him and said, "I don't know why, but the good Lord only gave me one son, and you happen to be it, which means the future of our company and the Cogsworth name will depend on you and you alone. The company has prospered since your great-great-grandfather Adolphus Cogsworth started it, from one generation to the next, and one day it shall fall to you."

Otis blinked, said nothing.

"Honestly, if your sisters weren't girls, I'd feel much better about them taking over, but we must play the hand that God gave us in His infinite mystery. So, Otis, all this will be yours, and you had better not fail."

Otis was six when this happened.

The solarium looked out onto the reflecting pool, which looked out onto the Atlantic, a placid blue void this morning. In the middle of the pool, a dozen brass dolphins spit bullet-sized water pellets from their smiling mouths. The Cogsworths' household assistant, Andre, had already set up a coffee service and tuned the television to CNBC.

Otis sipped his coffee and turned up the volume. On the screen, two pundits sat at a table. *Empty, talking heads*, he thought. One of the analysts, bearded and bespectacled, looked like he taught Econ 101 at a community college. The other was a CEO who was most famous for running six companies into the ground before becoming a cable news pundit who specialized in talking about how to grow a business.

The Cogsworth International logo flashed on a screen behind the men, stopping Otis in mid-sip.

The professor said, "My sources tell me the Department of Justice is considering an investigation because at least eight hundred semiautomatic pistols traced to crimes in Chicago have been manufactured by Cogsworth International Arms and sold by its distributors."

The CEO nodded knowingly. "Today could be a bumpy ride for Cogsworth stocks. We'll keep our eyes on it."

There were some phrases Otis preferred not to hear while sipping his morning coffee, and certainly not on national television. Those phrases included, but were not limited to, "Department of Justice," "investigation," "bumpy ride," and "Cogsworth stocks."

He pulled a phone toward him and punched in a number. After a few rings he heard an inappropriately cheerful "Helloooo" from his nephew, Bruce Cogsworth Davies.

"Conference call in an hour," Otis said brusquely. "You, me, and Sunny McCarthy."

2

A sabogue mayor Lois Liebowitz pedaled her bicycle against the steady breeze blowing off the ocean. Her short legs pumped rapidly, and she emitted small, determined gasps and grunts. A burlap tote bag from a recent ACLU conference banged against her waist. Sweat had beaded on Lois's cheeks and gradually dampened her cropped gray hair beneath her trademark straw hat. No one would have blamed her for being miserable during her commute—she was seventy-four, short, flabby, and out of shape—but Lois loved it.

Her daily ride to Village Hall allowed her not only to see the village but to *feel* it: to taste the salty ocean air on her tongue; to hear the sounds of the merchants sweeping the sidewalks outside their shops on Main Street; to pedal by the organic community garden and check the daily level of the giant community fund posterboard thermometer.

Lois turned her face into a gust of wind that swept down from Billionaires Bluff and pedaled harder, trying her best not to think about the Bluff for too long. To Lois and her neighbors, Billionaires Bluff was merely a barrier that separated downtown Asabogue from its own white beaches. It was created by an ancient glacier that must have slowed just enough to deposit additional earth for the privileged few who would one day call it home. It rose subtly, but may as well have been the Great Wall of China. When people asked Lois what it was like being the mayor of the prestigious Bluff, she often answered by saying, simply, "I play in my sandbox and they play in theirs." Their sandbox, of course, was raked and cleaned every morning and dotted with signs that read "NO PUBLIC BEACH ACCESS."

Louis saw the first sign of trouble that morning at the intersection of Route 27, a commercial corridor that plowed straight through the village, and Asabogue Bluff Lane, a private road that curved gracefully up a steep and winding hill.

A streetlamp at the intersection was flickering in the morning sun, which meant that by nightfall Asabogue's most dangerous intersection in absolute darkness. For months Lois had asked the Department of Public Works to repair the light. For months the department ignored her. She composed a memo in her head: "If you don't fix it, I will."

She turned away from the Bluff and continued pedaling.

More trouble ahead, at Veterans Park, a grassy expanse in front of Village Hall, with a few tall oak trees shading two wooden benches. At the center of the park was the International Pole of Peace, a seven-foot granite obelisk engraved with the word *peace* in dozens of languages. (There had been some controversy when Lois had agreed to a request by the Long Island Alliance for Togetherness and Harmony to install the pole. An editorial in the *Asabogue Bugle* had opined that since the village didn't conduct foreign policy or maintain a standing army, it shouldn't display a pole dedicated to world peace, no matter how virtuous the cause. On the Bluff, there had been a clucking of tongues about whether Lois was too busy saving the world to run the village. She shrugged it all off. After all, she thought, who could be against world peace?)

Two empty beer bottles had been propped against the base of the pole. Lois glided her bike to a stop at the small circular brick-work that surrounded the monument. She pulled a small trash bag from her ACLU tote, snapped it open with a flick of her wrist, gingerly picked up the bottles, and placed the bag back in the tote, ignoring the throbbing in her lower back. She resumed her ride to Village Hall.

Lois Liebowitz, she thought. *Mayor. Giver of streetlight. Sanitation crusader. Global peace envoy.*

Lois arrived at Village Hall. She rested her bike against the stand she'd installed with funds from the modest Asabogue capital budget, without locking it. This was a matter of immense pride to Lois. Her village was so safe you didn't need bike locks. She dropped the bottles into a blue plastic bin with ASABOGUE RECYCLES stenciled on it in white, and pushed through the building's squeaking front door.

The wooden floors, original to 1750, groaned as she entered. Portraits of past mayors, old and white and heavily bearded, peered suspiciously from their perches high on the wall, as if to ask, "How did she become one of us?"

The historic Old Sitting Parlor had been converted to a reception area and was now dominated by a long wooden counter cluttered with tourist brochures for nearby attractions: wineries, museums, art galleries, and the famous Montauk Lighthouse, which had glowed at the tip of Long Island since George Washington was president. Sunlight streamed through a bay window, heating the room despite the wheezing of a wall-mounted air conditioner.

"Good morning, Sam!" Lois said cheerfully.

Sam Gergala, the part-time village clerk, leaned against the counter. He was tall and lanky and tanned from a lifetime as a local potato farmer. A few years before, his farm had succumbed to a development of mini mansions. *Domus erectus*, he continued to tell anyone who'd listen: *a highly invasive species*. Developers were like weevils, Sam explained. They chewed through acreage, leveling the land, turning rich soil into infinity pools for the rich. Lois had stood at Sam's side during the battle that took his farm, and Sam had stood with Lois ever since, although both had to crane their necks to make eye contact.

"Good ride this morning, Mayor?" Sam asked, as he did every morning.

"Oh, Sam," Lois said. "The knees are creaking. The ankles hurt. The back is going. But I keep pedaling. When will DPW fix the light on Asabogue Bluff Lane? Are they waiting for a major accident?"

Sam shuffled through a stack of papers. "They're getting to it, Mayor."

"They've been getting to it since last winter. Just get me a ladder."

Sam smiled.

"What else is on the agenda today?"

"You've got that charity function at Jack Steele's."

"I can't believe he's letting me in his house. I thought liberals were banned."

"It's for the East End Animal Welfare Alliance. I doubt they even told him you're invited. I wish I could see his face when you show up." Sam smiled mischievously.

"What other fun have you planned for me?"

"Councilman Kellogg called, demanding to talk to you about malfeasance and corruption in the Planning Department."

Lois suppressed a shudder. "That man gives me the creeps, Sam. Did you know he carries around a pad listing all his enemies?"

"Pretty sure we're on every page."

"What else?"

"That actress, Caitlyn Turner, is coming in. Again."

"Now what?"

"She wants us to remove the new stop sign near the front of her house on Asabogue Bluff Lane."

"Why?"

Sam shrugged. "Says if traffic slows, it'll give people time to gawk at her front gates. Her exact words were, 'Slowing down is one thing, but coming to a full stop should be completely out of the question.'"

Lois wondered whether Caitlyn Turner had given as much thought to stopping versus slowing as she had. For Lois, slowing for even one moment was anathema. If she didn't pedal as quickly as possible to work, if she didn't respond to complaints as soon as she could, if she didn't attend every single civic meeting held in the village, no matter how inconsequential or unproductive, Lois knew she'd lose. She'd lose valuable ground. She'd lose sight of the future, and if that happened, she would then, inevitably, slip backward into the sad memories of her past, back to that night long ago when her husband, Larry, casually informed her that he was having an affair with a movie star who lived on the Bluff, as if letting her know he'd decided to switch breakfast cereals. Slowing down would cause Lois to think, endlessly, about the struggle of raising two children in a modest house near Main Street, in the scruffy neighborhood where the "year-rounders" lived, far from the Bluff where celebrities stole the natives' husbands. Slowing gave her time to remind herself of the mistakes she'd made, now buried by the passage of time and lost in the wake of Lois's perpetual motion.

One paralyzing year after her divorce had been final, she had shed a final tear and plowed into her new life, volunteering for various civic causes including the Asabogue Historic Preservation Society and the Village Improvement Association. She'd landed a job as office manager at Asabogue Realty and represented the company at meetings of the Asabogue Chamber of Commerce. Those commitments had kept her out most nights of the week, sometimes with her two sullen children in tow, and Lois considered this busyness a blessing compared to the slow, lonely year she'd just endured. Before long, she'd propelled herself to what she'd thought at the time was the very zenith of local civic power: chairwoman of the Beautification Committee of the Asabogue Civic Association. Every Tuesday night she was required to attend sessions of the Village Board, facing a technicolor dais of plaid sports jackets, pink ties, green slacks, and what she privately thought of as Civil War hair: blue and gray. She fought overdevelopment, opposed pesticides, combatted sprawl. She became a permanent presence at Village Board meetings. When one ancient councilman publicly referred to her as "that annoying little Jewish woman," some had gasped, but Lois loved it. It broadened her smile. It added pep to her step. It propelled her forward, away from all the pain in her past.

Then came that one hot summer, which locals called, only half jokingly, the Battle of Billionaires Bluff.

An octogenarian multibillionaire by the name of Sidney Schwartzman had purchased three contiguous properties on the Bluff. He'd intended to build a home for himself and his new wife, an actress best known for her artistry in various soft-core porn series on cable television. Schwartzman had told his architects he wanted his home to "rival the Taj Mahal!" and it quickly became clear that he meant "rival" in the literal sense. His plan was to build an exact replica named "Taj Too," right there on the pristine shores of eastern Long Island, blocking the oceanfront views of his neighbors.

It turned out, however, that billionaires, who could afford to fly their private planes to India to view the original Taj Mahal, didn't appreciate the convenience of being able to stare at it from their homes on Long Island, and therefore, overnight, the oft-forgotten and mostly ignored Asabogue Village Zoning Code became the most important document in those billionaires' lives. The code, in addition to making it virtually impossible to expand sheds or erect neon storefront signs, was blessedly clear in prohibiting full-size replicas of the Taj Mahal within village boundaries.

Schwartzman was undeterred. All over the world his hotels, shopping malls, and office buildings provided multistory steel-and-glass testaments to his victories over the "not in my backyard" crowd. Though, in this case, the crowd bobbed near the top of the *Forbes* Richest People in America list and their backyard was the Atlantic Ocean.

The battle commenced. And when the residents of Billionaires Bluff had needed a commander in chief, they found one in Lois Liebowitz.

Schwartzman had met his match. Lois knew every word of the Asabogue Village Zoning Code. She could recite chapter, verse, and even legislative intent. She wasn't cowed by Schwartzman's threats to sue her for everything she had, because, as she told him, she had nothing. When he switched tacks and offered to make her a highly paid consultant to Schwartzman Global Properties, she counteroffered a spot as office assistant at Asabogue Realty Associates. Starting salary: minimum wage.

That summer the war cries of "Stop Schwartzman!" had permeated the hot ocean air of Asabogue. He threatened. He bullied. He litigated. He retreated. And the following year, the seasonal residents of Billionaires Bluff and the year-rounders in their small cottages downtown showed their appreciation by electing Lois Liebowitz mayor of Asabogue, replacing a longtime incumbent who many believed had first run during the Hoover administration, and breaking the village's 130 string of consecutive Protestant, Republican mayors.

Lois Liebowitz, that "annoying little Jewish woman," had been mayor, undisputed and unopposed, for the four terms since.

But that was about to change.

Now, in Village Hall, with Sam staring at her, Lois returned to the crisis of rubbernecking at Caitlyn Turner's. "Stop sign or not, people can't see past her hedgerows."

"Well, she's pretty steamed."

"Maybe she's just nervous about whether she'll be nominated for an Oscar next year. Imagine having the best actress living right here in Asabogue."

Sam nodded absently, not all that impressed at the prospect. Best actress. Best billionaire. Best hedge fund executive. Best fugitive Russian tycoon. That was the Asabogue yellow pages.

Sam glanced at a television mounted on a wall behind the counter. "Look what's happening in Chicago. Makes a stop sign here seem pretty silly."

Lois glanced at the screen. Images of violence in Chicago had dominated the news all summer. Now she watched footage of yet another shooting, interspersed with shots of flashing police lights, angry residents, and the indignant mayor. The corporate logo of the gun manufacturer Cogsworth International flashed onto the screen, and the words "Justice Dept Investigation Rumored" crawled beneath it.

Lois suppressed another shudder.

On the fringes of Asabogue, Councilman Ralph Kellogg was convening a meeting.

Twice a week, Ralph met with his small cadre of supporters in the unfinished basement of his modest Cape Cod on a lonely back road leading out of Asabogue. The floor and walls were concrete; the room was heavy with the odors of mold, age, and the occasional flood. The only decoration was a faded 1980s movie poster of action hero and now Asabogue resident Jack Steele, across the top of which was scrawled in red Sharpie, "*To Ralph, My Partner in Crime!!!*" An entire wall of shelving displayed an arsenal of firearms, including Stinger surface-to-air missiles, man-portable, shoulder-fired grenade launchers, flamethrowers, and an assortment of military assault rifles and submachine guns. Tucked in a corner, under a tangle of copper pipes and a lightbulb that hung from a chord, were Mrs. Kellogg's washer and dryer, which, evidently, were the most heavily guarded laundry appliances on the planet. A basket overflowing with Mrs. Kellogg's underwear— beige and white and large enough to be confused with burlap sacks—sat nearby.

In the center of the basement, Ralph had arranged some circa 1960s living room furniture acquired on a clandestine excursion to the Asabogue Village dump, pieces in garish orange and lime green with stains blooming on their various surfaces like algae. For his guests' reading pleasure there were tattered back issues of *Modern Militia* fanned out across red plastic TV-dinner stands with wobbly legs. There was also an old RCA television in a faux mahogany console, usually tuned to military history documentaries on Ralph's favorite channel.

Ralph called this group the Organization, but it wasn't so much an organization as a small alliance of semi-dependable half-wits willing to help Ralph with special "projects": distributing smear literature, intimidating political opponents, extorting, and bundling illegal and semilegal campaign contributions.

If the Asabogue High School Class of '78 had had an award for Most Likely to Secede, Ralph Kellogg would have won convincingly. During his senior year he'd run, unsuccessfully, for senior class president on a platform of withdrawing from the Model UN and arming the marching band. The campaign was marred by allegations of dirty tricks and became the subject of the first lunch money for votes scandal to be formally investigated by a state Board of Elections.

At seventeen, Ralph Kellogg retired from politics and began a long period of embittered simmering. At twenty-five he joined Kellogg & Kellogg, the family insurance business, and began to dabble in various hobbies: fishing, hunting, right-wing militias, and paramilitary groups. Fortified by 9/11, he developed a particular dislike for Muslims, and although Asabogue had no Muslims, Ralph stood guard.

Behind every act of political mischief in Asabogue were Ralph's heavy hands. When anonymous fliers circulated, everyone knew they were authored by "Crazy Ralph." When candidate signs were swiped in the dead of night by a figure serpentining from lawn to lawn in military fatigues and night-vision goggles, people shook their heads and said simply, "Ralph." When ballot boxes were stuffed, everyone knew Ralph was to blame.

For most of his life, Ralph's reputation had prevented him from seeking political office. Generally, voters who cluck their tongues when they see you coming don't want to put you in charge of things. Then, one fateful year, a dozen separate candidates had run for the Village Board, the normal candidates had split the normal vote, and the remaining crazy vote had elected Ralph Kellogg with a plurality of twelve percent. It was a campaign upset that upset most of Asabogue.

Since that election, Ralph Kellogg had taken it upon himself to keep an eye on things in Village Hall. This was, of course, the suspicious eye of a conspiracy theorist who saw plots in every zoning variance and deck expansion supported by the Liebowitz administration. This eye darted constantly in search of cover-ups, corruption, and Muslims. And slowly, enough of Ralph's fellow conspiracists had come out of the woodwork to form the paranoid coalition that had come to be named the Organization.

Ralph had deputized two of his followers.

There was Louie Delmarco, Parks Maintenance Assistant III in the Asabogue Parks Department, whose job description might as well have been "looking busy while idly leaning on a rake." Louie's body was short and round and seemed built to conserve all the energy it took not to rake. Louie put the "no show" in "no-show job."

And there was Bobby Reilly, recently fired from Southampton

Hardware, which he'd managed to burn down when he accidentally overturned a can of turpentine, and, in annoyance at his own clumsiness, flung his cigarette butt at the spilled contents. Bobby wasn't much in the common sense department, but he was everything Ralph needed in the willing to take extreme risks department.

For this morning's meeting Mrs. Kellogg had put out plastic bowls of Cool Ranch Doritos, and Ralph provided the beer. Louie munched and slurped, and Bobby chain-smoked from a carton of Camels. The Battle of Stalingrad was being waged on the RCA. Ralph had just finished reading a *New York Post* article about the banning of guns in Chicago. Now he paced urgently in front of the laundry appliances, arms crossed against his barrel chest, eyes burning with anger. "Guy's name is Rodriguez. Need I say more?"

The Organization nodded collectively, signifying the need for Ralph to, indeed, say more. And since Ralph Kellogg fancied himself a motivational speaker, inspired by a VCR collection of great war movies that were rubber-banded in an upstairs closet, he continued.

"It's that Islamex conspiracy I've been telling you about. The Mexicans infiltrate our country. Open up our border to the Muslims. Next thing you know we're bowing to Mecca instead of saying the Pledge of Allegiance." Overcome with agitation, Ralph turned off the television, which signaled that the day's meeting of the Organization was thereby in session.

That morning's agenda was a rumor in Village Hall that Mayor Liebowitz would soon be proposing a law that would expand commercial recycling to every household. "She's turning us into the People's Republic of Asabogue! When will it end?" The thick veins in his neck pulsated and his hands clenched into fists. Ralph conceded that recycling was, he supposed, good for the environment, but what he was unhappy about, and what he couldn't abide by, was the prospect of serving in some slave labor camp separating newspapers and glass.

"Fuck Liebowitz," Louie said through a mouthful of Doritos, crumbs spraying from his mouth like a cluster bomb.

"Little blue bins in front of every house," Ralph continued. "Next thing, she'll put our women in headscarves."

Louie popped open another beer. "What do you want us to do about it?"

Cigarette clamped at the side of his lips, Bobby said, "We could take out the recycling center? Lotsa flammables there." For effect, he exhaled a long plume of smoke.

Ralph sighed as the meeting arrived at this familiar roadblock. He had the Organization but no plan. They swilled beer and devoured junk food and aired their grievances against Liebowitz, liberals, Muslims, Jews, blacks, Mexicans, gays, Wall Street, the Federal Reserve, the media, you name it—but it always came down to the same thing. Bobby wanted to blow things up. Louie wanted more Doritos and, apparently, to learn about something called the War of the Austrian Succession on the TV.

Ralph looked at his watch: ten thirty. He had to be at Jack Steele's for a party by eleven and felt a soft twinge of anxiety in his stomach. He and Jack were kindred spirits, bonded by love of country and a variety of right-wing conspiracy theories, but Jack's parties troubled Ralph. Usually they amounted to nothing more than a bunch of snooty billionaires who looked down their nose jobs at him, judging him, mocking him silently, thinking "Crazy Ralph" whenever he spoke.

Soon, Ralph promised himself, as he always did when he felt himself becoming discouraged, *they'll all be on their knees, begging me. When the Muslims cross the Mexican border and take over the country, and USA stands for United States of Allah, and the Constitution is replaced with Sharia law—then they'll know! How the whole thing was planned. An inside job. How the government took our guns away so we couldn't defend ourselves from the invasion. How the Federal Reserve manipulated our currency to enrich the petrodollar states and bankroll the caliphate. How corrupt judges and the ACL-Jew let mosques get built*

right under our noses! Then they'll all say, "Maybe Ralph wasn't so crazy
after all. Maybe we were the crazy ones." And they'll all want to come to
Asabogue. Because I protected my town.

Ralph pulled from his shirt pocket the tattered red three-by-five spiral memo pad he carried everywhere. The pad comprised page after page of people, places, and things Ralph considered threatening, sometimes written in a vengeful scrawl, sometimes in cool and precise block letters. Enemies of Ralph and Asabogue, enemies of the state, current enemies in Village Hall, and past enemies from high school. Even friends of friends were potential enemies, at least in Ralph's book. He wrote: *recycling*.

He stuffed the notepad back in his pocket. "I have to go to Jack Steele's," he announced miserably.

"Bring back some of those mini egg rolls," Louie said as Ralph climbed the basement stairs.

3

S unny McCarthy sat in her robe on a balcony high above Washington, DC's Penn Quarter, sipping her morning espresso. The robe fell open above her knees. It occurred to her that some voyeur might have been gazing at her from the multitude of windows nearby, but that morning she had bigger problems in the exposure department.

Her iPad had already tracked nearly three thousand media references to her employer, Cogsworth International, two dozen unfavorable references on morning news shows including *Morning Joe, Today, Good Morning America* (but not *Fox & Friends*; it wasn't that bad yet), plus blogs and tweets that were trending about a zillion to one against Otis Cogsworth.

Sunny brushed a lock of blond hair away from her face and smiled at her tablet's screen. *Gonna be a bitch of a day*, she thought happily.

Her cell phone rang, its screen flashing the name Bruce Cogsworth Davies. Sunny rolled her eyes. Otherwise known throughout the ranks of Cogsworth International as "the idiot nephew," Bruce was incapable of performing any job at Cogsworth International without shooting himself or others in the foot, so to speak. He bore the title Vice President for Public Affairs.

"Good morning, Sunshine!" Bruce chirped. His appropriation of her formal name rankled Sunny twice over, once because hardly anyone called her Sunshine and a second time because she'd asked Bruce repeatedly to call her Sunny. Still, he persisted in ignoring her request as part of what Sunny sensed was some misguided form of flirtation. "How are we doing this fine day?" he asked.

"Um, let's see," Sunny said matter-of-factly, "our company's biggest seller was just involved in yet another massacre, the DOJ's going to start serving us with subpoenas any minute, the latest polling says seventy percent of Americans want to ban our product, our stock will have sunk like a rock by the close of the markets, 'Cogsworth' is now in first place for most despised search word on the Internet, but other than that, oh, what a beautiful morning." She let out a harsh laugh, a combination of contemptuous cackle and annoyed growl.

"Well," Bruce said, unfazed, "that's why we pay you the big bucks. Right?"

"I want a raise."

"Hey," Bruce said. "You already make more than me, and I'm a vice president."

"But I'm *worth* so much more than you," Sunny replied, and laughed her double-edged laugh again.

After a few seconds of uncomfortable silence Bruce got down to business. "Otis wants a conference call in one hour," he told Sunny. "Can you do that? If you'll be in the shower or something I can—"

"I'll be on the call," Sunny said abruptly, hoping she'd extinguished the visual that had clearly been forming in Bruce's mind.

"Right. I'll text the conference number and password. Bye, Sunshine."

Sunny pressed END CALL.

She rose from her chair and walked through the sliding glass door into her apartment, a designer four-bedroom condo that glittered above downtown DC. It was a tasteful blend of granite, porcelain, and stainless steel. Floor-to-ceiling windows framed the Capitol dome in the distance. Spacious closets were crammed with clothing plucked from Georgetown's top boutiques like fruit from the grocery store. The walls featured photos of Sunny with celebrities and senators and various presidential candidates. There was a framed cover of *Washingtonian* that read, "SUNNY & HOT: MEET DC'S SEXIEST LOBBYIST." There were photos of the famous and the powerful. Formal and informal; candid and posed; grips and grins (she learned how to grin through some senators' lecherous grips). There was not, however, a single family picture.

She gazed out a window toward the Capitol, already shimmering in Washington's early-morning heat. There was a time she'd been inspired by the sight. Now she thought of it as merely a massive cash register sheathed in marble. She put money in; she took money out. Her national anthem began and ended with "cha-ching."

She sipped her espresso. It had turned cold and bitter.

An hour later, showered and ready for the day's fight, Sunny entered the bedroom that she'd converted into an office. A bank of television screens on one wall offered muted images from the major news networks. Three separate screens were tuned to various C-SPAN channels, because one wouldn't want to miss a live oversight hearing of the House Subcommittee on Bee Pollination. Bookshelves were crammed with congressional almanacs, congressional directories, and congressional quarterlies. The largest piece of furniture was a beaten leather couch that Sunny had hauled to

DC from her childhood home. It was really the only reminder she had of her roots, and now it served as a combination newspaper recycling bin, clothes hamper, and file cabinet.

The landline on her desk flashed to indicate three missed calls, all from that morning, all from the same person: her mother.

The number triggered a pang of guilt in Sunny's stomach.

Call her back later, she thought at first. *Get it over with now*, she then argued. *Ugh*. She decided to wait until after the conference call with Cogsworth.

She punched a number on the phone, hit speaker, announced her password, and listened to the theme music from *The Magnificent Seven*. Bruce was surely on the line, too, but presumably he knew better than to try and flirt with Sunny when his uncle was about to get on the call. Soon an operator's voice said, "Stand by for Mr. Otis Cogsworth. Go ahead, sir."

Otis wasted no time. "We're in a shitstorm," he told them, and Sunny wondered whether he thought she didn't know that. "How are we gettin' out of it?"

This, she thought, *is why he'll never be appointed ambassador to any foreign country. The diplomacy genes are definitely missing.*

Bruce began reading talking points prepared by some assistant idiot. "Condolences have been sent to the families in Chicago. We released a statement noting that Cogsworth International is voluntarily assisting state and federal authorities in various gun trafficking investigations and reiterating our significant financial support of school safety programs and mental health outreach—"

"Blah blah blah," Otis said. Sunny imagined him kneading the temples of his balding scalp, wishing his nephew away. "What about the Feds? What's our status, Sunny?"

She sat back. It was her favorite position: sitting back, arms folded, and taking charge. "So far about a hundred tweets blasting us from the usual Members of Congress. Four scheduled press conferences, to announce various bills to regulate us. And forty House Democrats are releasing a letter to the U.S. attorney general demanding an investigation of us, specifically why so many of our products are ending up . . . where they're ending up."

"Good Lord."

"I'm not bothered by tweets no one reads and bills no one will pass," Sunny said. "But that letter to the attorney general, that's a problem."

"Big problem," Cogsworth said.

"Why?" asked Bruce.

Sunny rolled her eyes. "The attorney general is leaving the administration to return to California," she explained patiently. "He's going to run for governor. As a Republican. Which means he can only win statewide by persuading Democrats to vote for him. And the best way to prove to them he's not just another Republican is to take on the gun industry. You're about to be a poster boy, Otis."

"Goddamnit!" Otis shouted. "I told the president, 'Don't appoint that guy!' You know what he said? 'Don't worry, Otis. He may be from California, but he's a Republican.' To which I said, 'Mr. President, he may be a Republican, but he's from California.' He should have listened to someone who knows what he's doing."

Sunny laughed. "Someone . . . like you."

"Exactly."

"The problem with President Piper is that he does listen . . . to the last pollster who whispers in his ear."

Otis grunted his agreement, then said, "We cannot have the Justice Department pokin' its nose into our business. This is still America!"

Bruce said, "I have an idea."

Brace yourself, Sunny thought.

"Let's fund a twenty-four-hour toll-free hotline to help—"

She couldn't hold back another laugh, in part because Bruce's idea was truly laughable and in part because she knew nothing shot down a ludicrous trial balloon faster than the machine-gun fire of her own withering cackle.

"Stop right there, Bruce," Otis said. "Do you realize we're staring down the triple barrels of a threat to our survival? We've got an attorney general who thinks he's getting elected governor with our scalps, a mayor of Chicago who runs for president by kicking us in the balls, and the fake news outlets that boosts its ratings by shoving every gun crime up our ass."

Well, that broke a record for anatomical references, Sunny thought.

Bruce, wisely, didn't respond.

"And your strategy is a toll-free helpline?"

"Hotline," said Bruce.

"We gotta stop this investigation," Otis said. "We're in a goddamn war! I need strategies, not helplines."

"Yes, s—"

"I need this stopped dead in its tracks. I'm paying you people a fortune. I gotta get ready for some charity function at Jack Steele's house, but when I come back, I want a plan to fight back and fight back hard. You got it?"

Sunny said, "We'll have something for you."

All she heard was a dial tone.

4

Otis and Lucille Cogsworth climbed into their Range Rover and glided down their long stone driveway. They turned right on Asabogue Bluff Lane, drove slowly west for approximately ten seconds, then turned right again and passed through the massive wrought-iron gates of their next-door neighbor, Jack Steele.

"What's the charity du jour?" Otis grumbled as he waved off a parking attendant and began the winding ascent up a gravel driveway.

"The East End Animal Welfare Alliance," she said. "And please be nice."

But nice wasn't a tool in Otis's toolbox, especially the one he brought along to Asabogue charity functions. He detested these events. Never in history had so many eyes made so little contact. Whomever he finally, begrudgingly entered into conversation with, they were constantly peering over Otis's shoulder to see if there was anyone better to corner. Their eyes scanned and darted in search of more fame and bigger fortunes. A clash of raw egos in refined dress, circling as gracefully as sharks.

Particularly annoying was that today's soiree was a Jack Steele production, which meant Otis would at some point be held captive to the aging film star's right-wing ramblings. Steele had become the iconic celebrity spokesman for a number of high-profile conservative crusades: taxes and spending, abortion and regulation, drilling here and bombing there. His proudest title was National Chairman of the American Gun Owners Defense, or AGOD, the chief spokesman for the God-given right to bear arms without pesky background checks. Otis agreed wholeheartedly with Jack's politics. He just thought there were better, more productive ways to express these opinions than sounding like the keynote speaker at the reunion breakfast of the John Birch Society.

Otis maneuvered the car up the narrow driveway, tires rumbling loudly on the loose gravel. Dense woods crowded the path, and heavy tree branches arched low overhead, casting a foreboding shade. Signs were posted prominently, warning NO TRESPASSING and PRIVATE PROPERTY. One read, IF YOU CAN READ THIS YOU'RE IN RANGE. Finally, Villa di Acciaio rose in front of the Cogsworths. *This man's home literally is his castle*, Otis thought. There were dark gray stone and medieval turrets and even a gurgling moat. It seemed built to defend against an invasion of tourists, jihadists, and most registered Democrats. They parked in a courtyard. Lucille balanced a blueberry pie from the beloved local farmstand, Marion's, in one hand, and Otis cradled a gift-wrapped Cogsworth Crusader 9-millimeter in the crook of his right arm. Because how do you go to your neighbors' without bringing a little something?

They entered the main hall, where Jack Steele movie posters were mounted on high granite walls: *Jack Steele in Hard Steel*, *Jack*

Steele in Sharp Steel, Jack Steele in Steel Medal. Guests circulated, clinking champagne glasses, blowing air kisses, and coming close enough to hug without actually touching. Everyone was awaiting the grand entrance of the star of this show.

The first person Otis recognized was Councilman Kellogg, who was towering over the crowd. *Crazy Ralph*, Otis thought, shaking his head and avoiding eye contact. Lucille drifted into the fray, cooing over her pie with a few of the other Bluff wives.

Suddenly a voice ricocheted off the stone walls from the top of the grand stairway. "Carpe diem!" it announced sternly. The guests clapped and oohed and ahhhed because this was the catchphrase that signaled the end of every Jack Steele film, usually accompanied by a sneer and the deliverance by Steele of some final blow to the film's villain: a cold-blooded push out of an airplane door or a heartless hurling over a canyon's edge. The voice was now raspy after all these years, but it was unmistakably Jack Steele's.

There he was in living color: tanning-parlor bronze. For today's gathering Steele wore his trademark cowboy hat with a purple checkered shirt, black jeans, and monogrammed snakeskin boots. His face was taut, his parchment skin stretched surgically over hollow cheeks, but his eyes glowed icy blue and his perfectly aligned teeth sparkled through those famously thin lips, like the glinting edge of a razor-sharp knife. As Otis took Steele in, he contemplated the fact that he always thought of Steele as mildly stooped with age, but in fact the man stood ramrod straight and, at six foot six, was easily the tallest person in the room, with a spine seemingly made of, well, steel.

Steele's wife, Amber, stood beside him, her head turned anxiously up toward his. Her blond hair was tied back in a sleek ponytail, and she wore a short white summer dress that clung to her petite frame. "She wore that two weeks ago." Otis heard one of the wives hiss at another. Twenty years earlier, Jack had plucked Amber, then Amber Jankowsky, from anonymity as an extra in

Forged Steel. She was forty years Steele's junior, and remained perky and blond. As far as Otis could tell, she spent the majority of her time acting as lead cheerleader and caregiver for her husband.

She quickly whispered something into Steele's ear, and he narrowed his eyes at a small card cupped in his hands. "Welcome to Villa di Acciaio. We are here today to raise money for . . ."

Amber whispered.

". . . the East End Animal Welfare Alliance, a cause I relate to because I made some real dogs in my career."

Obligatory laughter rippled through the main hall.

Jack then spoke of his love of animals, which, he recounted, had been kindled with his horse, Swifty, on the set of *Gunslingers of Tombstone*. He segued into his usual monologue about how "they don't make action movies like they used to" and how "Sly Stallone could kill a bunch of gooks on set but the man would weep at the sight of a puppy" and "that time Sly stuck a whoopee cushion under this blond actress with big tits. Can't remember her name but, God, do I remember the tits," all to the accelerated kneading of Amber's fingers and the nervous shifting of feet of the East End Animal Welfare Alliance staff. Amber placed a slender hand on Steele's forearm and, as if a director had yelled "Cut!," Steele's eyes snapped back into focus.

"So let's dig deep into our pockets and support our animals and—"

Steele stopped, and for a moment Otis assumed he'd lost his train of thought again, but then the old actor's blue eyes locked onto someone in the crowd and narrowed menacingly. Slowly and en masse, his guests turned toward the object of Steele's scorn.

Otis saw her immediately, right there in plain sight, a villain who'd somehow infiltrated Steele's home: Mayor Lois Liebowitz, sporting her droopy straw hat and ACLU tote and sipping a mimosa.

Otis turned back to Steele, who took a quick, audible breath, smiled icily, and said, "Carpe diem, Madam Mayor."

Villa di Acciaio grew cold.

Later, Otis found himself engaged in small talk with the owner of a mineral and gas mining company whose inherited position didn't disqualify him from lamenting the leeches who sucked the system dry by collecting unemployment insurance because they didn't understand the value of hard work. Otis was nodding numbly when he felt a tight squeeze around his forearm.

"Follow me," Jack Steele ordered.

They cut through the crowd and strode out onto a glittering marble terrace that extended toward the beach. They passed a massive swimming pool whose floor featured various scenes from Jack's films in mosaic tiles. On the far side of a perfectly man-icured rolling lawn was a large red-roofed guest cottage, nestled amid trees that blocked Jack's view of the billionaire next door, or, for that matter, anyone else on earth. Otis always wondered how Jack managed to build so close to the property line, but the answer seemed clear: Jack Steele didn't bother with such nuisances as per-mits, variances, and approvals.

They arrived at a weathered wood railing that overlooked roll-ing sand dunes, dotted with beach grass that rippled in the soft breeze.

Steele squinted toward the blue horizon, slowly turning his head as if scanning for an incoming threat. Then he closed his eyes and sucked the ocean air through his lips. Otis watched Steele's rigid chest expand and contract as he exhaled a long, raspy breath. His eyes fluttered open and he said, "Only in America do you get a view like this."

Otis chose not to debate the likelihood of similar views in countries with certain features. Like coasts.

Steele stared at the ocean. "'On such a full sea are we now

afloat,'" he said. "'And we must take the current when it serves, or lose our ventures.'"

"That from a movie?" Otis asked.

"It's Shakespeare," Steele said. "I was classically trained."

That explains Guts of Steele Two, thought Otis as he wiped his sweaty neck with a handkerchief.

Jack leaned against the rail and sighed. "Otis, if this country continues its course, we'll lose our ventures. The ship of state is sinking, brought down by people like . . . that woman." He pronounced "that woman" the way he might say "that virus."

Otis didn't respond. Steele knew he was a compatriot when it came to loathing Lois Liebowitz.

"I don't even know how Liebowitz got past my guard dogs," Steele went on. "That animal rights group must have invited her. You know how they are. They shelter homeless animals and hopeless liberals." He laughed at his own joke, a shallow cigarette smoke–infused gurgle from deep in his chest. "I don't mind her in my house, but I can't stand that she's in Village Hall. Christ, this is a conservative town, Otis!"

"Well, she did stop Schwartzman," Otis said.

"That was a goddamn lifetime ago!" Steele rasped. "Things were simple then. All about the quality of life. Now it's about *our* way of life. It's us versus them, my friend." He underscored *them* by thrusting his forefinger at the horizon, in the general vicinity of the rest of the world. "And us, Christ we're getting softer than the jellyfish on that goddamn beach."

Otis felt it wasn't a good time to remind Jack that Mr. Tough was hosting a fund-raiser to benefit stray kitties.

"We're being taken over, Otis," Steele went on. "Those illegals, pouring through the border. Soon as they get here they drop their anchor babies and pick up their ACLU membership cards."

"Jack—"

"Infiltrating our society. Taking over our institutions. *Habla español*, Otis?"

"I don't—"

"America's changing, Otis. Did you watch the news this morning? The story about your little . . . problem? With the Department of Injustice?"

Otis let out a growl. "I saw it on CNBC. The administration's going to screw us."

Steele smiled. "And you're surprised? Republicans, Democrats. They're all the same. One big jellyfish party. Want to know what I think?"

Otis nodded grimly.

"Instead of the Feds investigating you, someone should investigate the Feds, investigate how they allow our citizens to go defenseless, how our government lets criminals have guns and law-abiding Americans get shot at."

Otis cocked his head, realizing Steele was actually, finally, coming around to some point.

"Know what I'd do if I ran this country?" Jack asked. "I'd give 'em all guns."

"What are you talking about?"

"Every time there's a shooting, the politicians stampede to the cameras to announce more gun control bills. It's time to turn the tables. Instead of passing laws taking our guns away, pass laws giving them out. Everyone gets a gun. Annie gets a gun. Andy gets a gun. Two cars in every garage and a gun in every pot."

"Jack, we're having a hard enough time playing defense in Washington."

Steele smiled, and soft creases spread across his tanned face. He pulled his cowboy hat lower on his forehead. "Otis, don't you watch my movies? How does every one of them end? I'm half dead. My bones are broken. I'm sliced and diced. I'm outgunned and outmanned. But what do I do? I go from a losing defense to a winning offense. I stop taking punches and start throwing them. Bad guys lose. Good guys win. Fade to black. Roll credits. End of story."

Otis stared at the horizon. Half of him wished Steele would simply shut up and let him enjoy the view, but the other half was interested—not that he'd let Steele know that.

"Your problem is you spend too much time on defense, Otis. Start fighting back. Before it's too late. Carpe diem!"

The waves rolled in and out. The breeze refreshed Otis. His heart beat faster.

He said, in soft assent, "Carpe diem."

The familiar number flashed on Sunny McCarthy's cell phone, and each flash was a kick to the gut. Her mind warred with itself: *Don't pick up. At some point you have to talk to her. I don't need this right now. She won't stop calling.*

Sunny declined the call and let out a long, fatigued breath. She began twisting locks of hair between two fingers, the only nervous habit she had. In the hours since the conference call with Otis, she'd sat at her desk, staring at the flood of television coverage from Chicago, racking her usually nimble mind for a response, but she was coming up unusually empty.

The crisis management textbooks instructed that when the shit hit the fan, you changed the direction of the fan. Deflect. Dance. Distract. At this point, however, changing the subject would be no less herculean a task than changing the Earth's rotation. The textbooks further instructed that when you couldn't change the narrative, you approached the controversy directly, with hands above your head. Acknowledge. Admit. Apologize. Use language like "We will strive to do better," followed by heartfelt pleas for forgiveness from a) family, b) the public, c) God, or d) all of the above. But Sunny knew that remorse wasn't in Otis's repertoire. She no longer proposed acknowledgments, admissions, or apologies to the man who'd been known to belt out "My Way" in the shower every morning.

She glanced at a split screen on CNN. On one side, Chicago police were stretching yellow crime scene tape around a convenience store shooting. On the other, Mayor Rodriguez was performing his regularly scheduled sputtering about Cogsworth International.

Sunny's cell phone rang again: Otis, wanting to know what she'd come up with, no doubt. She sighed and answered. "Hello, Otis, I'm still working on a response. I promise—"

"I got one."

His voice was fuzzy and distant, which meant he was driving somewhere on Billionaires Bluff.

"You do?" Sunny's mind raced. Was he messing with her?

"Yup," he said. "And it's a beaut!"

Oh, God, she thought.

His next words were drowned out by static. Sunny strained to listen, picking up references to Jack Steele and "best defense is a strong offense" and something about carpe diem.

"Whoa, Otis," she said. "Slow down."

There was a pause, and just when she wondered if the call had been dropped, Otis said, "I want a bill introduced in Congress requiring that every American own a gun."

Sunny let her boss's words linger on the line between them. Otis had never been shy about offering bad ideas, and her usual technique was to let him talk himself out of them. He paid her handsomely to do damage control, and some of Otis's own suggestions could be, well, catastrophic. So she waited for Otis to shift into reverse.

He was silent.

"A law actually requiring gun ownership?" she asked.

"Yep. Mandatory gun possession. With fines if you're caught without one."

All she could come up with was a noncommittal "Hmm."

"Don't you see?" he continued. "We turn our shitstorm into *their* shitstorm! Let the administration explain why they refuse to give law-abiding Americans the tools to protect themselves from criminals! Instead of coming after us, we turn the attention on them."

Sunny straightened in her chair and glanced at the television. His Honor was now hysterical, demanding new federal investigations of Cogsworth International for gun trafficking, tax evasion, and multiple other violations of local, state, and federal law. She wondered whether an international war crimes tribunal was next.

"We have enough friends in Congress to pass a bill, don't we?" Otis asked. "I mean, good Lord, I'm like the U.S. Mint with all the contributions you make me send!"

The third lesson in the crisis management books was to frame expectations. Sunny knew that Otis's strategy had a dangerously high risk and a distinctly low probability of success. It would anger a president who didn't exactly like having his squishy spine being forced against a wall. It would ignite a clash of special interests and require tens of millions in paid media. It would enjoin powerful Members of Congress, enflame the liberal editorial boards, empower the gun lobby and its millions of supporters. It would force gun control proponents back on their heels. It would be the gun control battle to end all gun control battles.

It was perfect.

Still, Sunny needed to temper Otis's enthusiasm. "I think it's a good message piece," she said coolly. "Great, actually. But let's not kid ourselves about passing a bill. I mean, legislation requiring Americans to own a product?"

"Obamacare!" Otis shouted. "That abomination said every American had to purchase health insurance! Why can't we require that every American purchase life insurance? A gun!"

There had been moments in Sunny's political career when someone said something, usually in the offhanded way that Otis just did, that lit a strategic path through the dark. These moments were rare. Washington strategists and consultants basically got paid to regurgitate old plays or perform political rain dances to summon good luck, but Otis Cogsworth had stumbled onto an idea which, properly executed, could be ingenious.

So Sunny said the only thing she could say: "Let me get to work."

Several miles away, Air Force One landed at Joint Base Andrews with a barely noticeable thud. This concluded President Henry Piper's surprise visit to Iraq, which caused, well, quite a surprise.

The idea had two presumed benefits. First, with domestic gun violence escalating, Congress fighting, and the economy breaking apart, a few days in a war zone didn't seem like a bad idea. Second, the president's political advisors assured him that visiting his troops would jump-start favorability ratings that weren't just anemic, they were clinically dead.

The strategy backfired. The carefully orchestrated backdrop of adoring troops behind their commander in chief didn't account for the fact that prolonged exposure to Piper's circumlocutory oratory in a stifling airplane hangar near a desert could be categorized as a violation of the Geneva Conventions. By hour two, the cameras were focused on usually steely soldiers in various stages of gaping yawns and eye rolls. One, Staff Sergeant Charles Gatto, nodded off and toppled from the stage, resulting in the headline "WOUNDED INACTION."

That was par for this president's course. The former navy admiral found himself in command of a ship of state, trying to avoid comparisons to the captains of the *Titanic* and the *Lusitania*. That old mariner's technique of sticking a finger in the air wasn't helping matters against swirling gale-force winds.

As Air Force One taxied toward Marine One, the president sprawled in his stateroom, watching the latest news. There was Mayor Rodriguez, demanding that the president do something— anything—to stop gun violence in Chicago. The broadcast was interrupted by a commercial by a group called the Second Amendment Crisis Network demanding that the president do something—anything—to stop gun control in America.

At that point, Henry Piper was tempted to order his pilot to return to Baghdad.

5

The next morning, Lois Liebowitz was seriously distracted. In addition to a heat wave that had brought Asabogue to an early-morning swelter and the air conditioner in the Old Sitting Parlor drawing its death-rattling breaths, there was the new matter of helicopter traffic over Billionaires Bluff, the overnight violence in Chicago, and the potentially violent Ralph Kellogg flexing his fingers on the other side of the conference table, all of which triggered a dull ache between Lois's eyes and a nervous churning in her stomach.

A delegation from the Bluff had descended on Village Hall to protest the nuisance of helicopters flying low over their compounds, and they were now impatiently awaiting Lois's response. Her eyes kept drifting to the television high on the wall. One network had upgraded the grizzly news from Chicago, assigning it its

own funereal theme music and the stylized ever-present logo "CHI-
CAGO MASSACRES."

The room was crowded, which increased the heat and forced
everyone to fan themselves with papers.

A hedge fund executive pounded a fist on the table, snapping
Lois's attention back to the room. "It's like Grand Central station up
there!" he was saying. "Helicopters right over my compound, back
and forth, day and night!"

A commercial real estate developer dressed in tennis clothing
nodded. "I'm not paying obscene taxes to live through something
out of *Apocalypse Now*," he said.

"And one of those birds," said a reclusive actor in oversized
sunglasses, "is gonna hit a CIA drone someday."

The general nodding around the table ceased, and Lois saw a
few brows furrow in confusion. At the far end of the table Sam Gergala said, "A CIA drone? Over Asabogue?"

"Over everywhere, man," said the actor.

A real estate tycoon shook off the tangent. "Listen, Mayor," he
said. "We've raised a couple million dollars for something we call
SHAA: Stop Helicopters Abusing Asabogue. We're going to lobby
the FAA to divert the helicopters. They can fly north. They can fly
south. Anywhere but Asabogue."

Almost everyone scribbled that down for its bumper sticker
potential.

Lois looked up at the television again and mumbled, "Just ter-
rible."

"Exactly!" said the hedge fund executive. "Deafening!"

Lois sighed. "I mean what's happening in Chicago."

Heads turned to the screen—a crawler said there had been another six shootings overnight—then back to Lois and the urgent
matter of helicopter noise. Against war, disease, and poverty, Lois
thought, the people of Asabogue raised money at cocktail parties;
but against invasions of their quality of life, they rose up, prepared,
as Kennedy once said, to "pay any price, bear any burden, meet any

hardship, support any friend, oppose any foe" in defense of their values. Property values, specifically.

"Mayor?" said the actor, perhaps sensing that for once he wasn't the most spaced-out person in the room.

Lois frowned and sat up straight, anxious to end the meeting. "All right," she said. "I'll contact the neighboring mayors. There's strength in numbers. We'll meet with our congressman. Ask him to pressure the FAA. I'll do everything I can."

Convinced that there would be peace and quiet in their time, the group adjourned and went their separate ways back up to the Bluff.

Lois went to her office, aware that she was under the suspicious gaze of Councilman Kellogg.

In Washington, Sunny bent over her laptop, reviewing whether there was any precedent for a federal law requiring citizens to own guns. But, nothing. On the issue of mandating Americans to carry guns, Congress had been strangely silent, which meant Sunny would have to find someone crazy enough to champion it as a new cause, but not so crazy as to trigger a rolling of eyes and chuckling of the cynical Washington press corps. According to her research, there was really only one possibility: freshman congressman Roy Dirkey of Arkansas. Sunny had already booked an appointment with him and Otis for the next day.

Dirkey had defeated a popular Democratic incumbent with the Dirkey American Dream Twelve-Point Plan, the twelve points of which were the dozen federal departments he proposed to abolish. Their functions, he promised, would be transferred to state and local governments as well as Walmart Service Centers (Walmart's headquarters just happen to be in Dirkey's congressional district). That would leave two Cabinet departments intact: the Defense Department and Agriculture (Arkansas, after all, had farms, and Dirkey had statewide electoral ambitions). Dirkey's NRA rating was one hundred percent, with the notation "If we could give bonus points, we most certainly would!" He had potential.

The phone rang, and Sunny answered without giving herself a chance to back out. "Hello?"

"Sunshine? It's me. Your mother."

"I know, Mother," Sunny said dully. "How are you?"

"Have you been watching the news? From Chicago?"

"Of course, Mother. I happen to be the lobbyist for the company that's making news in Chicago. Remember?"

"All those innocent people being killed. Children! It said on the news that almost ninety percent of child gun fatalities in industrialized nations happen in the U.S."

"Well," said Sunny, twirling a lock of hair, "maybe people who don't like gun rights should just move to those countries and—"

"Sunshine."

"Mother, we've been through this, and I'm pretty busy right now. As you know. From watching the news."

"They're saying your company may be investigated by the Justice Department. That worries me."

Sunny struggled to control herself. Her mother wasn't worried about her. She never worried about Sunny. She was worried about what people would think of a daughter who'd gone from Sunshine to the Queen of Darkness, which wasn't what her mother had expected. Sunny often visualized her sitting at the elementary school play, leaning in to a neighbor, and whispering, "See that little blond girl? Playing the fairy princess? That's my daughter! One day she'll grow up to be a corporate lobbyist for the largest gunmaker on the planet. I'm so proud!"

"Why don't you leave Cogsworth and go into business with your brother?" her mother went on. "No one's investigating his company."

True, Sunny thought. *Starving artisanal chocolatiers in Vermont have somehow managed to escape the attention of the DOJ.* "Mother," she said, twirling her hair. "Let's not do this."

"Do what?"

"I have to go to a meeting. I'll talk to you next week." Sunny knew that next week meant at least several weeks.

"Sunshine . . ."

There was an uncomfortable silence, the same one that had permeated nearly every conversation between Sunny and her mother since she'd left home that day long ago and shortened her name from Sunshine Liebowitz-McCarthy to the simpler Sunny McCarthy.

"Good-bye, Mother."

"I love you, Sunshine."

Sunny hung up on Lois Liebowitz.

6

B efore we begin," Congressman Dirkey said in his soothing Arkansas drawl, "may we pray?"

Sunny and Otis, sitting opposite Dirkey on one of
his office's enormous blue leather couches, exchanged
a quick glance, then followed the congressman in bowing their
heads.

"Lord Jesus, bless this meeting that we may be inspired by your
divine guidance. Give us the strength to deliberate in accordance
with your teachings. Bless our nation. Amen."

"Amen," mumbled Sunny and Otis, but as they lifted their eyes,
Dirkey continued.

"One more thing, Jesus. Please, Lord, help us defeat the Mc-
Cullom substitute amendment to the Coal Power Plant Tax Credit
Extension Act, which, as you surely know, is scheduled for a vote
later today. In your name, Jesus Christ, we pray. Amen."

Having sought divine intervention from above, Dirkey now set his eyes on the divine inspiration immediately in front of him. Sunny watched his gaze begin to slide down her blouse, catch itself, and return to her face. She dug her stilettos into the plush blue carpet and thought, *Not my idea of congressional oversight.*

Otis shifted restlessly next to her. He wouldn't stop his squirming, she knew, until his private jet went wheels up later that evening and he was a safe distance from the nation's capital.

Roy Dirkey's office was decorated in Dirkey. Beige walls displayed framed Dirkey action shots: Dirkey waving to a cheering crowd on election night; sitting across from the president in the Oval Office; speaking to school children in Little Rock; dominating a panel of freshmen representatives on the set of *Meet the Press.* On a separate wall, positioned above a mahogany credenza: Dirkey in mud-splattered Special Forces fatigues in Afghanistan; Dirkey in Oakley sunglasses, leaning against a Humvee, flashing a thumbs-up; Dirkey receiving the Purple Heart.

Sunny noticed that he'd kept his black hair trimmed neatly and still sported a ring from West Point. No wedding ring, she noted, but she already knew that from her research. Also noted was that when Dirkey smiled, he revealed a slight space between his two front teeth, conveying a sense of boyish amiability, and that when he was listening to someone, he cocked his head and narrowed his eyes as if to say, "*This* is the most important thing I've heard all day."

Morning prayers over, Dirkey approached the subject at hand. "Mr. Cogsworth," he said, "my daddy taught me how to shoot with your guns. It's an honor to meet you."

Otis cleared his throat. "Congressman, the honor is mine. It's refreshing to see someone in Washington who truly understands this country's Constitution."

Dirkey smiled, revealing, again, that space between his teeth. Goofy, thought Sunny, but approaching cute.

"Thank you, sir," he said. "When I was deployed to Afghanistan

I took my oath to protect and defend the Constitution. Got shot at for it. Thought if I could take on the Taliban in Helmand, I could take on a bunch of liberals in Congress." Here his jaw seemed to twitch, and his dark eyes grew sullen. "I'm sure you heard, Mr. Cogsworth, how I took that bullet in Helmand, and how Christ and the Constitution saved my life."

Sunny knew that Otis hadn't heard, although she included it in the briefing memo that Otis annoyedly tossed aside with a groan when she picked him up at the airport. So she leaned back and let Dirkey mesmerize her boss.

Dirkey slipped a hand into his jacket pocket and produced a pamphlet-sized Constitution. It was soiled and tattered, and right through the center was a bullet hole.

"Everywhere I went in Afghanistan," he explained. "I kept this pocket Constitution taped to my chest, close to my heart. One day we're defending a village down there in Helmand, walked straight into a Taliban ambush. Next thing I know, I'm shot. Bullet passes right through my body armor and my pocket Constitution. Just a flesh wound, as they say. But I believe the Constitution and the good Lord saved my life."

"Good Lord!" Otis echoed, clearly as moved as Sunny expected.

"That day," Dirkey said, "Jesus told me if I got out of Afghanistan alive, I should go back to Arkansas and run for Congress in the third district."

"Jesus said that, specifically?" asked Sunny, unable to help herself.

Dirkey nodded. "It's what I heard, ma'am."

I'm Jesus Christ and I approve this message, she thought.

Dirkey stared vacantly at his polished loafers for a moment, then refocused on his guests. "So what can I do for y'all?"

Sunny took that as her cue to get down to business. "Congressman, the Constitution is under attack again. Not by the terrorists, but by the Democrats in Congress who want to take guns away from law-abiding citizens."

"When will they learn?" Dirkey asked. "If they would only find Jesus—"

"If Jesus had a PAC, maybe," Sunny said. "But if the choice is the possibility of eternal salvation or the guarantee of the next reelection, I'm pretty sure salvation will wait."

Dirkey frowned.

"Do you remember the shooting in that school in Connecticut? In 2012?" Sunny asked.

"I do."

"After it happened, politicians raced to pass new anti-gun laws. Obama, the House, the Senate, governors, mayors—just about everyone. Except the city of Nelson, Georgia."

"Go on," said Dirkey. He leaned his body forward and folded his hands on his lap so that his gold cuff links peeked from his jacket sleeves.

"Nelson, Georgia, went the other way," Sunny continued. "They passed a local ordinance actually *requiring* their citizens to possess firearms."

Dirkey whistled. "Gutsy move."

Now Sunny leaned forward, too. "There's a Constitution in your pocket with a bullet hole that says you have guts yourself."

Sunny and Dirkey locked eyes and sized each other up. She felt Otis fidget beside her. Finally Sunny said, "We want you to introduce the Nelson city ordinance in Congress. Federalize it."

Dirkey whistled again. "You want a law requiring every American citizen to own a firearm?"

"I can promise you our allies will be with us on this, Congressman. Big time. Everyone from the NRA to the Annie Oakleys."

"Annie Oakleys?"

"Pro-gun Girl Scout troops. We funded a little outreach project. Emphasis on little."

Another whistle.

"We're creating a movement here, and we need a leader for that movement. Think of the visibility! Think of the opportunities!"

Sunny loved that word, *opportunities*. Spoken in a congressional office, it meant different things to different Members. It was an all-purpose word, meant to stoke the embers of whatever hidden agenda the Member nurtured. For some, it was to public good or good press. For others, better fund-raising or running for higher office, up to and including president. It was a word designed to activate congressional salivary glands and hasten the beating of congressional hearts.

So imagine her surprise when Congressman Roy Dirkey leaned back in his chair and said, evenly, "I'm honored you'd ask, but I'm gonna pass for now."

At this Otis stopped squirming. Actually, he seemed to freeze. Sunny fought to hide her surprise. "Really?" she asked. "We thought you'd jump at this."

Dirkey narrowed his eyes, rubbed his chin, and smiled slyly. "Not jumping right now, ma'am, but I'll give it some thought."

"Of course," Sunny said, regaining her composure. "How much time do you think would be reasonable?"

"Few days," Dirkey said, still rubbing his chin.

"Just so you know, we were planning to discuss the idea with Congressman Pratt."

Dirkey's toothy grin spread wide across his face. "From Kansas?" he cried. "Oh, he's your *man*! Heck, I may be on the Judiciary Committee, which has complete jurisdiction on guns, and he may be on the Small Business Committee, which has no jurisdiction whatsoever, but he's been here a whole lot longer than me. And while some of my colleagues say old Fred's run outta steam, he's highly respected for his—now what do they call it—institutional memory. So I believe you should give this to old Fred Pratt. If that's what y'all want."

Sunny sensed that something was clicking into place. Dirkey, she realized, wasn't some freshman hillbilly who just liked to put the shiny Member of Congress pin on his lapel every morning. He had an agenda of his own after all. And now he was pulling *her* in. She willingly took the bait.

"Well, Congressman, I think the question is, what do you want?"

He gave her a look of mutual understanding that only skilled political operatives recognize. "I'm leaning against. But I never make a final decision without prayerful consideration."

Thank you, Jesus, thought Sunny.

Sunny and Otis walked out of Dirkey's office into a broad marble corridor echoing loudly with wandering tourists and scurrying aides. Otis looked defeated. "Good Lord!" he whispered loudly. "What just happened? We lost him!"

Sunny smiled. "We didn't lose him. This guy knows what he's doing. He's dealing."

"But he said he's leaning against."

"Otis, in this town, leaning 'no' is just another way of saying yes."

"I'll never understand Washington," Otis grumbled.

It didn't take long. Just as Sunny had expected, the call came in a few hours.

"Ms. McCarthy? This is Natalie from Congressman Dirkey's office. The congressman was hoping to meet with you later to follow up on today's discussion. How's Acqua Al 2 at seven?"

Sunny arrived early and sat at a table in accordance with long established protocol that Members of Congress don't wait for anyone. They showed up late and were whisked into rooms, a stiff breeze of self-importance trailing behind them. The restaurant was dark and packed with the usual crowd of insiders, press, and pundits. They were all engaged in intimate conversations that bubbled to a dull roar, laced with sweet nothings like "motion to recommit," "markup," and "conferee." Large white dinner plates were mounted on the walls, autographed in neon Sharpie by celebrities making their public relations pilgrimages to Capitol Hill to prove that beneath the Botox was a heart that bled for orphans in Africa or sperm whales in the Atlantic.

Finally Dirkey arrived, flashed that waggish grin, and clasped Sunny's hand. She sensed his eyes commencing another cleavage dive, but, again, he caught himself. *Like some kind of recovering addict*, Sunny thought. He ordered a beer, prefacing it with "I'm just a country boy who doesn't know much about fancy drinks but, please, order whatever you want."

Sunny ordered a bourbon, which seemed to surprise the Arkansas country boy. Pleasantly.

They engaged in the customary niceties that preceded most conversations at Washington restaurants: the humidity outside, whether Republican Speaker of the House Frank Piermont would be overthrown by his caucus, and, of course, whether the Transportation Authorization bill would reach the floor before the Highway Trust Fund was fully depleted. Scintillating stuff.

When the drinks arrived, Sunny wondered whether an opening prayer was required. She was answered by the sound of guzzling from Roy's glass. Sunny eased into business and casually asked whether the congressman had considered her proposal.

"I did," he said, nodding. "And I have concerns."

"Would you like me to try to address them, Congressman?"

"You can call me Roy."

She nodded, smiled.

He pulled his chair forward, planted both elbows on the table, and leaned toward Sunny, hands partially obstructing his mouth in case, Sunny assumed, any journalists were sitting within earshot. "You want me to introduce a bill that will make me public enemy number one with the liberals and gun haters. The Hollywood and New York City crowd will spend whatever it takes to beat me next election."

Now we're getting somewhere, Sunny thought.

"And I will have the profound satisfaction of taking yet another bullet for the Constitution. Ms. McCarthy, I may be a war hero, but I am not the recipient of unlimited luck. When you survive one bullet, the rule of thumb is don't stick around for another."

He threw back a healthy gulp of beer.

"Congressman—"

"Roy," Dirkey reminded her.

"Roy," she said. "We'll defend you."

"What kind of defense are we talking about here, Ms. McCarthy?"

"Mr. Cogsworth would like to host a fund-raiser for you at his summer estate on Long Island. Our PAC, the Fund for Straight Shooters, will throw a DC fund-raiser for you this quarter. Also, as you know, Mr. Cogsworth sits on the board of the National Rifle Association. He's already made some calls. They're very fond of you."

"How fond?" asked Dirkey, tenting his fingers in front of his chest.

"National e-mail solicitation to their donor list fund," Sunny said. "Keynote speaker at their Golden Circle of Freedom Gala fond. And while I don't know for certain, there are rumors they're Super PAC fond. Rumors of a three-million-dollar television ad buy on your behalf in your district."

Roy nodded, stone-faced. "That's enough to chase out any opposition."

"It's enough to lock down your district for life."

To Sunny's annoyance, Roy seemed disinterested in the prospect. His eyes wandered to a nearby table, where CNN's Dana Bash listened to the whispering of a source she likely would soon describe on air as a "senior Democrat."

Sunny barreled on. "We'll build out national grassroots support. American Gun Owners Defense. Gun Owners of America. The Gun Owners Parent-Teacher Association. Gays for Guns."

Dirkey winced. "Not sure I like the last one."

"Maybe one day you'll run for president, Roy. Don't write off the gay vote."

Dirkey shrugged. "I have no interest in running for president."

Sunny laughed and arched an eyebrow to show she wasn't fooled. There wasn't one Member of Congress who didn't look in the mirror and see a future president staring back.

"I mean it," Dirkey said. "President? No, ma'am. This country can't be managed. Debt's exploding, Social Security's running dry, pensions can't be paid, terrorists running around everywhere." He took another swig of beer and leaned closer to Sunny, crossing the official border, Sunny acknowledged, between business and flirting. "Governor," he whispered, then looked around to ensure he hadn't been overheard. "That's the job for me."

Sunny suppressed a satisfied grin. She'd stoked the embers and found one that glowed a deep, hot red. "You'd be a great governor, Congressman. Time frame?"

"Three years. Just gotta get past my first reelect to the House."

She nodded. "Running for governor of Arkansas as the national leader on gun rights. Seems like a smart strategy, Roy."

He stared at her for a moment, then smiled. "You know I'm just a country boy from Arkansas. Never pretended to be smart."

"Don't play dumb with me," Sunny said, smiling. "I've figured you out." She meant it. She'd spent her career sitting across the table from politicians like this. Members of the House and members of the Senate. Members of the Democratic Party and members of the Republican Party. It didn't matter. As far as Sunny was concerned, they were all members of the "Me" Party, with love of country but greater love of self. Conniving and calculating; plotting and planning. Most arrived as Jimmy Stewart in *Mr. Smith Goes to Washington* and left as Machiavelli. Sure, she admitted, there were those who slaved to feed the poor, to put solar panels on every roof, to beat swords into plowshares. Those honorable few may have been revered, but they were irrelevant. They sat on the back benches, not across the table from Sunny McCarthy. The price of a seat with her was the ability to wheel, deal, and deliver, to understand that the world was shaped by brute power, not the power of ideals. It was a tragically unfair world where children were shot in Chicago and where the Otis Cogsworths lived safely behind gates on high bluffs while the Mother Teresas lived in squalid poverty. And where some mothers were too busy to care for their daughters.

Sunny finished her bourbon.

"So did you to speak to old Fred Pratt?" Dirkey asked. "About sponsoring the bill?"

"Oh, Roy, you know the answer to that."

"Mind if I order a bourbon?"

"You know the answer to that as well."

When his drink came, they toasted to the Constitution, the next governor of Arkansas, and to the American Freedom from Fear Act or, as they christened it, "AFFFA."

7

Mayor Michael Rodriguez's motorcade rolled through impoverished, boarded-up neighborhoods in West Garfield Park, resembling a military escort winding its way through Baghdad. Police barricades blocked intersections. The *thwap* of helicopters cut through a grim gray sky. Surplus military Humvees and armored vehicles idled at curbs. There were occasional bursts of gunfire. The Windy City was a war zone, its air acrid with gun smoke. The hottest items at the upscale boutiques on Michigan Avenue, about ten miles away, were Neiman Marcus flak jackets.

None of this seemed to faze the mayor. He sat in the backseat, staring out a darkly tinted window. No leg thumping or cursing. In fact, His Honor was in a rare good mood.

"What media's showing up?" he asked.

Next to him sat a pretty twentysomething press assistant. She wore horn-rimmed glasses and clutched two cell phones in one hand. "Oh, everybody, sir. CNN, MSNBC, Fox, SOSNews, all the broadcast networks. Your plan is sheer genius!"

"Yes, it is." His Honor smiled, another rarity.

John Ashcroft Elementary School was barely visible in the smoky haze ahead. Ashcroft, born in Chicago, had served as the attorney general of the United States, the highest law enforcement officer in the land. This was fitting because the school bearing his name now resembled a prison, with gloomy red brick, barred windows, and high fences coiled with razor wire. Security guards in neon yellow vests were posted on the perimeter, ready to offer students "safe passage" through potential crossfire. The motorcade rumbled into the parking lot, a snaking line of black armor and swirling lights, then came to a brake-squealing stop at the main entrance. Rodriguez sat motionless, waiting for the signal: three knocks on the door indicating it was safe to emerge.

"Let's do this!" he barked to no one in particular.

The air in the gymnasium was thick and asphyxiating from fresh coats of varnish applied the day before, thanks to a generous (and last-minute) grant from City Hall. The assembled media impatiently awaited Rodriguez's arrival. Two dozen mayors from across the country fidgeted on a multilevel platform like a chorus about to begin its spring concert. Mayor Donnelly from Boston was there, plus Hackenrush of Denver, Kim of San Francisco, and Swati D'Antonio-Serrano-Goldberg of New York. Finally, Rodriguez entered the gym to a smattering of obligatory applause. He centered himself opposite the phalanx of television cameras. He heard the urgent shuffle of the mayors behind him, squeezing their bodies into the range of the cameras. Rodriguez knew that nothing terrified a politician more than the cold-hearted crop of a photo editor. He tried to erase a wry smile. This was serious business: his declaration of war against guns.

This was his "Chicago Compact."

A standard political theory is "strength in numbers" (or, as Rodriguez thought, "Misery loves company"). Now Rodriguez would show his constituents that they weren't the only bull's-eyes on the block. Gun violence was a national crisis requiring a national response. And if the federal government refused to protect its citizens, a new alliance of local mayors would do it instead. Each signatory to the compact pledged to pass ordinances within their own jurisdictions to ban the sales of certain guns, bar the use of certain ammunition, and blackball any pension funds that invested in gun company stocks. They were aiming at the gun manufacturers' profit margins, an ever-widening target.

A parchment was spread on a blue-draped table next to Rodriguez. He swept a pen dramatically across the page. Then, one by one, the other mayors added their names, to the flashing of cameras inside the gym and the distant *pop-pop-pop* of gunfire outside.

When the ink was dry, Rodriguez ended the press conference with an invitation to other local officials to join the Chicago Compact. His call was heard across America, in big cities and small towns; in counties, villages, and parishes; urban, suburban, exurban; by commissioners, council members, supervisors, and mayors. From the West Coast all the way to a lonely living room in eastern Long Island, lit only by the dim flicker of an old television.

Late that night, Sunny McCarthy sat in her bed, draped in an oversized Washington Redskins T-shirt, staring at a grainy photo of Mayor Michael Rodriguez on her laptop. She was propped against a mountain of pillows. Her head was drooping, and her eyelids felt heavy. Twice already she'd drifted to sleep, only to be jolted awake by the memory of Otis Cogsworth's panicked voice over the phone earlier that evening. He'd been watching the channel-to-channel coverage of Rodriguez's outrageous Chicago Compact and handling a torrent of calls from board members woozy from the afternoon's roller-coaster ride of Cogsworth stocks. "This gun ban could kill us, Sunny," he'd told her gravely, as if it hadn't occurred to her. "When do we go on offense? Where's our legislation? When will President Do-Nothing sign it?"

"Otis—"

"Why can't we move any faster?"

Sunny had sighed. She could have explained that this particular Congress operated at one of two speeds: glacial and gridlock. She could have described the almost interminable process for introducing a bill, attracting sponsors and cosponsors, holding committee hearings and markups, negotiating language, considering amendments, whipping votes, voting in the House, then the Senate, sending the bill to the president, overriding a potential veto. However, the yipping on the other end of the phone didn't exactly suggest Otis had any patience for "Intro to the American Legislative Process." So she let him continue until finally he ended the conversation with an exasperated "Good Lord!"

Sunny had spent the rest of the evening plodding through her to-do list. Tomorrow—or was it already tomorrow?—she'd meet again with Congressman Roy Dirkey to discuss the official rollout of AFFFA. Meanwhile there was the matter of Mayor Michael Rodriguez. She'd already retained her favorite opposition research company, 3D Associates, part of the vast network of political operatives at her command. The Ds stood for Digging, Drilling, and Dredging. They'd use their mud-stained fingernails to pry open the scabs on Rodriguez's life, probing for signs of infection: late taxes, debts, defaults, assignations, litigation, speeding, jay walking. They'd drop a FOIA bomb, filing Freedom of Information Act requests on every government agency with possible records on the mayor, back to and including his kindergarten report card.

For now, Sunny's delicate fingers simply clicked through the Internet as she tried to get a vague idea of what 3D might track down. The life and times of Michael Rodriguez appeared on her screen: three separate grand jury investigations, two acquittals, one indictment that was dropped when it worked its way to some judge who was some other judge's brother-in-law. *So what else is new*, she thought. *It's Chicago*.

Sunny glanced at the cell phone on her nightstand, still flashing two unanswered calls from her mother. She yawned. Outside her bedroom window, a soft orange dawn slowly edged across the twinkling lights of DC. She moved her laptop aside, settled her head on the pillows, took a long, anxious breath, and closed her eyes.

She found herself standing in the old house in Asabogue, when she was eighteen. A setting sun cast the kitchen in a faint orange glow. On the yellow Formica counter steam swirled from a pizza recently delivered from Gino's Pizzeria, she and her brother Jeffrey's favorite restaurant. The sound of a raucous television audience drifted in from the living room, where Jeffrey was watching a children's game show. Directly in front of Sunny, the old kitchen table was buried under piles of her mother's work: black binders containing the Asabogue Village Zoning Code, maps, blueprints, stacks of Village Board agendas, faded newspaper clippings, tattered manila folders. Mother was moving piles across the table like a shell game, her arms whirling frantically.

Sunny quietly took a seat at the table and tried to sense an opening to capture her mother's attention. She struggled to get her words past a giant lump stuck in her throat, a lump that had been there since her father left years before. That was when Mother had gone from paralyzing sadness to a frenetic anger aimed at the rich and powerful, at everyone from warlords in Africa to landlords in Asabogue, at the thieves and cheaters, like that woman from the Bluff who took her husband away. Sunny knew that the outrage helped her mother overpower her misery, but it seemed to plow through other parts of her life as well. Sometimes when her mother was particularly distracted, particularly overcome with aggressive, righteous energy, Sunny pictured an angry wave from the nearby beach crashing into their home, then withdrawing, taking everything in its wake.

At the table Sunny twirled her hair. The nervous habit was acquired after her father left. Her nails were chipped and bitten. Mother didn't have time to take her for a manicure. Mother barely had time to plop a take-out dinner on the counter.

Finally Sunny said, "Mother, can we talk?"

Mother continued her work. "About what?" she asked distractedly.

"About Brad."

"Brad who?"

"Brad," Sunny said, trying to steady her voice. "My boyfriend, Brad. Brad McCarthy."

Mother paused. Her eyes met Sunny's for just a moment, then darted back to the table. "The one from the Bluff?" she asked. "He's just going to disappoint you, Sunshine. Believe me."

Now the lump in Sunny's throat cleared and she felt a surge of anger. The words spilled out. "Brad wants to get married."

Lois stood still, staring at the piles on the table, avoiding eye contact, her arms suspended momentarily in midair, as if she were a conductor about to cue her orchestra to begin. "We'll discuss it another time," she said at last. "I'm late for my meeting. Another big hardware store wants to open in town. As if Kripsky's isn't good enough." She resumed combing through piles, then said, "Stop playing with your hair, please."

Sunny's eyes fluttered open in her dark bedroom. She lay breathing, willing her pounding heart to slow, assuring herself of her surroundings, of the life she'd built on the ruins of her past. The laptop had been pushed precariously close to the edge of her bed. Groggily, she sat up, pulled a robe from a chair near her nightstand, wrapped it around her, and took note of her perfectly manicured nails. She stepped onto the balcony, high above the early stirrings of Washington. A warm breeze washed over her. A few taxis slowly roamed the otherwise empty streets below. She could hear the distant thunder of the first planes of the day taking off from Reagan National Airport.

She surveyed her domain, far from Asabogue.

She turned and went inside. She had work to do.

8

C ongressman, feel free to share your passion. In less than one hundred forty characters."

Roy Dirkey sat behind his lustrously polished desk and cocked his head at Sunny. The morning sun streamed through parted red drapes, falling ethereally on the congressman. The desk was cleared of everything but a dog-eared Bible and an untouched stack of legislative memos. A television suspended from the ceiling broadcast a live hearing of the temporary Select Investigative Panel on Planned Parenthood, its temporary mission now creeping into a second decade. Members spewed, scorned, pointed, and jabbed from a wide dais.

Dirkey's senior staff hovered nearby: the chief of staff, press secretary, deputy press secretary, and senior legislative assistant—all part of the large team that Dirkey assembled in his war for smaller government.

On the subject of large, Sunny noticed something about Team Dirkey. With the exception of a rather slovenly chief of staff, the assembled personnel—Ashlee, Katie, and Tiffany—had certain attributes that might not have been fully described on their curriculum vitae. Evidently, for Representative Dirkey, hiring inside the Beltway was decided a short way below the belt. This could be the Federal Office of Blond & Buxom.

"I still don't get why I'm going to announce the American Freedom from Fear Act in a tweet," Dirkey protested. "I was planning a major speech on the House floor."

"That's so Henry Clay," Sunny said. "Have you heard there's a new way of communicating? It's called the Internet."

"Real funny."

"It's all arranged," Sunny continued. "You'll do a tweet. The NRA will retweet it to their hundreds of thousands of followers. Then it goes viral."

"Then a speech on the floor?"

"Then a post on Facebook. We retained the best online consultants in politics: Daniel Webster Associates. They're expensive but totally worth it. They'll integrate digital platforms to build out a national audience. Drive search engine optimization, arrange list swaps, penetrate blogs, increase the number of followers and likes."

"But when do we do real press?" Dirkey asked. "The kind where I actually announce the bill and reporters actually report on it."

Sunny sipped from a bottle of water sourced in Dirkey's district, a place she mentally renamed Tepid Springs, and said, "You'll formally unveil AFFFA in an informal two-minute Web announcement. After we've built out our virtual community, you'll give the speech of your life. Roy Dirkey's Gettysburg Address!"

Roy winced. "We gave some good speeches on our side of the war, you know."

His staff nodded earnestly.

Sunny shrugged.

"In any event, when do I speak in Congress?"

"You don't. We have a much better venue."

"Arkansas!"

"Nope."

"Where, then?"

"Chicago. City Hall."

Roy whistled. "That's enemy territory. Will I have any air cover?"

"We made a few calls," Sunny said, smiling.

CNN anchor Beth Burroughs locked eyes with the camera. "A group calling itself Patriot Protectors is mobilizing on the border of Indiana and Illinois," she told her viewers, "reportedly to, uh . . . defend Chicago! CNN's Joe Cook is on the scene with an exclusive interview."

Joe Cook, dressed in a blue blazer and crisp khakis, stood in the parking lot of a dreary strip mall containing of a fast-food taco franchise, a Dollar Boots & Shoes, several vacant storefronts, and something called Big Bob's GunArama, fronted by a giant neon M16. A couple hundred people scurried behind him, dressed in military garb, brandishing firearms of all shapes, sizes, and types and loading crates of provisions onto an idling convoy of flatbed trucks.

"Joe," Burroughs said, "the last time I saw a scene like this was at the border of Kuwait and Iraq."

"That's right, Beth. Only it's not Kuwait. It's Stutsville, Indiana. And I'm with one town resident, Bob Stork of Big Bob's GunArama."

A very big Bob stood next to Joe. An NRA cap sat far back on Bob's bald scalp, and a black polyester polo shirt barely covered the pale overhang of his corpulent belly. He stared vacantly into the camera, his hands folded awkwardly at his crotch.

"Mr. Stork—"

"Bob. Owner of Big Bob's GunArama. Where our aim . . . is customer satisfaction." He smiled nervously.

Joe nodded briskly. "Okay, Bob. So tell us what's happening here."

Stork leaned heavily into the microphone. "What's happenin', Joe, is we're movin' out to protect women and children in Chicago now that the mayor up there just surrendered."

Behind them, a small crowd waved exuberantly at the camera. The 1970s hit "The Night Chicago Died" blared from loudspeakers.

"Surrendered?" asked Cook.

"Absolutely, Joe. His people are gettin' shot at and his answer is to take away their guns. What would you call it?"

"You seem heavily armed."

"Better be, Joe. You can't win a war with a peashooter. Need heavy artillery. Which we have at GunArama! Includin' the Cogsworth AR-15 Justifier, on sale this week."

Joe Cook was visibly annoyed at this brazen attempt at unpaid advertising. He put his hand on Big Bob's spongy elbow. Bob took an alarmed step back.

"Now," said Cook, "some would argue that what's happening in Chicago isn't war. It's crime. And that we should let trained police deal with that. How do you respond?"

Big Bob gave Joe a look that said *Can you get me someone from Fox News?* "What's happinin' in Chicago *is* a war," he replied. "And the crime is that innocent people are defenseless. If the government won't protect 'em, we will."

The crowd behind him cheered "USA! USA! USA!"

Joe Cook turned to the camera. "Brooke, you just heard it. Here in Stutsville, people seem to be taking matters . . . into their own hands."

The matters in their hands were handguns, shotguns, and rifles: single action, double action, semiautomatic; sporting and tactical; bolt, lever, and pump; five rounds, ten rounds, twenty and thirty. In walnut and maple, in black polymer and composite camo. They were made by Colt, Glock, Ruger, Remington, and Smith & Wesson. They were named "Protector," "Defender," and "Repulser." And the Cogsworth AR-15 "Justifier."

Available at Big Bob's GunArama.

While supplies last.

Sam Gergala walked in long strides down Main Street, hands dug into his jeans pockets, eyes fixed low on the redbrick sidewalk. Looking left or right on his way to work made Sam uncomfortable. What used to be Kripsky's Hardware was now the Wick & Whim. It sold scented candles and pricey signs made to look old and cheap proclaiming, LIFE'S A BEACH! and ASABOGUE USA! Tony's Barber Shop was now a sleek real estate office, its windows plastered with glossy photos of East End "compounds" and "retreats" featuring "waterfront vistas," "vineyard views," and something called "sexy free-form pools." Even Joan's Main Street Bakery had changed. Sam used to be able to walk in and order coffee and a buttered roll. Now it sold coffee in endless syllables that tied Sam's tongue. On Sunday mornings the rich descended from the Bluff to buy croissants and baguettes, then rushed back with their *New York Times* cradled under an arm. They wore Panama hats and flip-flops, and parked their open-air Jeeps and Range Rovers under shade trees that seemed to slump in sad resignation.

Sometimes, he'd duck into the stores just to stand on the original wood floors, stare at the tin ceilings, and sniff at the musty past. He'd recall how farmers used to plant their stained hands on the dusty glass counters and gab, how the starchy scent of potatoes would cling to their clothing. Today, Sam just kept walking. He wanted to get to Village Hall and organize things before Lois arrived.

He unlocked the door to Village Hall. The Old Sitting Parlor was fusty and dark. The floorboards groaned under his mud-caked boots. He switched on the recently repaired air conditioner, which seemed to hiss in protest before commencing a shallow whine and some weak gurgling. Then he reached toward the television mounted above the counter. It flickered onto the scene in Stutsville, a place far away and of no interest to Sam, especially given the local urgencies he'd planned to discuss with Lois this morning. There was the defective streetlight on Asabogue Bluff Lane. Joan's Main Street Bakery had submitted a special use permit for outside dining. The community fund was stalled at thirty-nine thousand dollars. Plus, Caitlyn Turner, the actress, was threatening a multi-million-dollar lawsuit if the village didn't remove the stop sign that she claimed had been arbitrarily planted near her front gate. This was a particular concern to Sam. He assumed that Turner's budget for Beverly Hills lawyers exceeded Asabogue's budget for, well, everything. He positioned several piles of paperwork for the mayor to review.

The front door opened. Sam realized his mistake.

In the past few weeks he'd noticed Lois's fixation on the news from Chicago. Her eyes would drift to the television and her thoughts would wander from Asabogue. Before long she'd pucker her lips, which, Sam knew, meant she was thinking about something unpleasant.

He stretched his long arms toward the TV's power switch, but it was too late.

"Good morning," Lois wheezed. Her face was flushed and glistening under her floppy beach hat. She hugged her ACLU tote bag to her heaving chest.

Sam dropped his arms and hoped that somehow the mayor wouldn't notice the news. "Good bike ride this morning, Mayor?"

"Not bad. That streetlight is still . . ." She gazed at the television and asked, "What's going on?"

Sam glanced at the Patriot Protectors boarding their vehicles. "Just some idiots playing army. We have a lot of work—"

Lois sat in a chair with a soft groan and stared miserably at the screen, cupping her chin in both hands.

"Turn it louder, Sam."

"That streetlight—"

"Sam."

They watched the coverage from Stutsville: Big Bob and Joe Cook, the brandishing of guns, the blaring of horns, the revving of engines.

CNN went to commercial. Never before had Sam been so relieved by an erectile dysfunction ad. But he saw that Lois's lips were so puckered that she seemed to be swallowing her own cheeks.

"Sam, this cannot continue," she said quietly.

When Lois said that something couldn't continue, it meant she was about to start something big. It could be a battle against a housing subdivision, a Taj Mahal replica, a chain drugstore, or maybe the entire gun industry.

"This isn't our business, Mayor," Sam said carefully. "Things are safe here."

"What about the rest of the country? America leads the civilized world in gun deaths."

"Let them figure that out in Washington."

"You and I both know that Washington won't solve this, Sam. We have to do this ourselves. Like those mayors who signed that Chicago Compact."

Sam focused on the smoothing of the piles, making sure there were no loose edges.

"Sam?"

He stared at the pile and listened to the rattle of the air conditioner and the ticking of a nearby clock. That clock had been on that wall ever since he was a boy, marking the uniquely slow passage of time in Asabogue, when the days seemed longer and the potato farms stretched to the horizon, when ordering coffee didn't involve more than two syllables, and guns were handed to sons with pride. He could still feel the warmth of the wood and texture of the grain. He could still see the glint of pride in his father's eyes.

"That's a bad idea, Mayor. We're not Chicago. People like their guns here."

"They don't need assault weapons here, Sam."

"Government starts banning some firearms, you never know where it stops."

Lois's eyes widened. "Oh, Sam. Now you sound like the NRA!"

There was a long and uncomfortable silence. CNN returned to its coverage of the caravan winding out of Stutsville, headed for Chicago.

"You go after our guns, you'll lose this town," Sam muttered. "You'll lose the year-rounders who stood by you all this time."

Lois narrowed her eyes on Sam, as if challenging him. "What about you, Sam? Do I lose you?"

He stayed silent.

For the next hour they tensely reviewed the business of Asabogue, the little village where ACLU tote bags and NRA Lifetime Membership cards mixed in an uneasy alliance.

9

They called it Gunstock.

Thousands drove to Chicago in a mid-June heat wave that brought the blacktop routes to a shimmer. They jammed the roads in a rumbling procession of spewing RVs, SUVs, motorcycles, and pickup trucks, from Stutsville, Indiana, and also Wisconsin, Iowa, Michigan, and as far away as Arizona and Florida. No matter where they came from, they had one view, plastered on their bumpers in various iterations:

MY OTHER AUTO IS A 9MM!
KEEP HONKING, I'M RELOADING!
BULLETS ON BOARD!

Twelve thousand people occupied Grant Park, penned between the tall gray office buildings lining one side, and the blinding sparkle of Lake Michigan on the other. They wore their hearts not on their sleeves but on T-shirts of all sizes and colors:

YES LADIES, I'M PACKING!
FROM MY COLD DEAD HANDS!
GOD, GUNS, GLORY!

Discordant music—Nugent, Springsteen, Skynyrd, and Greenwood—blared from hundreds of radios and from giant loudspeakers hoisted on steel columns on a large white tented stage in front of the lake. They planted flags that drooped in the searing heat, revived only by the occasional tepid breeze. The flags were red, white, and blue; bright yellow, sprouting like dandelions, warning, DON'T TREAD ON ME; and black flags with thick white letters that read COME AND TAKE IT! They cooked on portable grills, filling the air with the scent of lighter fluid, charcoal, and sizzling meat. They dug their arms deep into ice-filled coolers of beer. Vendors sold survival gear, holsters, scopes, and souvenirs on card tables. There were also complete selections of ammunition in different shapes and calibers: soft point and armor piercing; lead round nose and full metal jacketed; 12-gauge shotshell, 8mm Mausers, .38 Specials, .44 Magnum, .45 Colt Pistol, .22 Long Rifle. The bullets were lined up like miniature rockets on a launchpad, the sun glinting off the brass, nickel, and steel casing. "All bullets kill, but some bullets kill better than others," a vendor bellowed.

So many organizations converged on Chicago that day. From AGL (American Gun League) to ZAG (Zionist Americans for Guns). There was GROAN (Gun Rights Owners Action Network), and GROWL (Gun Rights Owners Women's League). The Second Amendment Foundation was there, along with the Second Amendment Institute and the Committee for the Second Amendment but Not the Sixth. There were Mothers Against Gun Control and Grannies Against Gun Control, Armed Paraplegics of America, and the Armed Postal Workers Union Local 42, AFL-CIO. There was the TSA Watchlist Gun Rights Network, plus a distinctly small but noticeable group called Nuns With Guns (NWG).

The CPD (Chicago Police Department) showed up as well, dressed in their riot gear finest. They positioned themselves in a perimeter defense around the park, like nervous observers at a high school dance. They realized that if all hell broke loose, they were massively outgunned. And out-acronymed.

A few blocks away Mayor Michael Rodriguez, who had by now returned to his natural state of agitation, sneered at a video feed in the Crime Command Center. He pounded his feet to a stream of multilingual muttering. It was like a Santana concert.

Sitting beside him, the city counsel opined, "Not a prudent combination. The purchase of beer and bullets on city property, I mean."

"Then why the fuck did you issue assembly permits?" snapped the mayor.

Learned counsel considered the question through several puffs of his pipe. "They do have the right to protest, Mr. Mayor, do they not?"

"I do have the right to return you to the Zoning Board of Appeals. Do I not?"

Counsel's thick pink lips slumped around his pipe.

Roy Dirkey sat on a metal folding chair behind the Gunstock stage, nervously fanning himself with a hard copy of the most important speech of his career. He'd been guzzling from water bottles, but his throat itched and his forehead percolated with sweat. Plus there was that noose-like clenching of his neck muscles. *I'd rather be in Afghanistan*, he thought, and reached for more water.

Gunstock organizers in headsets and black T-shirts rushed around in the hot, dim space around him, shouting orders over a voice that blared onstage. Dirkey's Divas stood nearby, studying e-mails and exchanging anxious glances. Sunny sat across from Dirkey in a short floral skirt, her hair tied back.

"Ready?" she asked.

"Ready," Dirkey replied as bravely as he could. But his voice quivered. Sunny leaned forward, gently squeezed his arm, and said, "Remember. Just be yourself, speak from the heart . . . and read it exactly the way I wrote it." She gave a small laugh, triggering a weak smile from Dirkey.

Hours of rehearsals had nearly broken the congressman. Sunny forced him to fit his slack tongue around her sharp words; to say "freedom" instead of "fraaay-dum" and "you" instead of "y'aaaalllll." She barked at him to "speed it up" and then to "slow down," as if he were shifting gears in a sputtering old car. She adjusted his body language, pestering him to "stand straight, but not like that, you look like a Nazi." During one frustrating practice, Sunny remarked, "I wrote a Winston Churchill speech that's being read by Gomer Pyle."

Onstage, Dirkey heard Jack Steele readying the crowd for his national debut. The Borscht Belt once had Georgie Jessel, the Bullet Belt had Jack Steele. For the past hour Steele had been introducing warm-up acts: obscure politicians, minor celebrities, and several pro-gun musical acts including the favorably received heavy metal band Sweating Bullets. Now Dirkey watched as Steele raised his arms to quiet the audience.

"Friends! Are you ready to meet a real patriot?"

"Ready!" the crowd hollered in unison.

"You know, we got a bunch of people over there in Washington—"

Booing rolled across the crowd.

"In three branches of government," Steele went on. "Gutless, useless, and clueless! All three could repeal the Second Amendment in the bleeding heartbeat of a liberal! Good news is, there's one guy who knows a little something about our Constitution . . . Took a bullet for it in Afghanistan! Please welcome CONGRESS-MAN! ROY! DIRKEY!"

Dirkey summoned a smile, trying to ignore the tremors across his cheeks. Sunny brushed a hand across his back as he stepped on-stage. He was assaulted by the sweltering air, the blinding sun, the deafening roar, and by Jack Steele, who wrapped the congressman in a bear hug that squeezed his ribs and lifted him a few inches off the ground. Roy grunted, and Jack set him down.

"Knock 'em dead!" Jack rasped into Roy's ear. Then, "But do it fast. I have a plane to catch."

Roy tugged at his blue suit jacket—no tie, Sunny had advised—and stepped up to the podium. He squinted at the heaving mass of bodies that stretched across Grant Park, whooping and yelping, stomping their feet and creating a thick haze of dust in the stagnant air. Roy placed his sweat-smudged speech on the podium and adjusted the microphone.

He caught Sunny peering at him from just offstage. She was twirling her hair.

"Thank you!" he bellowed, surprised at the thunder of his own voice, which seemed to bounce off the distant buildings and shake the entire park. He waited for the crowd to quiet, then resumed soberly. "There are so many important people to recognize here. But one in particular. My most important leader . . . Ladies and gentleman, whatever your affiliation or faith may be in this land of religious liberty, please join me in thanking Our Lord, Jesus Christ."

The crowd clutched their guns and bowed their heads, all except for the RAG (Rabbinic Assembly for Guns), who seemed uncertain.

Dirkey continued. "Now, I may just be a country boy from Arkansas, but I do know a little something about Chicago. America's first skyscraper was built here. Route Sixty-Six began here.

Abraham Lincoln was nominated here. And today, here in Chicago, you and I will make history again. We won't build a skyscraper, we won't nominate a president. But we will keep the American people safe. Once and for ALL!"

The crowd roared as one. Fists pumped.

Just as practiced, Dirkey breezed through the story of the brave pioneers who settled Chicago, of how they crossed mountains and rivers, settled on farms and tilled fields, paved roads and built skyscrapers, how the generations that followed crossed oceans, stormed beaches, and made the world safe for democracy. "And through it all," Dirkey declared, "Americans have always kept two things at their sides. GOD . . ."

He paused, raised his right hand in a tight fist.

". . . and GUNS." Dirkey punched quickly at the air. "GOD!" he repeated, punching on each word. "AND! GUNS! GOD! AND! GUNS!"

The sprawling crowd responded exactly as Sunny had promised they would. The chant was slow and scattered at first, then it built like merging waves and crashed resoundingly onto the stage, sweeping over Dirkey: "GOD AND GUNS! GOD AND GUNS! GOD AND GUNS!"

Dirkey allowed the chant to peter out. Now he went on to paint a different picture of America, one of crime-infested cities, terrorists lurking in communities, students walking in fear to school. The nation that won the Cold War was now in a cold sweat, intoned Congressman Dirkey. "And how do the liberals propose to keep our children safe? Well, I'll tell ya! SURRENDER! Arm the criminals and disarm America! SURRENDER! Give up our guns and retreat from our streets! SURRENDER! Go from the home of the brave . . . to cowering in our homes!"

Contemptuous boos filled the air.

In the Crime Command Center, Rodriguez was now shattering the world record for foot thumping.

Dirkey trumpeted, "Here's my message to them: WE are Americans. We do NOT surrender! WE are Americans. WE fight back! WE are Americans. WE don't wave the white flag. WE wave the red, white, and blue!"

Gunstock erupted into a deafening cacophony of war cries, high-pitched shrieks, and primitive grunts. Dirkey noticed that even some of the police were agreeably nodding their heads. He stole a glance at Sunny, now grinning offstage. He rocked back from the microphone and waited. Sunny had told him that it wasn't a speech, it was a seduction. You don't read the words, she'd said, you read the audience. They'll tell you when to continue and when to pause, when to whisper and when to shout. Pay attention to the way they pitch forward to devour the next word, or lean back to chew on what they heard, how they cup their chins or nod their heads, how their eyes narrow or widen. Then, when you own them, she said, you make them beg for more. So he waited, for what seemed like forever, as the crowd went from a hot boil to a smolder. He lowered his voice, forcing them to quiet themselves, as if to ensure that not a single word escaped into the hot air and drifted into Lake Michigan.

Then he announced that he was returning to Congress the next day to introduce the American Freedom from Fear Act. He demanded that the Speaker of the House pass it *immediately* (a word seldom spoken by the Speaker) and that the president sign it. Then came the rhetorical jab that had always brought delicious giggles to Sunny in their rehearsals. It was the ultimate punch line, hitting right at the sentimental soft spot of the anti-gun Left.

"You know, a, uh, great Democrat"—even now Roy's tongue stumbled over the words *great* and *Democrat* so close together—"a great Democrat once said, 'The only thing we have to fear is fear itself.' Well, he was right then. And he's right now. America, we will be FREE FROM FEAR!"

He pounded his fist on the podium.

"FREE FROM FEAR!" he repeated, with another pound of his fist.

He kept pounding, just as Sunny taught him, like a drum major establishing the rhythm, until the twelve thousand people all across Grant Park, men, women, children, in midwestern twangs and southern drawls, in dialects and accents from around the world, chanted with him:

"FREE FROM FEAR! FREE FROM FEAR! FREE FROM FEAR!"

"God bless y'all," Dirkey shouted as loud as he could, but his words were swallowed in the approving roar.

He swept his arms in wide triumphant arcs as he ambled off the stage. Just before exiting, he stopped, fixed his hands on his hips, and turned toward the crowd. He soaked in their adulation, the surging of their bodies toward him, the ringing of twelve thousand voices, the judder of the stage beneath him. He felt an inescapable gravitational pull between leader and followers, a surge of adrenaline intoxicated by hundred-proof power. Dirkey waved his final farewell, arms thrust high above his head, fingers splayed. He stepped off the stage.

Before Sunny could say a word, he wrapped his arms around her and pulled her in. "I did it!" he said, hoarse and breathless. The sweat on his face brushed against her cheeks; his lips pressed briefly against hers.

She was speechless.

All the next day, the words "Freedom From Fear!" crawled across the bottom of America's televisions, accompanied by images of Roy Dirkey in his army uniform. Newspapers printed "FREEDOM FROM FEAR" on front pages, in type size previously reserved for "MAN WALKS ON MOON!" There were editorials insisting that Congress and the White House drop whatever they were (not) doing and blaze AFFFA to passage.

The *New York Times* also noticed. They ran a story headlined "GUN RIGHTS RALLY IN UNLIKELY VENUE." It was on page A15, under a story about an Army Corps of Engineers project threatening something called the bog turtle. The article failed to mention that the U.S. Congress was about to consider a new law requiring every man, woman, and child in America to carry a gun.

10

Three days after Roy Dirkey's speech—hailed by Sean Hannity as "perhaps the greatest oration in Illinois since the Lincoln-Douglas debates"—Mayor Lois Liebowitz rapped her gavel against the old wooden dais in the meeting room at Village Hall and called the Asabogue Village Board to order.

The room seemed airless, baked by a sun beating through old, thin windowpanes. A coffee urn gurgled next to now-empty cartons of jelly donuts that had been donated by Joan's Main Street Bakery. Behind the dais a bright orange banner was stretched across the wall, bearing the village seal: a Native American clasping hands with a white settler, above the Latin words "Nos Relinquens." Loosely translated it meant, "We're outta here!"

Even before the meeting began, many of Lois's fellow board members were, well, bored members. They shuffled in and slumped into worn leather chairs. Their eyes were glazed and their heads drooped. Lois thought it might be a quick meeting because her colleagues would want to hurry home for the *Golden Girls* marathon later that afternoon, but Councilman Ralph Kellogg was in no such rush. He took his usual seat, appropriately at the extreme right of the dais. He leaned forward, ready to pounce on any evidence of corruption, conspiracy, or crime by the Liebowitz administration.

Get ready, Lois thought.

A handful of residents scraped metal folding chairs against the wood plank floors as they sat. It was the usual crowd: the curmudgeons and critics, the watchdogs and gadflies, united that stifling day by the powerful combination of free jelly donuts and nothing better to do with their time. Lois noticed that no one from Billionaires Bluff was present, probably due to the fact that there were no proposals to place stop signs near their gates or limit the height of their hedgerows.

Usually, Sam Gergala mingled with residents, draping his long arms over their shoulders, laughing at their jokes, and scurrying back and forth to the dais to make sure Lois had everything she needed. Today, however, he sat sullenly in the front row, staring blankly ahead, avoiding eye contact with Lois.

Next to him was Petey Scrafel. At age twenty-two, Petey was editor in chief, high school sports reporter, and director of advertising and circulation at the *Asabogue Bugle*. He also happened to be the publisher's son. He was tall and gangly. The last vestiges of acne were slowly retreating from his forehead under tangled clumps of curly blond hair. Petey aspired to one day write for the *New York Times*. For now, it was "all the news that's fit to print" in six pages once a week.

They recited the Pledge of Allegiance—Councilman Kellogg's voice boomed at "under God" as usual—and proceeded to the official agenda. They "wherefored," "whereased," and "resolved" their way through the meeting. By consistent votes of four to one, they authorized the mayor to procure road salt for the coming winter ("American salt or foreign salt?" Ralph Kellogg demanded to know); they approved a storage shed on the property of Al and Wendy Knickrehm; and they permitted limited outdoor seating at Joan's Bakery (which explained the complimentary donuts that day, a possible act of bribery that Councilman Kellogg seemed to ignore, as evidenced by the powdered sugar clinging to his mustache).

They reached the end of the agenda. Lois heard her colleagues push back their chairs.

"Hold on," she said. "I have one more matter."

She passed across the dais copies of a resolution she'd typed herself earlier: Village Board Resolution 52: Authorizing the Mayor to Execute an Agreement Re: Chicago Compact.

"What is this?" Councilman Kellogg asked indignantly. Flakes of donut powder fell from his mustache like light snow.

Lois answered, "It's just an intermunicipal agreement to—"

"To ban guns in Asabogue!" Kellogg said, his voice rising.

"To ensure public safety," Lois responded calmly.

Ralph thumped his fists on the dais, jolting everyone in the room. His cheeks turned bright red. He stood slowly, the fists pumping, jowls quivering in rage.

Sam Gergala also stood, ready to move protectively toward the mayor.

"Wake up, people!" Councilman Kellogg boomed, his voice rattling the windowpanes. "Don't you realize what she's doing? It's just like Ted Nugent said! Raping the Constitution! Urinating on the vision of our Founding Fathers!"

The audience stirred uncomfortably. Outdoor dining and domestic road salt were one thing, but raping the Constitution and urinating on the Founders certainly seemed to exceed the jurisdiction of the Village Board.

Lois stared forward, puckering slightly. She clenched her fingers around the gavel and said, "Thank you, Councilman Kellogg. Now, let's vote. All in favor?"

Lois was joined by three somnolent "ayes."

"Opposed?"

"Noooooo!" Ralph thundered, alone.

"The motion carries."

Lois clacked the gavel and pretended not to notice Ralph Kellogg's tightening fists and crimson cheeks. His eyes narrowed menacingly, but he said nothing.

The next morning, Otis enjoyed breakfast in the solarium while watching CNBC, and thought, *My troubles are over.* There were no mentions of federal investigations into Cogsworth, the American Freedom from Fear Act had enjoyed favorable coverage, and the prospect of a new national law requiring Americans to buy guns was having a salutary effect on Cogsworth stocks. On the screen, some unknown Member of Congress was blathering about the trade deficit with China in the cavernous rotunda of a congressional office building. His words ricocheted off marble columns and echoed in his own ears, ensuring, Otis supposed, that he was making sense to at least himself. Otis's bagel was perfectly toasted to a golden brown. The sun warmed the beach. CNBC warmed his heart. It was a good and peaceful morning.

Then the phone rang.

Otis heard Andre's muffled voice, then rapid footsteps against ceramic tile.

"It's Mr. Steele, sir," said Andre anxiously. "He says it's urgent."

Good Lord, thought Otis. He picked up the phone. "Hullo, Jack."

"Have you read this morning's *Bugle*?" asked Steele in his signature rasp.

Of course. I begin every day with the Asabogue Bugle. *Then, if there's time, I turn to the* Wall Street Journal *and the* Economist. "No," said Otis.

"Christ, man! Don't you know what's happening in your own backyard?"

Otis scanned his own backyard. The ocean horizon was shrouded in a serene morning haze. "Tell me," he said resignedly.

"That woman! She just dropped a bomb right down our stove-pipe!"

Otis blinked.

"The village is signing that Chicago Compact! Banning your guns! Going after your stocks. Right in your hometown!"

Jack Steele rattled on about Lois Liebowitz's threat to civilization, but Otis tuned him out and slumped in his chair. Otis didn't really care about civilization. Otis's concerns were of a more personal nature. He imagined the conversation at the National Association of Firearms Manufacturers annual golf outing. *That's right, I'm from Asabogue*, he heard himself saying. *The little town that banned my product and tanked my stock. But the beach is nice and property values have held steady. May I play through?* He groaned into the phone. "I'd better have my people look into this."

"Look into it? Sure, Otis, that's what I always did. When the terrorists had me hanging out of an airplane at thirty thousand feet, I looked into things."

"What do you suggest?"

"The Jack Steele way, my friend. None of this eye for an eye bullshit. You take out my eye, I chop off your head. With my good eye."

Otis wondered from which Jack Steele film that line came. Or was it Shakespeare?

"Otis, I'm getting rid of Liebowitz."

"Jack—" Otis hoped Steele wasn't talking about what he thought he was talking about, and yet he wouldn't put it past Steele.

"I'm taking her out!" he said with a snarl.

"Good Lord, Jack! You can't!"

"Christ, Otis, calm down! I'm not gonna kill her. I mean, physically. It's gonna be legal. By the books. My lawyers found the solution right there in the Village Code."

"I'm listening."

"A recall election. All you need is five hundred signatures on a petition to recall the mayor, and an election is mandatory." He pronounced *mandatory* with relish, drawing out each syllable and clicking on each consonant. "We get her out of Village Hall and put in one of our own."

Otis assumed that "one of our own" would be Jack's protégé, Ralph Kellogg. He winced, then asked, "How long do we have?"

"Couple of weeks. If we get those signatures, the recall election is in November. We'll bring in the top political operatives. Spend whatever it takes. I need your best people. You in?"

Otis briefly considered the potential indelicacy of asking Sunny McCarthy, his best operative, to help "remove" her mother. Then he mumbled, "Yeah, I'm in."

"Carpe diem!" Jack barked.

Fade to black, Otis thought.

11

I n the Capitol dining room reserved for Members of Congress and guests, Roy Dirkey bowed his head, clasped his hands, and said grace. Sitting across from him, Sunny ungracefully peeked at her e-mails.

Sunny regarded the Members' Dining Room as one-star dining for five-star egos. It was regally adorned in gold and blue and brightened by a crystal chandelier that sparkled from a high ceiling. It was crowded with Members of Congress chewing the fat, literally, at white-linen tables. Nearby, the lobbyist for the American Council of Big Oil and the chairman of the House Ways and Means Committee devoured slathered heaps of pork sausages, with a generous helping of tax subsidies on the side.

Famous on the menu was the navy bean soup. According to congressional lore, in the early 1900s, Speaker of the House Joe Cannon requested the soup for lunch. When told it wasn't available that day, the tyrannical Speaker ordered that navy bean soup appear on the menu every day until the end of days. Suffrage and civil rights would wait. But the right of the people to slurp overly salted brown glop would not be denied or delayed.

After a quick "Amen," Roy started on his bacon and eggs. Sunny noticed his eyes narrowing on every forkful and the forceful bobbing of his jaw, as if he was rushing through a meal ready-to-eat before battle.

Between gulps, he shared the parts of his bio that didn't make the *Congressional Directory*.

His father had owned Dirkey Chevrolet, known throughout North Little Rock for its interminable, grating commercials: Roy Sr. dressed as Dirkey the Duck, quacking into the camera about Dirkey Deal Days as the feathers of his low-budget costume flittered in the air. Roy wanted to join the military to serve his country and, he admitted, avoid taking over a business that required him to quack on TV. He secured a congressional nomination to West Point, graduated, then deployed to Afghanistan. Within a year he returned to a hero's welcome in Bentonville, where running for the House fulfilled his lifelong dream of not running Dirkey Chevrolet. "I guess I found the one job less popular than a used car salesman," he said, "I'm a Member of Congress."

Sunny was sure he'd used that line before.

Roy seemed momentarily lost in a life-size oil painting that dominated a far wall. It was Constantino Brumidi's depiction of the British surrender to George Washington. Sunny thought that the Brits looked positively happy to be leaving America. Washington, on the other hand, wore the severe grimace of someone who knew what a shitstorm awaited. Or, maybe he knew about the navy bean soup.

Roy said, "I keep pinching myself that I'm here. I mean, if someone had told me that I'd be in Congress, I never would have believed it. I guess this is exactly the democracy our Founders had in mind."

Sunny shrugged. "That's one theory. I have another."

He cocked his head.

She sipped some coffee, which had grown stale and cold. "The guys in that painting basically didn't like paying high taxes to the king. But, they had a problem. They couldn't recruit an army willing to fight the most powerful military on earth on a 'tax and spend' message. So they sprinkled in some 'inalienable rights,' a dash of 'all men are created equal,' and a pinch of 'we the people.' Of Thomas Jefferson's many inventions, political spin was his greatest."

Roy looked hurt. "That's pretty cynical, isn't it?"

She thought, *You're in the U.S. Capitol. They sell cynicism snow globes in the gift shop.*

Roy pushed his now-empty plate forward. "So, I told you the story of my life. When do I hear yours?"

Sunny drained the last of her rancid coffee and said, "I could use a refill."

"C'mon now," he coaxed.

She sighed. She needed to prepare Dirkey to unveil AFFFA to the entire Republican Caucus the next morning. At the moment, however, he clearly had other interests. *Let's get this over with*, she thought. She whisked back her hair and lowered her eyes to the empty coffee cup.

"I was married, but we didn't make it to our second anniversary. Name was Brad. I lived on the poor side of the tracks, his family had their own helicopter pad. Brad's father was managing partner at a white-shoe law firm. Daddy-in-law, by the way, did not do commercials dressed as any sort of waterfowl."

Dirkey laughed. Sunny traced the lip of her coffee cup with her index finger.

"Anyway, we moved to Manhattan. Brad went to work for his father, who pulled some strings and got me a job at a PR firm that handled crisis management for his . . . special clients. Special, as in under investigation by the U.S. Attorney, the SEC, the IRS, you name it. You think Afghanistan was tough, Congressman? Try image rehab for a hedge fund billionaire with a twenty-one-count indictment for tax fraud."

"Bet you nailed it," Roy cooed.

"That particular client eventually had to deny rumors of pending sainthood."

She waved at a waitress, who waved back cheerfully, not quite grasping the international signal for "more coffee."

"So what happened? With Brad?"

"We had our differences. So dear old daddy-in-law flew us to the Dominican Republic for an all-inclusive weekend, including a quickie divorce. I got a decent payout and some very lucrative client referrals, including Cogsworth International Arms."

"That was generous."

"Noooo. Those were my demands. I learned that Brad the fair-haired son was screwing Stephanie the big-boobed summer associate. So I turned what could have been a very ugly trial into a beautiful settlement. As they say, the rest is"—she pointed at the painting—"history!"

Dirkey nodded his head sadly. "I'm sorry."

"I'm not. It's worked out nicely."

Sunny turned toward the nearby table. She watched the Ways and Means chairman shake hands with the oil company lobbyist and wondered just how much that little breakfast was costing the U.S. Treasury. She calculated about thirty dollars for the meal and ten billion for the deal.

"So who's the future First Lady of Arkansas?" she asked abruptly, sending the conversation back to Roy.

He smiled, revealing that subtle space between his teeth. "For me, marriage is a sacred institution. I'm just waiting for the right one."

Sunny noticed his eyes lingering on her. It wasn't the usual leer, but more of an evaluation. She wondered whether Dirkey might be imagining her in some kind of below-the-knees, pastel Sunday church getup, surrounded by five mini Dirkeys whom she would chauffeur to Bible class on her way to delivering homemade cupcakes to the United Daughters of the Confederacy bake sale.

I'm not that kind of woman, buddy.

Her thoughts were interrupted by the soft ping of her phone. She glanced at URGENT in the subject line and scanned the text.

She blurted, "I'm going to kill her."

"Who?"

"I have a situation. Back in two minutes."

Sunny rushed into a dimly lit corridor, its high vaulted ceiling muraled with American history scenes. She read the e-mail again, under an image of the British burning down the Capitol in 1814, which seemed appropriate given the fire in her chest.

To: SBM@Cogsworth
From: BIG-GUN@Cogsworth

Sunny—see attached *Bugle* article about your mother. Good Lord!! This will get messy. I know you're in a tough position. If continued work on AFFFA is a problem, I understand.

She thought, *"I understand"? That's what they say when they don't understand! A patronizing tap on the head. "I understand you won't be able to work with us, little girl. Not to worry, we'll find someone else with, shall we say, more suitable familial ties. Now, go away and let the big boys take it from here. Understand?"*

Each word from the *Asabogue Bugle* article churned in Sunny's stomach. Her usual crisp and cold-blooded thinking was turning slow and molten. She folded her arms, leaned against a wall, and struggled to manage her anger. She watched an intern guide tourists up a wide marble stairway known as "the Bloody Steps," pointing to faint splotches of blood dried into the marble. Sunny had heard all the legends, conspiracy theories, and ghost tales, but loved the real story of a nineteenth-century public relations crisis.

In 1890, a newspaperman was reporting on the serial scandals of Kentucky congressman William Preston Taulbee. One day, Taulbee decided to add his own spin, literally, by shoving the reporter in a corridor just outside the House chamber. The journalist scurried from the Capitol to the taunting of Taulbee and his colleagues. Hours later, he returned with his gun, and on those very steps, shot the gentleman from Kentucky in the eye.

Sunny stared at the stains, imagined the scene: the blast echoing through the austere halls of the Capitol, the screams of the bystanders, the acrid odor of gunpowder. She visualized Taulbee, staggering down the steps, clutching his face, blood pouring through his fingers and splattering on the marble, soaking in to become an indelible exhibit on guns in the People's House. American history was displayed on the high painted ceilings above, and soaked into the marble steps underfoot.

She remembered that Taulbee's killer was acquitted on grounds of self-defense.

Sunny took some deep breaths.

You can manage this.

Take control.

She poked Otis's number on her cell phone.

"This is Ot—"

"I'm resigning," she snapped.

"Whoa—"

"No, Otis. If you don't think I can do my job on AFFFA, fine! I'm done. I'm sure your barely competent nephew Bruce can take it from here!"

"Sunny—"

"It's truly been a privilege, Otis. Now I think I'll go to work defending child slavery. That's a challenge I'm up to."

Sunny imagined the sweat trickling down Otis's puffy red cheeks as he struggled to find the right words, pressing his fingers to his wide forehead. She began counting to herself, until Otis finally blurted, "Good Lord, I was just trying to . . . be sensitive."

Sunny burst into that prolonged spitfire laugh, which rattled through the corridor. "Otis, you're good at some things. Being sensitive isn't one of them. So let me be clear: I do not let my mother's politics affect my business. And my business happens to be keeping you in business. Do you understand?"

"I understand."

"Good! Just one more thing."

"Okay."

"Never say 'I understand' again."

Sunny returned to the Members' Dining Room.

12

S peaker of the House Frank Piermont puffed on his fifth cigarette of the day, and it was only 7:45 AM.

He sat in the rear seat of a smoke-filled SUV, accompanied by a two-person security detail that was required to take regular lung X-rays. Piermont was in his usual position: clamping a cigarette to his lips with one hand and a cell phone to his ear with the other. The security detail informally called him "Two-fisted Frank," but his official code name was "Smokestack."

That morning, Smokestack was repeating into the phone "No way, no way, no way," through gurgling hacks.

On the other end, his chief of staff said, "But sir, it's a political grand slam."

"No way!" the Speaker insisted.

The "grand slam" was the introduction of the American Freedom from Fear Act by the distinguished gentleman from Arkansas (who wasn't distinguished enough for Piermont even to recognize his name). The bill would be discussed at that morning's breakfast meeting of the House Republican Caucus.

"Forcing people to own guns is just . . . well . . . it's nuts," Piermont whined. He immediately regretted the use of the word *nuts*. In that session of Congress, *nuts* had become the most overused word in his vocabulary. The entire caucus was marching off the deep end, and that end was far to the right. He often groused privately to friends, "Yeah, I'm Speaker of the House. The nuthouse!"

"Mr. Speaker—"

"Your grand slam has four strikes against it. One, arming every American is dangerous public policy. Two, even if we pass it, the Senate won't. Three, even if they do, the president will veto it. Four, even if he signs it, the Supreme Court will strike it down. So it's a total waste of time!"

Hack-gurgle-wheeze.

"Exactly, sir. This will never make it into law. Which is exactly why we should pass it immediately."

"Huh?"

"Look, Frank"— the staffer only called his boss Frank when they weren't within earshot of anyone else—"we're getting real close to losing the Speaker's gavel. The talk grows louder about a coup against your own leadership—I don't want to say they're vultures, but they're practically building nests next to your bed. Our conservative Members think you're a sellout."

"Because I negotiate? Because I compromise? The moderates still support me."

"There aren't enough of them to fill a Members Only elevator. Our caucus is breaking apart. We can't agree on taxes, spending, war, peace. But we do agree on one thing, Frank. Guns. Guns make us . . . us! Guns keep our caucus united. Behind you!"

Piermont expelled enough foul air to receive an EPA fine under the Clean Air Act.

"And it's not just our caucus, Frank. We need something to

excite our base. Give 'em a reason to vote in the midterm elections. We throw them a gun rights issue and they'll stampede to the polls. We expand our majority and you keep the gavel. With no chance that the Dirkey bill actually becomes law. It's just a message piece."

"Just a message piece," Piermont repeated. He gazed out the dark windows at the Capitol dome a few blocks away. In a few weeks, he thought, Congress would mercifully leave Washington for the July Fourth recess, when it would manage to do slightly less work than when it was in session. He took a long, hard drag on his cigarette, and muttered, "The crap I have to do to keep my hands on a gavel."

Roy Dirkey was hopelessly lost. For the past twenty minutes he'd wandered through a maze of dark tunnels, fathoms below the Capitol Building. They were crammed with thick overhead pipes and multicolored cables that snaked from low ceilings and echoed with the desperate footsteps of other lost souls searching for an exit.

After asking various Capitol Hill police officers for directions, Roy finally arrived, in a slight sweat, at the well-hidden meeting room of the House Republican Caucus. He was confronted by two preening staffers guarding a wide mahogany door. They gave Roy the usual scowl reserved for new Members, the one that said *You may be a congressman, but soon we'll be lobbyists making three times your salary, and you'll be groveling at our feet for a PAC check.* Then they nodded him in, as if dispensing a favor.

In front of Roy, two hundred and forty Members of Congress wriggled impatiently on metal folding chairs.

The Washington press corps called the weekly meeting of House Republicans "the Raucous Caucus." This was the battleground of the party's warring parties. They fought with sharp elbows, clenched fists, and foaming mouths. Particularly lively was the power struggle among their top leaders. Each represented a different faction of the caucus, united only by the desire to thrust knives in Frank Piermont's back, somewhere in the vicinity of his corroded lungs.

Roy glanced at the caucus leaders, slumped behind a white-draped folding table at the front of the room. There was Piermont, Majority Leader Tom Doolittle, Majority Whip Fred Stinson, and caucus chairman Bobby Blunk. They reminded Roy of one of those old photos of the Soviet leadership at the Kremlin Wall, only less jovial.

The Speaker looked particularly miserable. His eyes were in a frozen glaze, his hands cupped beneath a plunging frown. Roy assumed it was the recently enacted no-smoking rule (which, *Roll Call* reported, was instituted by Majority Leader Doolittle just to torture Piermont), or the no wine before noon rule (again, the Majority Leader). More likely it was the fact that at these meetings Piermont wasn't really the Speaker, he was "the spoken at." They formed endless lines at microphones, to preach and pontificate, beseech and bemoan, to lather the Speaker with praise while plotting how to skin him alive. Chairs were set up theater style for the rank and file. Or, as Piermont was reported to have once called them, "the crank and bile."

A dozen Members huddled in a corner, in a sort of perimeter defense. They had the look of hunted prey. In fact, they could have qualified for the Department of Interior Endangered Species List. They were moderate Republicans. They represented the last flickering orbs of purple on a national political map that burned bright red with tiny specks of blue. Political survival required certain evolutionary adaptations. Short necks—unpracticed at sticking out—sat low against shoulders. Hands were chafed from constant wringing. Tongues darted agilely to the left and right.

Roy headed straight for the breakfast buffet, set up at the back of the room. Nothing brought Republicans together like pork. Not the spending kind, the eating kind. Bacon, ham, and sausage simmered in aluminum vats above flickering Sterno cans, next to gloppy eggs, frittatas, and home fries. A healthy options menu—organics, granola, vegan—was available. All one had to do is become a Democrat and attend their caucus meetings. He heaped food onto a plastic plate, poured coffee into a Styrofoam cup, and found a seat.

The gentlewoman from Ohio was leading the caucus in benediction. She chaired the House Republican African-American Women's Caucus. She was also the only Member of said caucus. The meetings were lonely but lively.

She solemnly asked the assembled to bow their heads and pray for God's favor, particularly in smiting the Democrats' parliamentary motion on the previous question, which was expected to come up later that day.

"Amen!" they heartily responded.

Whip Fred Stinson briefed the Members on that week's legislative agenda. There would be votes on the American Jobs for American Workers Act, the American Tax Relief for American Small Businesses Act, and the American Support for American Troops Defending America Act. Plus, there were approximately three dozen bills to rename post offices in congressional districts from coast to coast. The Whip suggested aye votes on each because of their noncontroversial nature.

After eighty minutes of controversy, including the suggestion that the names of local post offices be bid on by corporate sponsors, Chairman Blunk banged his gavel and noted it was almost time to adjourn. "Is there any other business?"

Dirkey stood. Cleared his throat. He proceeded to explain AFFFA.

When he finished, the caucus was in rapture.

The distinguished gentlemen and gentlewomen high-fived one another and slapped Dirkey's back.

"Hallelujah!" cried the gentleman from Florida.

"God is our cosponsor!" proclaimed the gentleman from South Carolina.

"Proud to be G-O-P!" chanted the gentlewoman from Tennessee with a fist pump that accidentally landed on the chin of the gentleman from Alabama (her opponent in a caucus election for assistant whip).

For the first time in anyone's recent memory, Speaker Frank Piermont showed signs of a possible smile.

The moderates filed out of the room, like prisoners on death row.

Roy Dirkey couldn't wait to tell Sunny.

13

That evening, in Ralph Kellogg's basement, the Organization celebrated the news that Mayor Liebowitz might be removed from office, to be replaced by—who else?— Ralph Kellogg. Mrs. Kellogg had poured cheese-flavored party mix into festive red Tupperware bowls. Ralph had upgraded the beer selection. They puffed on Tiparillo cigars, swiped earlier by Bobby Reilly from a 7-Eleven, the smoke hanging like a dead wake in the already foul air.

Despite the revelry, Ralph paced anxiously, from the towering gray steel shelves propped against one cement wall to the laundry appliances in a far corner. His arms were locked against his wide chest and his eyes narrowed on each step. His cheek twitched. Ralph couldn't help but recall similar moments when the Organization was on the cusp of victory, only to drop the ball, miss a cue, or incinerate the wrong hardware store. He knew they were running out of time, that there were only so many felonies one could commit before losing one's seat on the Village Board for a bunk at the Suffolk County jail. Ralph sized up his men. Louie was shoving cheese puffs through orange-crusted lips. Bobby seemed hypnotized by the burning embers of his cigar.

The Organization was in a state of slovenly disorganization.

Time for a motivational speech, Ralph thought. An inspiring oration would rouse his men from their stupor.

He positioned himself under the dim lightbulb that flickered from the ceiling.

"Listen up!" he commanded.

Louie and Bobby fixed their glassy eyes on him.

"Gentlemen! This is our time. Change is coming. And we sure as shit can't fuck it up."

Not exactly Henry V at Agincourt, but then again, this wasn't a Shakespeare book club.

Ralph continued his soliloquy. "Now we know what Liebowitz was planning all along. The peace poles. The recycling bins. They were distractions. Her real plot was to take away our guns and leave us defenseless against the Islamex invasion!"

The Organization growled, punctuated with angry crunches of cheese mix and slurps of beer.

"The good news is we'll be rid of her soon. Here's how it's gonna go down."

They downed more beer.

"I checked with my brother-in-law, the village attorney. First, five hundred people have to sign a petition to demand a recall election. Next, the County Board of Elections certifies the petition. Then, they set a date for two votes. One vote to recall Liebowitz. The other to choose her replacement."

"Duh, wonder who that's gonna be!" Louie blurted. He scanned the room to make sure everyone grasped his clever sense of irony.

Bobby Reilly removed the Tiparillo from his lips and tipped

his beer can toward Ralph. "Here's to the new mayor! Can I be fire commissioner?"

"Hold on," Ralph said. "I appreciate your loyalty and believe me, it'll be rewarded. But I can't get elected mayor unless Liebowitz gets recalled."

"Five hundred signatures? I can do it in an hour." Louie wriggled his forging fingers, now orange tipped from cheese flavoring and saliva.

Ralph frowned. "Not so easy anymore. Ever since the incident." The incident was an election for Suffolk County sheriff several years earlier. The Organization attempted to influence the result by submitting hundreds of absentee ballots. Mildred Hagerdorn, an octogenarian employee of the Board of Elections, gasped and fainted when she opened one ballot and learned that her beloved husband, Fred, had voted for the Organization's candidate. Fred had never expressed an opinion about who should be sheriff, certainly not one strong enough to compel him to vote seventeen years after his massive and quite fatal heart attack. An investigation revealed that forty percent of absentee ballots had been cast from the grave, giving new meaning to the political phrase "low voter turnout."

"Liebowitz could get into an accident," Bobby suggested. "Sometimes bicycle brakes just . . ." He shrugged.

Ralph sighed. "We don't need that. For now."

Bobby looked deflated.

"Think!" Ralph insisted, then quickly realized that thinking was pretty low on the Organization's best practices list.

All he heard was sipping and munching and the soft buzz of the overhead lightbulb. His eyes wandered to the autographed Jack Steele movie poster taped to the wall.

"Hmmmm," he grunted. For years, Ralph had been Jack Steele's loyal sidekick in Asabogue. He dispatched village snow plows at the first dusting of Jack's endless driveway. He deployed General

Services Department employees to Villa di Acciaio for the occasional home-improvement project. Parking tickets were forgiven, code violations overlooked. All he asked for in return was Jack's crisp nod of approval, the glint of his teeth, and that soft snap: "Thanks, amigo." Being a friend of Jack's was the only reward he needed (plus the customary hundred-buck gratuity). Ralph smiled.

Now it was time for Jack to return those many favors. He briefly imagined the press conference announcing Jack's endorsement, the gobs of campaign donations from Jack's celebrity friends, the bunting and bagpipes at his inauguration. He visualized the official Asabogue village stationery, the official park signs, the highway department vehicle mud flaps, bearing the imprint:

HON. RALPH KELLOGG
Mayor

So close, he thought.
All he needed was Jack's support.
Loyalty worked both ways, right?

14

The next morning, the sky was a leaden gray and the air heavy. Lois Liebowitz mounted her bike, commenced a wobbly roll down her dirt-packed driveway, and steered left on Love Lane. She rattled past old homes with drooping roofs and dandelion yards. In her knees and hips Lois could feel soft twinges indicating a coming rain.

When she turned onto Main Street, she saw more immediate signs of trouble.

Ordinarily, downtown would be emerging languidly into the morning. Neighbors would sip coffee and peruse newspapers at Joan's Main Street Bakery. Merchants would tidy the redbrick sidewalks outside their stores. But this morning, Lois noticed strangers—uniformed in khaki shorts and bright red polos— scurrying down both sides of the street. They carried clipboards crammed with oversized green papers. They huddled insistently around residents, who shot uncomfortable glances as Lois rode by.

Lois thought, *Well, this is most certainly a violation of Village Resolution 771-1949: Restrictions on Outdoor Peddling and Solicitation.* Then she pedaled faster, drawing in short breaths and returning soft groans. She arrived at Village Hall and hurriedly angled her bike into a rack, just as the first drops of rain fell.

The door squeaked as she entered.

A gloomy Sam Gergala stood behind the counter. This time he made sure the television was turned off. Next to him was Asabogue's chief of police, Ron Ryan. He had red-gray hair, a thick rust mustache, and grim eyes that scanned constantly for incoming threats. He was sturdily built, wide and low to the ground. He fixed his hands on his hips, spread his feet, and pitched slightly forward—a vestige of his glory days as a defensive lineman at Asabogue High School. Chief Ryan had spent twenty years with the NYPD; now he commanded a Department of Public Safety with four full-time officers, three part-time summer employees, and three patrol cars (one of which was usually dispatched to Asabogue Service & Gas for repairs).

"Good morning," Lois offered. But by the look of things, the morning seemed pretty bad.

The chief frowned. "You notice our visitors?" He always spoke in a low, conspiratorial manner.

"Who are they?"

"Checked 'em out. They came in from Washington, DC. Outfit called Canvass Sneakers."

"Canvass Sneakers?"

"They sneak into communities. To canvass voters."

"Clever. What are they doing here?"

Ryan looked at Sam and Sam looked at Lois.

"Show her," Sam mumbled.

Chief Ryan pulled a folded green paper from the breast pocket below his badge and passed it to the mayor with a soft grunt.

Lois felt her cheeks grow warm as she read: "Recall Petition: In accordance with Asabogue Village Code Title 3, Section 1300.1, et seq, the undersigned request that an election be called and held for the purpose of recalling and replacing Lois Liebowitz, Mayor, Village of Asabogue, County of Suffolk, State of New York." Followed by a bunch of blank lines where voters could sign the death sentence to the mayor's career.

"Has the village attorney seen this?" Lois asked, eyes frozen on the petition.

"He probably drafted the damned thing," Sam muttered.

In addition to serving as chief legal officer of Asabogue, the part-time village attorney also happened to be the full-time brother-in-law of Councilman Ralph Kellogg. After Ralph's election as the candidate who promised to downsize Village Hall, he presented his supersized patronage demands to the mayor. It looked like the invite list to a Kellogg family reunion. Lois rejected most of the names, but extended an olive branch by appointing Ralph's choice as village attorney. Now the olive branch was being thrust through Lois's back.

"Well, no one will sign this silly thing," she said, passing the petition back to Chief Ryan.

She laughed, but she knew it sounded forced.

Sam said, "All they need is five hundred signatures."

"Good luck," Lois scoffed. "And even if they found five hundred people, who'd run against me?"

The chief and Sam exchanged worried glances. Sam groaned, "Who do you think? Kellogg!"

Lois felt that unpleasant taste on the back of her tongue, then waved dismissively. "Which is exactly why they won't get the signatures."

The weekend began unhappily for Amber Steele.

"But Jaaaack, it's Saturday. I have tennis!"

Jack studied her from just outside the door of her cavernous bedroom. She was reclining on a purple velvet divan in the far corner, her long calves curving behind her, knees pointed forward. She wore a short pink tennis dress that matched the angry flush of her cheeks. The way the dress crept above her knees, revealing fine stretches of firm bronzed thigh, aroused Jack. But he knew that these days sex with Amber—or anyone, for that matter—was worthy of an Oscar, something in the category of special effects.

"I know, baby," Jack cooed. "But the whole thing'll be finished in an hour. Besides, how many personal appearances do I make for you? All those puppies' rights dinners and horse liberation brunches."

Amber crinkled her nose as she considered Jack's point.

He continued: "C'mon, baby, you can play later. I'll buy you a new tennis outfit." Then he thought, *Something you can take off for Antonio, the pro you're shtupping.*

Jack went downstairs to check on preparations for the first and—he was sure—last Jack Steele Open House. Outside, white tents billowed in the ocean breeze. Linen-draped buffet tables were stocked and top shelf liquor was unpacked. In the grand foyer, floral arrangements were primped and a jazz quartet prepared to play renditions of Jack Steele film scores.

Jack positioned himself in front of the grand staircase, checked his watch, and scowled at the double front doors. Soon, he knew, the hordes would parade through, like tourists at Disney. He'd sign autographs and pose for those loathsome selfies. He'd watch them ogle costars from his movies. (The average age of these quasi-celebrities was eighty. The average body part was eight. Boobs were lifted, tummies tucked, lips tightened, teeth implanted, hips replaced.) His guests would peek into the twelve bedrooms of Villa di Acciaio, gawk at the gold-plated fixtures in Jack's bathrooms, study faded movie awards in glass display cases. They'd marvel at framed photos of Jack chumming with Schwarzenegger, Willis,

Bronson. They'd guzzle mimosas and Bloody Marys, and gorge themselves on the lavish buffets. Three hundred Asabogue residents were invited, with one price of admission: a distracted glance at a green slip of paper, which guests would sign with ambivalent shrugs as their eyes tracked the course of caviar platters.

Jack heard the rumble of vehicles approaching on the driveway and sighed. *The sacrifices one must make for democracy*, he thought.

The next morning, Otis called Jack and asked, "How many signatures didya get?"

"Over two hundred. But the village attorney thinks we'll need a thousand. The Suffolk County Board of Elections has to certify each signature. We need a cushion."

"Good Lord! Five hundred is hard enough! How you gonna get a thousand?"

"Carpe diem."

Later that day, the Friends of the Land honored Jack Steele for his "lifetime achievement in protecting open space." "Lifetime" was a stretch. Even "a few weeks" would have been overly generous. Actually, Jack's entire commitment to land preservation was the time it took to call his golfing buddy, John Palmer, who chaired the board of the Friends of the Land to offer to "raise a few bucks" for the charity. Now, several hundred people, seasonably attired with sweaters slung across shoulders and white slacks, crammed into a renovated gray barn to fete Jack.

Speeches were made and plaques presented. Finally, Jack, who passed the torturous time with ample amounts of North Fork wines, was introduced. He grabbed the mic and slurred, "I don't deserve this honor." (That may have been the most honest portion of his speech.) "But I do know this. This land is your land. This land is my land. From California to the New York island. From the redwood forest to the Gulf Stream waters. This land was made for you and me. God bless our troops."

He sat down to the polite applause and mild confusion of the audience. Before filing out, they were asked to sign petitions.

"Now how many?" Otis asked the following morning.

"Six hundred. And counting."

Jack's schedule was packed.

The Friends of the Dunes gathered to receive the largest donation for beach restoration in its history. They toasted Jack with biodegradable cups filled with organic red wine. Then they signed green petitions. Later that night, sixty people gathered in the newly dedicated Jack Steele Theater at the Asabogue Library. They took pictures of Jack presenting an enlarged white cardboard check. Then signed green petitions. Within a few short weeks, the beneficence of the Jack Steele Charitable Foundation had spread, along with green petitions, throughout Asabogue. Thirty-five signatures were scrawled at the dedication of a new truck for the Asabogue Volunteer Fire Department; seventy signatures at the Friends of the Osprey Annual Brunch on the Bluff; eighteen signatures at the Friends of the Riverhead Aquarium Gala Fashion Show honoring Amber Steele; and thirty-seven at the ribbon cutting of the Friends of the Colonoscopy Unit at Southampton Hospital.

So many friends, so few actual friendships.

But so many signatures.

Of course, many squirmed when the petition was slipped in front of them. In such cases, a clean-scrubbed Canvass Sneakers staffer politely explained that "this petition doesn't obligate you to anything. It simply gives the people of Asabogue the right to decide for themselves whether to elect a new mayor. If you support

Lois Liebowitz, you'll be able to vote for her. Sign right here for the opportunity to support the mayor."

On a Friday morning in late June, a white minivan pulled up to the Suffolk County Board of Elections, a dull brick building in a place called Yaphank. Three armed security guards opened the doors of the truck, and a team from Canvass Sneakers emerged. They briskly carried bundles of green petitions into the building They plunked them down on a counter and watched as a sleepy clerk stamped them in and scribbled a receipt. They paid, by certified check, a two-hundred-dollar filing fee and took a receipt for that as well.

Later, the Republican and Democratic Commissioners of the Board of Elections examined each signature against the voter rolls of Suffolk County. They searched for discrepancies—voters who were not registered, voters who were no longer alive, voters who didn't reside at the address indicated, voters whose signature on the petition deviated materially from their signature on file with the board.

Of 1,104 signatures submitted, nearly three hundred were tossed out due to irregularities, leaving more than enough valid signatures.

A recall election was ordered.

By green petitions signed, sealed, and delivered.

15

O tis Cogsworth had summoned Sunny and America's highest-priced political consultants to design a legislative strategy to pass AFFFA. Although they sat around a long conference table in the New York City headquarters of Cogsworth International Arms, Sunny wasn't sure what century they were in. Dark paneled walls displayed brooding portraits of Cogsworth's early executives in the popular style of their time: mutton chops. Funereal red drapes were closed against windows, casting the room in a morbid gloom and muffling the squawking horns of traffic on Park Avenue ten floors below. White-tie attendants stood stiffly nearby, ready to pour coffee into gold-rimmed china emblazoned with the Cogsworth family coat of arms: two 1920s Cogsy submachine guns crossed against a bull's-eye. The bull's-eye was encircled with the words "Tueri et Defendere." Protect and Defend. The room reeked from decades of cigar smoke baked into overstuffed red leather chairs. Sunny expected that at any minute Cornelius Vanderbilt would crash through the doors to acquire a railroad.

She also noticed that she was the only woman at the table of political consultants, which seemed to make her the object of a salivating focus group. She was tempted to ask, "Are you excited to see me or is that a poll in your pocket?"

She fidgeted with the top button of her shirt, making sure it was fastened, and tugged the lapels of her suit jacket over her chest.

Otis rapped his thick knuckles on the table and barked, "Let's get started. Sunny McCarthy is my gal on this."

Gal. She cringed.

"Passing this law should be a piece of cake," Otis continued. "The Speaker supports it and it has two hundred cosponsors. So when can we expect the president to sign it?"

Heads remained frozen while eyeballs pitched into violent rolls. Sunny suppressed a laugh, then said, "Otis, it's Congress. Even when they agree on something, they'll find a way not to do it. Every bill is a hostage drama."

He scowled. "It's a wonder this country's made it this far." Then slurped his coffee before an attendant rushed to refill his cup.

"Our first big challenge is Congressman Wilbur Overbay. Chairman of the House Judiciary Committee."

Everyone grumbled in agreement. Overbay was the last of the old guard in the House, occupying his seat for more than fifty years. He was legendary for both ego and libido raging inside a rapidly failing body. When a *Roll Call* reporter asked him under what circumstances he would leave the House, he indicated it would be in a pine box with a brief layover in the Capitol Rotunda for a state funeral.

"With Overbay, it's all about congressional seniority," Sunny explained.

"More like senility!" someone blurted, to an explosion of frat house giggles.

Sunny was annoyed. "Don't underestimate him. He comes across feeble but he's ferocious. And he won't tolerate some lowly freshman from Arkansas trying to move a bill through his commit-tee. Ransom's going to be high on this. He'll demand that his name go on the bill. Plus on whatever bridge, dam, or highway Congress will have to fund in the deal he cuts to pass AFFFA."

"Where's he from?" Otis asked.

"Upper Peninsula of Michigan," Sunny replied. Then she asked, "What's the cost of television advertising in his district?"

A media consultant sporting a black T-shirt, black jeans, black blazer, black sunglasses, and black scruff responded, "Dirt cheap. Three media markets. Traverse City, Marquette, and Alpena. For a few hundred thousand bucks we can saturate Overbay's district with pro-AFFFA commercials. I mean, it's the Upper Peninsula. They love their guns, right?"

"Love, love, love," Sunny clucked. Then added, "And while we're pressuring Overbay through the airwaves, we've got some pressure on the ground. Her name is Sarah Plunkett."

Everyone seemed to lean forward for the lurid details. Sunny imagined visions of bedroom videos, salacious texts, and carnal tweets flashing in that dark, damp part of their brains where con-spiracy theories flourished. "She happens to be a popular state senator in Overbay's district. She'd like a seat in Congress but can't have one because Wilbur Overbay refuses to retire. Or die. So, if he doesn't move our bill fast enough, she'll threaten a primary."

"Check and mate!" someone said.

Sunny continued, "Congressman Dirkey and I are meeting with Overbay in DC tomorrow."

"If he makes it that long," someone groaned.

Otis nodded his head and proclaimed, "Good plan!"

Sunny thought, *It's Congress. The national junkyard of good plans that met bad endings.*

The next morning, Roy Dirkey grabbed Sunny's elbow and pulled her into an elevator in the Rayburn House Office Building that was reserved for Members Only. She knew it was Members Only because of the incessant flashing of scarlet red letters that said "MEMBERS ONLY" and the stern recorded voice of a woman repeatedly warning potential elevator hitchhikers that "This elevator is reserved for Members only!"

"Should I be in here?" Sunny asked.

Roy grinned. "You're with me."

She felt his fingers linger on her elbow, then pull slowly away as the elevator whisked upward.

"Remember," she said. "Overbay's old school. Freshmen are seen and not heard."

"I'm not much of a seen-and-not-heard type of guy. I came to Washington to shake things up."

"You want to pass this bill, Roy?"

"Yes, ma'am."

"Then play nice."

"What if Overbay won't support us?"

"Leave that to me. Meanwhile, grovel!"

The elevator doors slid open with another reminder that only Members could take a privileged ride.

Welcome to Wild Kingdom, Sunny thought as they entered Overbay's lobby. Animal trophies peered from high walls: bears, moose, and bucks. Sunny gasped when she realized she was standing heel deep in the filleted fur of a dead grizzly, jaws open, eyes frozen.

"He keeps the trophies of his political opponents in the back," she whispered to Roy.

An intern who looked like she was on loan from the Norwegian woman's basketball team pointed to a leather couch draped with a leopard skin.

They waited. And waited. Roy checked his watch several times.

Sunny whispered again: "It's an old-school ritual. He's making you wait. Establishing his dominance. It's better than spraying urine."

Finally, a door opened. Overbay's chief of staff, Buck Messina, appeared. He was in his fifties, thin, with wiry gray hair, slightly crooked glasses, and the expression of someone who didn't particularly care for company. A congressional staff badge swung from a metal chain around his neck. "Mr. Overbay is ready for you."

The inner sanctum was like an intensive care unit. Overbay was propped in a wheelchair. Medical devices beeped, whirred, and blinked. A web of plastic tubes coiled around his frail body. His head was slumped into a hollow chest cavity and parchment eyelids fluttered as he wheezed shallowly. Skeletal hands trembled in a lap filled with the remains of his lunch. His face sported uneven patches of whiskers, as if he had shaved that morning with a weed whacker.

Sunny scanned the walls. She believed that in order to connect with any official, she didn't have to study the centrifugal spin of their official biography. Just read their walls, which Sunny knew were museum exhibits to the life and times of the people they surrounded. Walls revealed personalities and priorities, values and victories. Sunny had a knack for finding that one thing on a wall that sparked conversation, created solidarity, cultivated a relationship. Here, she was tempted to say, *Did you know they now have color photography?* Every framed picture was faded black-and-white. Overbay had run out of wall space somewhere in the middle of the Reagan administration.

The chief of staff roused his boss from his slumber. Or, Sunny thought, coma.

Overbay lifted his head and opened his eyes. They were sepia yellow and seemed to be draining fluid, like a rusty faucet.

Dirkey put out his hand, which Overbay ignored.

Sunny noticed that something else had captured his attention. His eyes were frozen on her ankles, then followed the curve of her legs to her hips. The beeping of his medical devices accelerated. His snakelike lips curled to a lewd smile.

It's a medical miracle, she thought.

Dirkey began: "Mr. Chairman, thank you for—"

Overbay waved him away with a trembling hand. "What do you do?" he asked Sunny in a tinny voice.

"I represent Cogsworth International Arms, Mr. Chairman. We—"

"Phillip Cogsworth?"

Sunny figured that somewhere in Otis's family tree there was a Phillip. Maybe he was on the Wall of Mutton Chops in New York.

Overbay continued, "Phillip Cogsworth and I used to hunt together. For many, many years."

Success, thought Sunny. She'd found a connection. "Was he a good shot?"

"The jackass almost shot me in the ass. Never liked the man."

"I don't believe he's with the company anymore," Sunny replied quickly.

"Well, I sure as hell hope not. I went to his funeral. Sat next to Hubert Humphrey. The man talked through the whole service. Never liked him either."

Well, isn't this going well!

Dirkey leaned forward and harrumphed, "Humphrey! You know those liberals!"

Overbay's eyes thinned. The beeping accelerated and the oxygen tank hissed. "What do you mean by that, son?"

Seen and not heard, Roy!

"Well, you know. They . . . talk. But—"

"Let me tell you something. In those days, talking was a virtue. We negotiated! Compromised!" His skeletal hands fluttered on his lap, scattering sandwich crumbs. "We yelled at each other by day, drank with each other by night, cut the deal by dawn! Your generation? You don't want a deal. You just want to destroy. Tear down this institution. I'd take Humphrey over you any day of the week! And Nixon and LBJ, too. Ohhhhh, now Lyndon. He was a dealmaker. And Reagan . . ."

Well, this is a nice tour down ancient memory lane.

Overbay's lips were moving, but his words were reduced to murmurs. He seemed to be drifting off. Sunny wondered whether he was dreaming about the time he negotiated the annexation of Texas with President Polk.

He snored.

Buck Messina, whose principal function seemed to be keeping his boss awake—or alive—said, "Thank you for visiting. See you next time."

"We'd like to discuss the chairman's support of the American Freedom from Fear Act," Sunny pressed.

"Not going to happen."

"But—"

"You're wasting your time. No one in this Congress has a better record on gun rights than Mr. Overbay. He's chairman of the Judiciary Committee for a reason. The NRA demanded that the Speaker appoint him. We have to rent a warehouse for all the awards they've given him. But this bill—requiring every American to possess a firearm—goes way too far. It's dangerous. In fact, it's going to backfire. No pun intended." He didn't laugh or smile. He just stared matter-of-factly through his thick eyeglasses at Sunny.

The only sounds were the beeps and hisses of Overbay's life-support system.

Sunny said, "Speaker Piermont and two hundred colleagues support it."

"Whoop-de-doo," Buck responded. "They can go home to their districts and beat their chests and boast about being original co-sponsors of your crazy bill. They can pad their NRA vote scores and look like heroes. But without Mr. Overbay's support, this bill dies in committee. And he will never support it."

"You're not worried about the pressure on your boss? As the one Republican in Congress who's blocking passage?"

"Five decades of NRA perfect scores. Remembered as the

congressman who led the vote to overturn Bill Clinton's assault weapons ban and defeated Obama's background checks. No, we're not worried. Does he look worried?"

A thin stream of tobacco-laced drool ran down Overbay's chin.

Sunny shrugged for effect. "Well, I suppose you have to do what you have to do." That was her way of threatening to do what she had to do.

The chief of staff responded, "This bill passes over his dead body."

A machine beeped erratically.

Two days later, Buck Messina pulled his car into his prized spot in the underground garage of the Rayburn House Office Building. Even here, in the darkest bowels of Capitol Hill, dark and nauseating with fumes, seniority mattered. Buck Messina's ten square feet of oil-stained paradise sat immediately next to wide gray doors that automatically swung open to a bank of elevators that whisked him up to his office.

His tranquility was disrupted by the unnatural sound of shrill phones ringing like alarms as he approached the office.

He pushed open the mahogany door to a besieged staff. They yammered into phones: "No, sir, Congressman Overbay is not taking your guns away"; "No, ma'am, I am not a socialist. I'm just an intern."

A press secretary emerged, frazzled. "You'd better see this." His voice was heavy, as if breaking the news that someone had died. Overbay, perhaps.

They went to a cubicle. It had a prized view of the Capitol dome across the street; but the view on the computer screen almost made Buck throw up:

A man at his kitchen table, staring into the camera. Crew cut. Flannel shirt. Steam rising from a cup of coffee. Forlorn piano notes playing softly.

"I've lived here all my life. Worked hard and played by the rules. But, not everybody plays by the rules. Criminals . . . and terrorists. So when I learned that Congress is debating a bill to let Americans defend themselves, I just assumed my congressman supported it. Now I've learned he may not. To me, that just seems . . ."

Dramatic pause.

". . . out of touch."

An indignant voice-over: *"Call Wilbur Overbay. Tell him to support the Second Amendment."*

Overbay's phone number flashed on the screen. Below it: PAID FOR BY AMERICANS FOR AMERICA.

The press secretary croaked, "They started running at seven this morning. In Traverse City and Marquette."

"How many calls so far?" Buck asked.

"Hundreds."

Buck gulped for an air of self-confidence. "I bet the worst is over. They did their damage. Nicked us. Let's not overreact."

"Who are they? Americans for America?"

"One of those Super PACs."

"Where they getting their money?"

"Donations are undisclosed. We don't know."

He thought of Sunny. "But we can guess."

Sunny sat on her balcony. She sipped her espresso and turned her head to the soft warmth of the morning sun. Then she gazed at the Capitol building and enjoyed the heat she knew she was generating inside, imagining steam coiling from the windows. She dialed Otis.

"Hey, can you convene a family meeting?"

Otis knew what that meant: raise more money.

"How much?"

"Another hundred thousand would do it. We want to cut one more spot."

"Where's the money going?" Otis asked.

"A group called American Crosshairs."

"Personal donations or corporate?"

"Corporate donations are fine."

"Will it show up anywhere?"

"Nope. American Crosshairs is a social welfare organization. They can accept corporate donations and not disclose the source. Thanks to the Supreme Court! Ain't democracy great?"

Otis said, "It's greatly expensive."

Days later, just when he thought it was safe to turn on the television, Buck Messina saw this:

Warm, syrupy music. Father and son. Little League. Fishing. Hunting. Then, the piercing sound of police sirens. Grainy black-and-white crime scenes in Chicago. Terrorists waving Kalashnikovs in Pakistan.

An anxious voice-over: *"Michigan families have always counted on Congressman Overbay to protect our way of life. Now, Washington liberals want him to stop a vote to protect the Second Amendment. Call Wilbur Overbay. Tell him: Protect Michigan values. Protect Michigan families."*

Overbay's phone number flashed on the screen. Below it: PAID FOR BY AMERICAN CROSSHAIRS.

Wilbur Overbay's pollster had one religion: data. He worshiped at the crosstab. His idea of eternal sin was the margin of error. And on this morning, his faith was challenged.

Overbay's numbers were sinking like a boulder in Lake Michigan. Every indicator was down: job approval, personal favorability, reelect. His reputation was plunging to the murky and unchartered depths of a possible competitive election in Michigan's first congressional district. For the first time in Wilbur Overbay's career, it looked like his career might be over.

An emergency conference call of the Overbay brain trust was

organized. The pollster reported that in a head-to-head choice between Overbay and State Senator Sarah Plunkett, the congressman was down by three points. Even worse, in a head-to-head between Overbay and anyone but Overbay, "anyone but" was a shoe-in.

"We can't ignore these Super PAC hits," the pollster warned.

"What do you suggest?" asked Buck.

"Send him to the district over the July Fourth recess. Mend some fences. We need to remind people that he's the Wilbur they know and trust. Do a listening tour. Live and in person."

Buck wasn't sure about the "live" part.

"When was the last time he was in the district, anyway?" the pollster asked.

"April, I think."

"Not as bad as I thought."

"April 2007."

"Time to go home," said the pollster.

Prepare the medevac, thought the chief of staff.

16

One week later, a plane banked over an endless expanse of evergreen trees and landed with a soft bounce at Overbay Regional Airport in the Upper Peninsula of northern Michigan, also known as "the UP." Overbay Airport had two distinctions. It was the recipient of nearly forty million dollars in congressional appropriations from its namesake. And it offered the fewest routes of any airport to or from any other airport in America. The FAA might as well have paved its single runway with gold leaf.

Congressman Wilbur Overbay was rolled in his wheelchair through a mostly empty terminal. A lonely gift shop featured two for the price of one T-shirts that read DO YOU YOOPER? and SAY YAH TO DA UP, EH! Two TSA guards—unsure why they had been assigned to this purgatory of an airport—read and reread the newspaper, waiting for the arrival of somebody to screen. Any live body would do.

Overbay was carefully lifted into a black SUV that doubled as a mobile surgical suite. The vehicle proceeded north on the Wilbur Overbay Causeway, across the Overbay Bay Bridge, in sight of the Overbay Sewage Treatment Plant. It continued on a thin ribbon of asphalt, meandering between towering pine trees and flat farmland, until arriving, two hours later, at Lake Overbay City, which wasn't much of a lake, or a city, but happened to be the hometown and political base of its representative in Congress.

The car pulled into the parking lot of the Overbay Senior Citizens Center, a little brick building with a cheerful red awning and plots of tulips and daisies meticulously nurtured by the senior center's "Garden Committee."

There was also a greeting committee of sorts.

Dozens of angry seniors waved handmade signs:

"DUMP OVERBAY!"

"GO HOME, LIBERAL WILL!"

"RIGHT TO BARE ARMS!" (Spelling was not one of the continuing-ed courses at the senior center.)

"Crap," said the driver, a twenty-two-year-old community outreach worker in Overbay's district office.

They surrounded the SUV, red-hot and white-haired. They waved canes and rattled walkers. They were energized by supplies of fresh air pumped from their oxygen tanks. They shook liver-spotted fists and rapped gnarled knuckles on the car windows. They chanted—panted, actually—"Keep our guns, keep our guns, keep our guns!" Two men in caps reenacted the famous scene from Tiananmen Square by maneuvering their motorized scooters in front of the SUV, defying it to move. The authorities of Wapamatum County didn't expect a riot that day at the senior citizens center, a facility whose only violence up to that point was a two-year silent grudge over possible cheating at a Parcheesi tournament. The only law enforcement officer on duty was one overmatched part-time county security guard/senior center bus driver named Hap, who seemed hapless.

There were, however, about two dozen television crews, tipped off to the untriumphant return of Wilbur Overbay by Sunny McCarthy. They recorded the brave veterans who stormed Normandy in defense of freedom, now storming Wilbur Overbay's car.

Inside, a rather startled Overbay, accustomed to being whisked into a VIP parking area at the White House for occasional meetings with the president, commanded his driver to "get the hell out of here!" Specifically he suggested that they "run the bastards down." The driver summoned his recent political training and properly assessed that vehicular homicide against the elderly might come up in a future candidates debate. So he began gently shifting gears, rolling the car backward and forward, inches at a time, until he could maneuver out of the crowd, and beyond the top speed of the motorized scooters.

The cameras captured the moment when Overbay's car lurched away, leaving behind shaking fists and mouths frothing with saliva and denture cream.

Congress returned to Washington the following week. In the ornate chamber of the House Judiciary Committee, Chairman Overbay wheezed into a microphone and feebly tapped his gavel. He read the Opening Statement of the Chair, as prepared by his staff: "Today the Judiciary Committee will consider the Overbay-Dirkey American Freedom from Fear Act, a historic step in ensuring the personal safety and freedom of all Americans."

The bill passed in committee. By a vote of twenty-six to eighteen. It was headed to the floor of the House.

17

On Billionaires Bluff, Jack Steele had asked Otis Cogsworth if he could borrow a few things. As a good neighbor, Otis was happy to comply. He sent over some pollsters, media consultants, campaign strategists, opposition researchers, and fund-raisers.

He didn't include Sunny McCarthy, although he had briefly considered it. He figured that a strategy session to plan her mother's destruction might be, well, awkward for Sunny. The man had a heart. Actually, Otis had come to an agreement with Sunny: she'd focus on passage of AFFFA in Washington and he'd help defeat her mother in Asabogue. It would be a firearms firewall.

Now Otis sat at a long glass table on the terrace at Villa di Acciaio. The early-morning shadows of turrets spread against marble tile. A soft ocean breeze rippled cotton shirts, gingham slacks, and blue table linens. Servers had put out crystal pitchers of Bloody

Marys, mimosas, and silver chalices of coffee. At each plate was a menu of breakfast selections prepared by Jack's personal chef. Jack's favorite was Freedom Toast (he despised the French). Otis chose the Jack Steele Sausage Links and a side of pastry puffs.

Jack tapped a silver spoon—not the one from his mouth at birth—against a champagne glass and raised it.

"To the demise of Lois Liebowitz. May she be gone . . . and forgotten."

His guests snickered, then slurped. Otis thought the toast might have been hard for Sunny to swallow.

Jack continued: "We're here to discuss how to defeat that woman in the recall election. We need a strategy. A budget. And someone to run against her."

Otis's assumption was that Councilman Ralph Kellogg would run. He found it strange that Kellogg wasn't present that morning.

"I've taken the liberty of assembling dossiers on prospective candidates."

An assistant scurried to the table. Otis assumed she was recruited from the Southampton Beach Club, Blond & Tanned Lifeguards Union, Local 200, AFL-CIO. She embraced a stack of color-coded folders against ample breasts then plunked them—the folders, that is—in front of Jack.

Jack waved the first file. "Councilman Ralph Kellogg."

There was satisfied agreement around the table.

Jack said, "Pros: he's my guy. He'll do what I tell him. I love him like a brother."

I second the nomination, thought Otis.

"Cons: I love him like a brother who's a juvenile delinquent. Christ, the man's borderline psychotic. Plus, we need him to stay where he is. The trusted ally of the man who will be mayor."

Jack always liked surprise endings, thought Otis. And this certainly was a surprise! Ralph Kellogg, disposed of efficiently, like some minor character in Jack's films. As Jack said in his toast: gone and forgotten. Without even a credit at the end.

They reviewed each folder. Civic leaders, town fathers and mothers, bankers, doctors, merchants. Jack vetoed each one. Too independent, too needy. Too loud. Too meek. Closet gay, closet liberal, closet filled with skeletons, real and imagined. When the last folder was put aside, Jack announced, "That leaves one candidate."

They looked around the table.

Jack stood, gazed at the ocean, then proclaimed, "It is not in the stars to hold our destiny but in ourselves."

Shakespeare, Otis knew. He translated for the group, blurting: "Jack's runnin' for mayor!"

Even some seagulls seemed to squawk their delight.

Jack's nomination secured, the candidate got right to business. "Let's talk money. What's it gonna take?"

The media consultant, still dressed in fashionable funeral black, jumped in. "New York broadcast media is the most expensive in the country. So we'll have to advertise on cheap cable television."

"I despise cable!" Jack snapped, perhaps because his movies were recently buried in the graveyard between RetroFlix and HasBeenTV. "Buy network! No one makes a four-star picture on a one-star budget."

The pollster said, "We need a benchmark poll. Then two, maybe three tracking polls. Some focus groups would be good. Probably about a hundred thousand dollars."

"Spend it!"

The mail consultant reached for the golden ring. "We're looking at about twenty mailings to likely voters. Hit pieces on Liebowitz. Positives on you. Total budget, including location shoots, creative, production, and postage . . . roughly three hundred thousand."

"Done!"

A third consultant pitched forward. "Field program won't be cheap. This isn't exactly a presidential election. We can expect massive voter drop-off. Half your supporters live in Palm Springs

or Beverly Hills. We'll have to register voters here, persuade unde-
cideds, turn out our base—"

"How much?" Jack asked impatiently.

"Two hundred thou—"

"Worth it! Leave no voter behind."

"Thirty thousand for an opposition research book on Liebowitz," said the opposition researcher.

"I'd pay anything for that!"

"Could be another ten thousand."

"Don't get greedy."

"Ten grand a month for a campaign manager," someone bid.

"Get the best in the biz. Get me the Spielberg of political campaigns. Just not Spielberg."

Heads bobbed happily around the table. Waves splashed on
the beach. The horizon was bright. In Asabogue's history, no mayoral campaign had ever exceeded thirty thousand dollars. That
morning, the nascent campaign of Jack Steele projected a total
budget of three million. An average investment of just under six
hundred dollars per eligible voter.

"A small price to pay for the defense of liberty," Jack beamed
before consuming another mimosa. "And besides, money will not
be a problem. I have friends."

Otis reached for his checkbook, delighted that he'd found an
Asabogue charity worthy of his support.

That night, Mayor Liebowitz convened her kitchen cabinet—in
her kitchen. They sat at her wobbly table, under a dim light fix-
ture, accompanied by the labored hum of the old refrigerator.
Sam Gergala wore a steep frown. Neighbors Patsy Hardameyer
and Vera Butane sullenly moved pieces of Vera's homemade blueberry cobbler across their plates. Vera was the Asabogue Blueberry Cobbler Queen from 1959 through 1974, when the contest

was discontinued. Technically, she still reigned. Coach McHenry, potbellied and still perspiring after high school summer football practice, nervously twisted his whistle lanyard around two puffy fingers.

They were in quiet mourning, surrounding the mayor as if she were a terminally ill patient drawing her last breaths.

"We'll win," Lois insisted.

Her neighbors exchanged glances, which Lois silently interpreted as *Poor Lois. Poor naive, unelectable Lois.*

Sam exhaled, "Jaaaack Steeeele," triggering the clucking of tongues and resigned shaking of heads.

Lois said, "All we need is a plan." She tapped a pen against a yellow pad. It was blank. She caught Sam narrowing his eyes at no one in particular.

"Maybe," he offered, "you should rescind that Chicago Compact. Then Steele will withdraw. You can put out a statement that it . . . deserves further study. Like they do in Washington."

Lois crossed her arms and leaned back in her chair. "Sam, you know I won't do that."

"You're making this an uphill battle," Sam muttered.

Lois knew Sam was right. The battle was uphill and the hill was about a mile away, past a broken streetlight, sloping luxuriantly to a sun-kissed plateau, where actresses stole husbands and now Jack Steele wanted to take her job. She watched Sam clench his fists on the table. She thought about the night at that table, long ago, when Larry matter-of-factly delivered the news that changed everything.

Lois wasn't surprised by her husband's announcement. She'd suspected an affair for months, though she was initially puzzled that the celebrity Valerie Verrine would fall for Larry from so rarified an eminence as Billionaires Bluff. But, Lois figured, that's how people behaved up there. When they owned everything, they took what they didn't even want, including Larry Liebowitz, a local real estate lawyer in the early stages of a midlife crisis, whom Verrine eyed at the closing of her newly acquired beachfront property. What maddened Lois that night was Larry's cloddish timing. Sunshine and Jeffrey were watching a children's sitcom in the next room, which meant that Larry pronounced the marriage dead to a televised laugh track in the background. "Please, leave," Lois ordered. "I'll tell the children." Larry exited, never to return.

Lois shuffled into the living room, turned the television off to the confused protests of Sunshine and Jeffrey, and broke the news. Years later Lois felt a chill whenever she recalled Sunshine's eyes, widening in disbelief, then narrowing as if squeezing out her rage. Sunshine raced out, the paper-thin screen door flapping violently behind her. Hours later, Lois received a phone call from Sam. He'd found Sunshine hidden in his barn. He'd take her to Joan's Bakery to "let her settle," then drive her home. Lois spent the rest of the night at the kitchen table, crying, until she heard the groan of the screen door. Sunny stepped through, eyes icy, cutting right through Lois, as if she wasn't there. As if this was Lois's fault.

Lois's thoughts returned to her neighbors. "We're just going to do whatever it takes to win."

"With what?" Sam asked incredulously.

"With us, Sam. Grassroots. I'll knock on every door in this town. We'll get volunteers. Who wants to volunteer?"

Her neighbors seemed engrossed in the orange sunflower patterns on Lois's dishes.

"No one? Just me? Fine."

Patsy Hardameyer sighed. "I suppose I can make up some lawn signs." At eighty-five years old, Patsy had a flair for arts and crafts. "Let's see . . . How about 'We Love Lois.' With a heart where 'Love' would be?"

Coach McHenry clawed at his whistle lanyard. "I'll ask some of the football team to stuff mailboxes after practice."

"Good! Now, we need a campaign manager. . . ."

Everyone looked at Sam, who focused sharply on the uneaten blueberry cobbler on his plate.

"Sam," Lois coaxed.

He mumbled in protest, which Lois considered assent.

She folded her hands on the kitchen table and proclaimed, "I promise—we . . . will . . . win . . . this . . . election."

The table wobbled, like the lives of those who sat around it.

18

Sidney Schwartzman ended the phone call with a satisfied smack of his thick wet lips and thought, *Life's a gamble. And the house always wins.*

He was sprawled on a chaise lounge on the high terrace of his penthouse at the King David Resort in Miami Beach. He was wrapped in an oversized white King David luxury robe ("Fit for a King. Available for $399 by Calling Guest Services"). His skinny legs protruded from the robe like withering branches on a gnarled tree. The Atlantic Ocean shimmered below him in the early dawn, and a warm wind washed over the few reedy strands of hair remaining on his scalp. Planes glided across an orange sky headed toward Miami International Airport, vaporous streams of revenue for Sidney's real estate empire.

Denied his Taj Mahal by the Village of Asabogue, Schwartz-man had retreated to other perches: the sprawling penthouse atop his resort, his private island in the Caribbean, the castles in Palm Springs, Palm Beach, and on Park Avenue. Still, Schwartzman wasn't the type to rest easy. He kept score of things: the insults to his honor, the acts of disrespect, the people who got in his way that he had to get out of the way, like that little woman in Asabogue who'd blocked him from building "Taj Too." She'd made him appear impotent to the actress for whom the dream palace was planned. No wonder she'd left! Now she was known as "ex-wife five." Or was it six?

No matter. The phone call would settle the score with Lois Lie-bowitz. He smiled.

Of course, Sidney believed there was more to life than win-ning personal grudge matches. There was Western civilization to save from the jihadists, environmentalists, socialists, leftists, and all those other "-ists" threatening America. The nation was being taken over by the bleeding hearts and weak-kneed who wanted to redistribute his hard-earned stock dividends before surrendering to a new world caliphate. Sidney thought of himself as free enter-prise's last line of defense. It wasn't cheap. He personally bank-rolled an outfit called FreedomWonks, which was comfortably ensconced in a redbrick town house on Capitol Hill's Massachu-setts Avenue. It was staffed by former deputy assistants and dep-uty assistant secretaries from long-ago Republican presidential administrations. Now they were called "distinguished fellows" and "senior policy analysts." Their "best of" analyses included:

"So Farsi, So Good: The Manageable Cost of a Nuclear Strike on Iran."

"Why Coolidge Was Right."

"Global Warming: Is It Chilly in Here or Is It Just Me?"

The reports weren't exactly candidates for the *New York Times Book Review*. But who needed the *Times* when Sidney had SOS-News, the latest acquisition in Sidney Oscar Schwartzman's ever-expanding empire. A FreedomWonks thinker had a thought, a theory, an opinion. Research was conducted, then accessorized with footnotes and draped in a laminate cover. It was shipped to an SOSNews producer, who would book the author to appear for an on-set interview. One minute your eyes are deep in statistical abstracts on the U.S. workforce in 1929, the next you're squinting at the harsh lights of an SOSNews studio listening to an anchor giddily praise your "trenchant analysis." All of this added a veneer of academia to the raw tonnage of Schwartzman's wealth.

One day, Schwartzman took his favorite Supreme Court justice for a few rounds of golf. Mr. Justice won the game, but justice lost. A few weeks later the court ruled that Super PACs could accept unlimited, undisclosed gobs of corporate money. Americans for America was born with an initial endowment of fifty million dollars spread across ten of the most competitive Democratic-held districts in America. All ten Democratic incumbents lost.

As Schwartzman said: "Never bet against the house, unless it's a Democrat in the House."

Sidney went on a spending spree. Buying up congressional districts across America in a real-life political version of Monopoly. "This message paid for and authorized by Americans for America" was the death knell of Democrats in competitive districts. They may as well have played "Taps."

And now, the phone call he had just completed with Jack Steele—another victory to savor!

Steele had sounded breathless. "Sidney. Remember that woman in Asabogue who stopped your building permit?"

How could I forget? he thought.

"I'm getting rid of her!" Steele proclaimed.

Sidney remained silent. Whenever he spoke on his cell phone he assumed someone was listening. The SEC, the FEC, the FCC, the FDA, OSHA, the Nevada Gaming Commission, various Arab intelligence services, the Democrats, the divorce lawyers. Those platypus lips were evolutionary, a protective layer against saying anything that could be used against him in a court of law.

"I'm running against her for mayor. We're going to beat her. But I need your help."

"How much?" Two of Sidney's favorite words.

"How much can you do?"

Such a foolish question.

"Why don't you fly out? I want you at my official announcement at Village Hall next week."

"Next week? Why so long?"

"Well, these things take time. Staging. Lighting. Press advisories."

Sidney shook his head. "No! No! No! I have a much better idea. You will announce tomorrow!"

He ended the call. Considered the empire he had built around him, minus one replica of the Taj Mahal in Asabogue. "Never bet against Schwartzman," he said as he speed-dialed SOSNews headquarters in New York.

Even under the searing studio lights, there was a cold war on the set of SOSNews. During a commercial break, Megan Slattery was wedged between fellow anchors Robert Thomas and Ashley Barnes on a curved red couch. They were so close that Megan could smell her colleagues' industrial-strength hairspray. It stung at her eyes. As usual, Robert was tormenting her with his disgusting off-camera rituals. He cleared his throat like a Jet Ski grinding on phlegm, and darted his jaw back and forth while tapping out some kind of Morse code with his teeth. Megan knew he was just waiting to roll over her lines with that exaggerated frat boy laugh. And Ashley—*Could you possibly hike that skirt any higher on those toothpick thighs? I mean, are you auditioning to host an infomercial on purging, girl?*

"Five seconds," a woman's voice snapped into her earpiece.

Those disembodied voices, she thought, commanding her from the black depths of the studio. Like gods, giving and taking away her time, choosing between darkness and light on millions of television screens, deciding between Megan Slattery and a commercial for motorized chairlifts.

Robert emitted a final hack, and Megan checked for pieces of lung that may have landed on her lap. Ashley crossed her legs and clamped her knees shut. Ashley's legs were fair and balanced, to use a competing network's favorite phrase.

"Three . . . two . . . one."

Upbeat music streamed into Megan's earpiece. She froze a smile and locked her eyes on the teleprompter beaming at her from the dark.

She read: "Welcome back. Now let's go to some quick headlines . . ."

She heard a swooshing sound. It ushered in the footage that accompanied each story, creating a sensation of fast pace and quick change. Sidney Schwartzman was in the news business to make money, which required him to sell the news at volume discounts. They crammed shorter stories between more commercials, tailored to the national attention deficit disorder. A country once engrossed in the Great Debates could no longer absorb any information exceeding an Instagram post. Every television remote was on hair trigger.

SOS. All the news fit to swoosh.

Of course, SOSNews bites were designed to bite into America's thinning skin. It was news based not on fact, but phobia. Wars erupting on America, on taxpayers, on capitalism, on Christmas; terrorists hiding in mountains and lurking in malls; bureaucrats raising taxes on hard-working Americans to lather welfare on illegal aliens; secularists chasing God from classrooms; the politically correct but morally bankrupt; the Muslims; and mayhem. No wonder it was called SOS. Not a tribute to Sidney Oscar Schwartzman, but a cry for help from a sinking civilization.

Swooooosh.

She followed the teleprompter: "Despite liberal outrage, conservative talk show host Rush Limbaugh has won the National Toddler Book Association's top award for *The Little Tax Cut That Could*. The—"

"Good job, El Rushbo!" Robert interrupted with that unctuous laugh.

I hope you choke on your lavaliere, Megan thought, smile in place.

Swooooosh.

She continued: "And outrage in Pennsylvania, where liberal authorities banned an opening prayer at Camp Hack-Ah-Loos-Ah's annual parent-child water balloon toss."

On a monitor below the camera, Megan caught a glimpse of a riot over the absence of a peaceful water balloon prayer. The balloons flew like Hellfire missiles, splattering against flesh in violent explosions of neon latex and water.

"Horrible!" Rob puffed.

"Poor kids!" Ashley sniffled.

Swooooosh.

"Now to some breaking news from a big star in a little village that's trying to ban guns. Let's go live to Sean Wagner for an SOS-News exclusive. Sean, seems like this small town is fighting back, right?"

A control room director snapped his fingers and Sean Wagner instantly appeared in front of Asabogue Village Hall, which looked particularly dreary that overcast morning. A gentle breeze rustled his lustrous blond hair. He wore "broadcast casual": a dark blue button-down shirt and khakis, and held a large SOS microphone under his square jaw. "Thaaat's right, Megan! I'm here in the Village of Assss-a-bogue, Long Island, with someone who knows a litt-ell something about fighting back: veteran film star Jack Steele!"

The camera pulled back for what the film industry once called "the Steele Reveal." There was Jack, hands perched on hips, elbows at sharp angles, spine stiff, stomach taut, eyes narrowing on the camera lens, as if sizing up every viewer individually.

Sean began, "Jack, people know you as the hero of action movies, but now you're taking on a new role."

"Yep." Jack kept his eyes on the camera and his voice to a raspy whisper. "I'm running for mayor. You know the joke: politics is show business for ugly people."

Robert bellowed. Ashley giggled. Megan smiled icily through her rising blood pressure.

Sean said, "You had a great career on the big screen. Why run for office in this tiny little village?"

"Well, first of all, because I love this tiny little village. And second, because the current mayor—Liebowitz is her name—wants to take away our guns." His pronunciation of "Liebowitz" was pitch perfect—if the pitch was low and to the right. Liebowitz: as in Jewish-sounding, loud-talking, left-leaning. He continued: "I suppose I could just sit back and enjoy my retirement. But I'll never sit back when our Constitution is being attacked. Not in my backyard."

On set, Rob oozed "Woooow" and Ashley cooed "Good for him!"

"You're talking about the Chicago Compact?" asked Sean.

"Yep. I'm fed up with liberal politicians forcing their agendas on the rest of America. If you don't like guns, move to Chicago. Their city motto oughta be 'Duck and cover.'"

Megan heard the slapping of Robert's palms against his knees.

"My point is, why can't these liberals just leave small towns like Asabogue alone? We're the real America."

Sean could have mentioned that not every real town in America had a median income of $2.2 million. But "median income" tended to lose viewers, except on CNBC.

"Now, when do you plan to announce your candidacy—officially?"

"Just did. It's Steele versus Liebowitz."

He shared the name of his newly designed campaign website and smiled, his teeth glowing like a bright beacon that cloudy morning.

Sean turned to the camera. "Megan, Ash, Robert, as they say in the movies, thaaaat's a wrap. From the litt-ell village of Assss-a-bogue!"

"Carpe diem Sean-o!" Robert bellowed.

Megan thought, *When they pull your earpiece out, can they see to the other side of your head?*

She read, "We'll be back after this break. Stay with SOS."

In her office, Sunny poked at the television remote, slumped in her chair, and exhaled sharply as the television darkened. She imagined millions of SOSNews viewers receiving the gospel about her mother as the political Antichrist, rushing to their checkbooks and computers to donate to Jack Steele's campaign.

Sunny knew this was only the debut of the Lois Liebowitz roast. This had docudrama potential. The networks devoted weeks of constant coverage to plane crashes. Now SOS would train its cameras on the spectacular crash and burn of Lois Liebowitz. Politicians would push each other out of the way to condemn her. Pundits would become studio armchair generals: analyzing, projecting, dissecting every battle in the Liebowitz-Steele election. Election bulletins would flash into America's homes, accompanied by the military cadence of drums and trumpets. The woman Sunny called mother would become a household name—vilified on SOS prime-time talk shows where there wasn't talking as much as there was trashing; debated and debased at dinner tables across America.

And when it was over—when Lois's dreams were incinerated by the licking flames of SOSNews—the network would simply cast her aside. Not a heave-ho but a ho-hum. The Lois Liebowitz show would imperceptibly fade from America's screens, replaced by a new ratings favorite: a terrorist, a flag burner, a book by a former subterranean-level Obama appointee admitting that, yes, the former president was a closet Muslim who secretly prayed toward Mecca in a White House closet.

Swooooosh.

No one would remember Lois Liebowitz. Except those who had to live with her, Sunny thought.

Sunny hated her mother. She never imagined the entire nation joining the cause.

Brought to you by SOSNews.

She twirled her hair.

19

I n a drab six-story brown and beige office building near the
foot of Capitol Hill, at the far end of a dingy corridor, was the
national fund-raising firm PAC It in Associates. There, an attractive raven-haired consultant with long freckled legs leaned
back at her cluttered desk and blew a delirious breath while thor-
oughly enjoying the chorus of her favorite song, "Click-Click Cha-
Ching . . . Click-Click Cha-Ching." The music played in her head,
but in the past few days it was as if the National Philharmonic was
right there with her.

Click—the sound of donors across America hitting a computer
link that said "Contribute to Jack Steele Right Now!" *Cha-Ching*—
the ring of the donation as it landed instantly in the Steele campaign treasury.

Since Jack's announcement on SOSNews earlier that week,
the clicking and cha-chinging had overwhelmed Jack Steele's

campaign website, crashing it six times. A grand total of $1.6 million was raised, in increments of $5, $35, $50, from rich people and poor, young and old, blue states and red. A contribution from Diane Fretzeil of Elmsville, Indiana, came with this e-mail: "I'm a senior citizen on Social Security and I struggle to make ends meet. But I'm a churchgoing grandmother who loves Jesus and my country. So here's five dollars to help you beat that gun-hating bitch!"

The fund-raising consultant, surrounded by photographs of the senators, congressmen, and governors whose political paths she'd paved with gold, thought, *We will, Diane! And by the way, now that you're in our database, consider yourself one of 62,800 close, personal friends of Jack! As part of our not so inner circle, you'll be hearing from us again. And again. Sometimes hourly. As a friend, we'll be counting on you, Diane Fretzeil! We'll be appealing, beseeching, and cajoling you for another five bucks. To match your first five. Or seven. Seven dollars is a small price to pay for Jack's friendship, right Diane? How about ten dollars, Diane? For your grandchildren? Those little angels that Liberal Liebowitz will expose to criminal thugs and Muslim terrorists? Would you consider twenty? Click here for fifty. Thanks, Diane. Your Steele Supporter bumper sticker is on its way.*

Diane would come through. She and 62,799 others would affirm and reaffirm their affection for their new best friend, Jack Steele.

One click and cha-ching at a time.

In Asabogue, the Organization met in the man cave, over some nacho cheese–flavored Bugles and a six-pack of Diet Dr Pepper. This time, Ralph withheld the beer—he wanted everyone completely clearheaded. Plus, he figured the diet soda would keep them in fighting shape. Louie Delmarco in particular needed to drop a good thirty pounds to perform Ralph's mission without collapsing.

Ever since hearing the news that Jack Steele had stabbed him in the back, Ralph had been plotting his revenge. The details clunked in his immense head, like the lumbering of Mrs. Kellogg's dryer. At night he sat at his desk in a spare bedroom upstairs, furiously scrawling on a yellow legal pad under the harsh beam of a gooseneck lamp. A cassette tape recorder warbled his favorite war movie theme songs. His prized possessions were tacked to a cork bulletin board above him: his Certificate of Election to the Village Board, his Soldier of Fortune wall calendar, and a black-and-white photo of his first swearing-in, when a seemingly petrified town clerk named Eloise Vanpin had him raise his gigantic right hand and swear to "follow the code and ordinances of the Village of Asabogue, so help me God."

The plan veered from that oath. Considerably.

Now he was unveiling it to the Organization. To avoid any distractions, he made sure Mrs. Kellogg had already completed the laundry. There were no baskets overflowing with her underwear, this time. Just a large map of Asabogue, fixed with black electrical tape to a rough cement wall.

For the occasion, Ralph was dressed in army camos and black tactical boots. A pair of knock-off Oakley sunglasses that he'd shoplifted from the Shade Shack were straddled across his scalp. Ralph enjoyed the look. This would have been his everyday dress had it not been for the army recruiter who scrawled "Mentally Unbalanced!!!" on his file so many years ago.

"Listen up," Ralph commanded. The crunching of Bugles ceased. He began pacing in front of the map.

"We have two enemies. Lois Liebowitz. And Jack Steele."

The words reddened Ralph's cheeks. Jack Steele! His friend and mentor, his comrade in heavy arms. For years Ralph handled Jack's dirty work in Village Hall, most recently arranging for that stop sign in front of the actress Caitlyn Turner's house to torment her.

And for what? Not a thank-you, but a fuck-you. Jack didn't even have the decency to inform Ralph personally of his candidacy. Instead, a phone call from one of Jack's buxom assistants informed him that "Mr. Steele is running for mayor and looks forward to scheduling a meeting with you to discuss your support." The words dropped like an anchor in Ralph's stomach. There must be some misunderstanding, he'd thought. But then he saw for himself: Jack announcing his candidacy live on SOSNews. He'd literally broadcast to the world that Ralph Kellogg had been thrown to the curb like an empty beer can, stepped on and crushed, like Ralph's dreams.

Schedule a meeting? Have your people call my people! I don't have people. Except for the Organization.

He stared at them. Sitting forward on that old stained couch, hanging on his next words, ready to accept the plan without question or pause.

Ralph folded his arms against his wide chest. "Two enemies. Two objectives. One: take out Jack Steele. Two: defeat Lois Liebowitz."

They nodded.

Ralph continued, "To save Asabogue, we're gonna have to burn it down."

Bobby Reilly giggled excitedly, a cigarette jiggling between his lips.

The plan was flawless. The planners were, well, flawed.

20

Congressman Roy Dirkey had been navigating through confusing and endless Capitol tunnels to a similarly confusing and endless hearing of the Subcommittee on Regulatory Reform, Commercial and Antitrust Law when his cell phone rang.

"Where are you?" his chief of staff panted.

"On my way to subcommittee. For my daily eye glaze."

"Turn around. Now. Go to the Speaker's office."

"Go where?"

"The Speaker. Wants you at a meeting. With the Leadership!"

The words landed with both urgency and majesty.

The Speaker.

Wants you at a meeting.

With the Leadership.

Roy had passed by the Speaker's office many times, off the gray stone alcove between Statuary Hall and the cavernous Rotunda. The corner of his eyes would catch the sign SPEAKER OF THE HOUSE FRANK PIERMONT. It might have well said NO FRESHMEN. He'd steal a glance at the long, forbidden corridor painted in regal red. He imagined the Speaker, behind those walls, pulling levers and twisting dials like the Great and Powerful Oz, complete with puffs of smoke and wheezing. Dirkey would then shift his eyes forward and continue walking, the echo of his footsteps clacking on the marble floor, punctuating the *oohs* and *aahs* of tourists as they craned their necks under the soaring Capitol dome.

Now he found himself inside and, he contentedly assumed, an insider. He sat under two massive crystal chandeliers at a lustrously waxed conference table reflecting the ghostlike images of the luminaries around it: the men and one woman of the House Republican Leadership. They were gray hued with metallic sheens, like silverfish. The Speaker had handpicked each from competing factions of the Republican caucus to maintain his precarious hold on the gavel. This was Frank Piermont's exquisite feat of political engineering—weights and pulleys, cogs and gears exerting equal force against each other, built so that he would last.

Or, as Piermont frequently described it, "a bunch of loose screws and wing nuts."

They awaited the Speaker's arrival, wedged around the table so that their elbows touched, engaged in the forced conviviality of rivals. Big egos conducted small talk, every syllable laden with artificial sweeteners. Most of them, however, sought distraction in their electronic devices. A profession once known for glad-handing and back-scratching was now consumed with hunting-and-pecking. Dirkey watched the most powerful people in America hunched over small screens, necks bent, eyes drooping, consumed by torrents of e-mails, texts, online subscriptions, and hot new apps. The state of the Union was ☹.

Piermont had once announced his temptation to put up a sign in the conference room: NO TEXTING WHILE LEGISLATING. His

Leadership team was like the House steno pool. Piermont would say something, fingers would tap on keyboards, and within minutes some television correspondent was reporting it verbatim from "a Republican Leadership source attending the meeting with the Speaker."

Which meant that the Speaker hardly spoke.

Roy eyed a painting that dominated the wall behind Piermont's vacant chair at the head of the table. It was a portrait of a young nineteenth-century congressman sitting where all anonymous freshmen sat in the House chamber: far in the back. His hair was slightly tousled. His elbow rested on a book on his desk. He had dark eyes, a cleft chin, and he seemed to be suppressing a wry smile, almost winking at Dirkey.

Congressman Abraham Lincoln.

Dirkey took in the painting, marveling that he'd landed in the same club as Congressman Lincoln. In freshmen orientation, he was told that about twelve thousand people had served in Congress since 1789. Names like Lincoln, Calhoun, Webster, Longworth, McCain, Kennedy, Pelosi. But also Smith, O'Brien, Marcantonio, Dickstein, and González. The mere mortals had no portraits on the Capitol walls, no names chiseled into marble buildings or national holidays on birthdays. Of the twelve thousand who'd served, nearly as many were now permanent members of the Congressional Obscurity Caucus. They were called "former Members," which was a polite term for "forgotten Members."

Not me, thought Dirkey.

He always knew his name would go further than a flickering neon sign above a Little Rock Chevy dealership. There was always that burning in his chest, a heart that pumped ambition like adrenaline. Those fights in the Pine Bluff schoolyards defending his father's duck costume had taught him not how to take a punch but how to dance around one. He'd developed a skin that wasn't as thick as it was adaptable, so protective that even a bullet in Afghanistan couldn't penetrate it.

On that score, Dirkey knew that plenty of soldiers got shot at in Afghanistan. But how many took a bullet right through a Constitution pressed against their chest? Sure, there were a few cynics in his unit who suspected Dirkey of embellishing the story. No one had actually seen him tape a copy of the Constitution to his chest. The hole in the pamphlet did look like a cigarette burn. But, hell, when you escape a Taliban ambush you don't counter each other's stories, you count your blessings. And really, in the heat of battle, who didn't layer on some added drama? Besides, Roy was a natural leader, with that toothy smile and aw-shucks charm, like the guy in the portrait.

"Public sentiment is everything," Lincoln had said. For Dirkey it was the nineteenth-century equivalent of his father's mantra, smooth like butter and melodious: "Son, you can't sell a Buick unless they think they're buying a Cadillac." It wasn't lying exactly, it was polishing. Like the streams of hot wax and buffing at Dirkey Chevrolet. Lincoln probably never even split a rail, thought Dirkey, just like George Washington never chopped down a cherry tree. Slight enhancements grew to embellishments, embellishments became myths. It was all designed to make a sale, advance an agenda, win.

Four muted televisions glowed from a mahogany console against a wall. Three news channels were covering recent comments by the bellicose president of Russia that "We have a score to settle with Napoleon." Another screen showed the current debate on the House floor: one Republican, one Democrat, and one nation not paying attention.

Dirkey heard a sudden spasm of coughing. A door opened and Piermont entered, led by his security detail and surrounded by staff, like pilot fish trailing a shark. He wore his usual blue suit and red tie. His face was leathery and dark, like an old catcher's mitt, and his silver hair looked shellacked. He slumped into his chair. Even at the opposite end of the room, Dirkey could smell pungent tobacco.

"Good morning," Piermont said, his lips already twitching for a cigarette.

"Good morning," everyone mumbled.

"I thought it would be useful to discuss the vote on this American Freedom from Fear Act. Where's Mr. Dirkey?" The Speaker swept his reddened eyes around the table, searching for someone he'd hardly met and didn't know. Then, with a shrug, said, "Tell us about your bill."

"Thank you, Mr. Speaker. I'm honored to—"

"It's a wonderful bill," Piermont interrupted. "Meticulously researched. Well constructed. Thoughtfully conceived."

Light to moderate applause encircled Dirkey. He nodded appreciatively and said, "Thank you. I—"

"But we need to discuss some . . . concerns."

Dirkey didn't like the tone of "concerns." As in, "I've seen your biopsy. And there are . . . concerns."

"Do you have any thoughts, Mr. Teabury?"

Piermont ran Leadership meetings like an orchestra conductor, a maestro of consensus. Pointing to different sections of the caucus to turn cacophony into harmony, or harmony into cacophony, depending on his objective. Guiding everyone to his conclusion as if it was their own, efficiently saving his own political capital.

Benjamin Teabury of Georgia cleared his throat. He wore a blue seersucker suit, a white sheen of hair, and round glasses that widened his sparkling eyes to the size of Georgia peaches. He was known for courtly manners and a melodic voice that lulled his colleagues into a legislative death grip. Teabury chaired the forty-member GGOOP Caucus: Get the Government Out of Our Pockets. "Mistuh Speakuh," he began. "The GGOOPs do agree with the intent of this very fahn meashuh."

Dirkey's heart rose . . .

"But ah regret to say we cannot suppoat it in its current fo-um," Dirkey's heart sank.

"Why is that?" the Speaker asked, as if he didn't know and as if almost everyone at the table didn't know that he already knew.

"Why it's a hidden tax, suh. If we mandate that everuh American own a gun—worthuh as that goal may be—well, guns, like buttuh, cost people money. And that, Mistuh Speakuh, could not have the support of mah felluh GGOOPs." Teabury smiled at Dirkey, who felt his mouth go dry.

"Hmmmmm," the Speaker mumbled, broken by a gurgling cough. "What do you think, Chairman Fogg?"

Hiram T. Fogg, chairman of the Ways and Means Committee, nodded. "I agree with the GGOOPs. But there is a solution."

"Oh?" said the Speaker.

"The government can help people pay for their guns. A refundable tax credit. They did that with Obamacare. If you couldn't pay the health insurance premiums, the government picked up the tab."

The mention of Obamacare seemed to send a low-voltage current through the room. Muscles twitched, skin crawled. Tears formed in some eyes.

"Ike, what do you think?" asked Piermont.

Congressman Ike Garvin of Texas was the chairman of the sixty-member ROBs: Republicans Opposed to Borrowing. He was a deficit hawk who looked the part: sharp, darting eyes and a long nose plunging to a bottom line. "Tax credits cost the Treasury money and increase the debt. The ROBs will oppose them. Unless you make them revenue neutral."

Ahhh, "revenue neutral." The sweet and seductive sound of it seemed to pump pheromones into the cold blood of the fiscal hawks, whose idea of soft-core were their tattered copies of the *Congressional Budget Office Manual of Long-Range Debt & Revenue Projections*. They were turned on by "offsets," their foreplay was "pay-fors."

Piermont rapidly tapped his tobacco-stained fingers on the table, a sign of nicotine withdrawal. "Millard Festersen?" he wheezed.

Millard Festersen was chairman of the TRACs, the Tax Reform Action Caucus. He proudly announced, "We have found an offset," as if proclaiming he'd discovered a cure for cancer.

The Speaker absently fished through his empty shirt pocket for his pack of unfiltered Camels.

Festersen continued: "Childcare! We're spending billions on tax credits for parents to put their kids into cold, heartless daycare warehouses instead of being nurtured at their mother's bosoms."

There was grumbling ascent in the room. The gentlewoman from Maine, Melanie Mills McMotten, suddenly found the bowl of peanuts in front of her wondrous, refusing to take her eyes off them.

Festersen leaned forward on his elbows. "Ending the childcare tax credit would free up billions of dollars. Which can be used to purchase firearms. We call them PSTCs—Personal Survival Tax Credits."

Gurgle-hack-wretch. Then, "Everyone agree?"

Teabury nodded his ascent. Fogg gleamed. Garvin smiled. Festersen gave a satisfied thumbs-up. Melanie Mills McMotten continued staring at the peanuts.

The chairman of the House Committee on Education and the Workforce asked, "Errrr, just checking here. Does the bill require everyone to own a gun? Without exception?"

Roy raised his hand, desperately seeking acknowledgment.

Piermont nodded in Dirkey's general direction. "What do you think, Bill?"

"Roy. I'm Roy."

Piermont scowled. "Yes, I know, Roy. But I was calling on Bill. Beaufort. Next to you."

Congressman William Jefferson Davis Beaufort shot an annoyed glance at Roy and muttered "rookie" under his breath, but loud enough for Roy to hear. He chaired the WACCs, the Women and Children's Caucus. The group was Piermont's idea to reverse a double-digit gender gap in the polls and blunt the Democrats' rhetoric about "the Republican war on women." And what better way to connect to women than a caucus of mostly white men whose idea of diversity was the color of their Brooks Brothers ties? Chaired by someone named William and Jefferson and Davis.

"Mr. Speaker, the WACCs could vote for this if it contains some exemptions. You shouldn't be required to own a gun if you're on the terrorist watch list or if you're a child."

One of the Speaker's aides hurried to his side, bent toward his ear, and whispered urgently. Piermont nodded, then said: "We'd better run that one by the NRA. You know, you limit the responsibility of anybody to have a gun, you limit the responsibility of everyone to own a gun. Camel's nose in the tent kinda thing."

And speaking of Camels, he thought.

Beaufort frowned. "Are we really going to hand out Colts and crayons in kindergarten?"

Hmmmm-hack-gurgle.

Hiram Fogg leaned forward. "We could give you an amendment on the floor to exclude children under thirteen."

Someone said, "Make it nine and you got a deal."

They clapped.

The bidding began.

Wheeling, dealing, logrolling, horse trading. Dirkey sat quietly, watching as his masterpiece was bloated with gaseous elements, including (and as the parliamentary lexicon stipulated, "but not limited to") a federal program for pre-K target practice; an American Gun Corps to retrain workers (in specified congressional districts) in firearms manufacturing; appropriations; authorizations; tax credits; grants; loans; subsidies; studies; pilot projects; demonstration projects; assistance for exports; duties on imports; fast-tracking; financing; funding and, inexplicably to some—but not all—a bridge in the Upper Peninsula of Michigan.

Since the Leadership was comprised of fiscal hawks and balanced budgeteers, everything had to be paid for. So they took their carving knives to the usual tonnage of fatty flesh in the federal budget: waste, fraud, and abuse. In this case, it was the waste of college tuition assistance, the fraud of climate studies, and the abuse of environmental regulations.

They feasted at the buffet table in the Speaker's office that morning. The GGOOPs and ROBs and WACCs and TRACs. It was the perfect Washington compromise—a give-and-take where everyone took and no one gave, as long as they had a seat at the table. They fulfilled their constitutional duty to provide for the common defense and ensure domestic tranquility in a more perfect Union (preferably without unions).

Roy sat silently as the deal was consummated under the portrait of young Congressman Lincoln, who now looked slightly queasy.

The Speaker adjourned the meeting and disappeared. In a puff of smoke.

Sunny McCarthy was reclining in her chair, her bare feet on her desk when Roy called. She didn't have the heart to tell him that four congressmen and two staffers had been sending her real-time text updates throughout the meeting. So she feigned awe at his triumph: how he set down his demands and refused to budge, how he slammed his fists and pulled concessions from the Leadership. He reported it in the hyperactive voice of the boy who hit a Little League home run and saved the game. Except, Sunny knew, he had never even got off the bench.

"So, how'd I do?" Roy asked.

"Am-aaaaa-zing, Roy." She smiled.

"We need a drink. To celebrate."

"Hold that thought. Until the bill actually passes. Anything can happen between now and—"

"Meet me later at the Republican Club."

"Roy. You have no idea how this town works."

"This town doesn't know how I work. Nine o'clock tonight."

Sunny sighed.

21

S peaker of the House Frank Piermont and Senate Major- ity Leader Horace Binslap cut their secret deals in plain sight: on an open balcony off the West Front of the Cap- itol with a sweeping view of Washington. That's where they met this sultry July evening, jackets off, ties loosened, sleeves rolled up. They reclined on wrought-iron patio chairs covered with plush green-striped cushions. Piermont puffed on cigarettes and sipped a merlot procured from his private stock. Binslap savored a fat Cohiba obtained from the U.S. ambassador to Cuba. Binslap, of Miami, despised Cuba. He waged his own legislative Bay of Pigs against the Cuban government, hitting them with waves of amend- ments to defund diplomatic relations. Cuba was evil, totalitarian, rapacious, and godless. Cuba was, to borrow a phrase from Trotsky, consigned to the ash heap of history. Meanwhile, he'd just have to enjoy its ash.

Tonight they discussed the fate of AFFFA.

The entire city lay at their polished wing tips. Lights twinkled against a pink-blue sky. The illuminated Washington Monument rose majestically in the distance. About one mile behind it glowed the Lincoln Memorial, and just beyond were the lights of Rosslyn, Virginia. They could hear the soft rumble of planes at Reagan National Airport, just a few miles southwest. Far below, knots of curious tourists stared at them, pointing at these two lonely figures on the Capitol balcony, assuming they had to be important.

Very important.

They were the kings of this Hill. Mr. Speaker and Mr. Leader. (In this Congress, Jills didn't make it up the Hill.) They met here weekly. Sympathizing, empathizing, commiserating about the ceaseless attacks from their own Members while pulling sharp objects out of each other's backs, like primates. They planned the legislative calendar, a complex minute-by-minute schedule of looking busy while accomplishing nothing and preassigning blame. It was alternate side of the street blame. Some days the House blamed the Senate. Other days the Senate blamed the House. Every day both blamed the president who blamed both in return. The bald eagle was being replaced by a scapegoat. Of course, all that finger-pointing required the appearance of discord between Speaker Piermont and Leader Binslap. So they dramatically played the part of congressional combatants defending their respective chambers. But this was Washington. In the city of mirrors, objects were closer than they appeared.

"Cheers," Piermont said, holding up a glass of merlot, clasping a cigarette between two fingers.

They clinked, then leaned back in their chairs, sighing contentedly.

Piermont opened with: "My Leadership agreed to bring that ridiculous gun ownership bill to the floor after the August recess."

Binslap scowled. "A horrible law."

"It's nuts."

Binslap expelled a heavy gust of former Cuban soil. He studied the smoke wafting lazily over Piermont.

Piermont asked, "How about you? Senate gonna pass it?"

Binslap shrugged. "Probably."

They fell silent.

"Well, one of us should kill it," Binslap said.

Piermont sipped, then said, "Damn thing saved me from a coup. Truth is my crazies are all fired up over it. Looks like it's up to the world's greatest deliberative body to stop it." He tipped his glass toward Binslap.

Binslap waved his Cohiba at the Speaker. "Not me. I have four senators running for president. Each trying to run to the right of the others. They're not going to allow a quiet Senate death for the bill. Ball's in the People's House." He winked.

Back and forth they went, in a polite parliamentary volley, until the sky turned purple then dark. The lights of the city glowed brighter and the tourists drifted away. Binslap's cigar became a wet and gangly stub and Piermont's bottle of merlot was drained to a thin red ring at the bottom.

Piermont stood, stretched, and lit another cigarette. "Looks like we're both boxed in. We could just pass it and send it over there." He pointed in the direction of a long horizontal gray gash that cut right through the city. Pennsylvania Avenue. At the other end, less than two miles, was the White House. The imposing Treasury Building blocked what would have been a clear view between the White House and its noisy neighbors in Congress.

Piermont continued: "The president will just have to veto AFFFA."

Binslap snickered. "When was the surgery?"

"Huh?"

"Vetoing AFFFA requires a spine. That is not part of this president's anatomy. The man is a study in invertebrate biology."

Piermont grunted.

"Besides," Horace Binslap continued, "even if he vetoes AFFFA, it comes right back here. For an override vote. You and I will be whipping votes to override his veto while secretly securing votes to sustain his veto."

"What else is new?"

Piermont walked to the edge of the balcony and leaned on the white granite balustrade. He took in the city. A helicopter glided on the horizon, its lights blinking persistently. "How is it that the two most powerful men in Congress can't stop Congress from passing a law we're both against?"

Binslap smiled. "The most powerful man knows to get out of the way of a speeding train, Frank."

Piermont knew exactly what Binslap meant.

The gun lobby.

"Well, maybe I can slow the train," Piermont mumbled. "I'm meeting with the president in a few days." He took a final drag on his cigarette and watched the smoke vanish in the still night air. In the city of smoke and mirrors.

22

Across town, lobbyists played the Washington fundraising circuit like pinballs, ringing up points whenever they made contact with a Member of Congress. Since it was impolite to eat someone's cocktails without bringing over a little something, they brought campaign donations of $1,000, $2,000, or $5,000, which is how Washington retained its world ranking in the category of "Most Expensive Mini Egg Rolls."

A black SUV dropped Sunny at the National Republican Club, a stately, white-brick expanse on Capitol Hill. This would be her final reception of the evening before meeting Roy for drinks. She strode under a long green awning, dressed in a blue skirt that clung tightly at her hips and swished well above her knees. Inside the darkened lobby, she scowled at the portraits adorning the walls: Coolidge, Eisenhower, both Bushes, to name a few. It was like a fusty museum of political history, she thought, back when a tea party at the Republican Club involved convivial nibbling of hors d'oeuvres after a pleasant day of bipartisanship instead of frothing at the mouth; when Congress was, well, the country's club.

She wondered, *What was so good about those good old days, anyway?* Republicans won elections, then rushed to lose reelection. They compromised—a word that tasted stale and spoiled on her tongue, making her want to gag. No wonder those portraits were painted from the waist up. The subjects had no balls.

For Sunny, politics was a blood sport where only one thing mattered: winning. The issues were irrelevant and the cause didn't count. The so-called moral high ground was a graveyard where the naive and powerless were buried by a few good mercenaries.

She turned her back on the paintings and found her way into a reception honoring Senator Peterson F. Tubbs, chairman of the Senate Subcommittee on Financial Institutions. Guests picked at crudités while gorging at the public trough. Hands were shaken, profits stirred. The room echoed with the familiar notes of the Washington Overture:

"Nice to see you."

"Nice to see you too."

"And you."

In other words, who exactly are you?

Chairman Tubbs stood on the far side of the room, lean, silver, and polished to senatorial resplendence. A long line of Wall Street lobbyists coiled toward him, as if he were an ATM, depositing PAC checks and withdrawing his good favor. He wrapped himself around his guests like a vine of ripened grapes, oozing sweetness. He recited industry acronyms—FHA, CFPB, FHLBB—like poetry, and turned small talk into exaggerated howls of laughter that seemed to rattle the wineglasses lined up on the bar. Sunny noticed that the lobbyist from the Association of Big Banks was there, plus the Association of Bigger Banks, and the Association of Banks Too Big to Fail. They all sought the senator's relief from un-American regulations that stifled their ability to create thousands of new jobs planting FORECLOSED signs on America's front yards.

Sunny whisked past the line and approached the senator.

She felt a sudden clawing on her shoulder.

She was spun abruptly.

Looming over her was the corpulent lobbyist for GUN (Guns Uniting the Nation). Everything about him was grotesque. He wore an expensive suit accented with his favorite red-and-black bull's-eye patterned suspenders and matching tie. His black hair was liberally slicked with gel. He had a wide, foamy smile that spread from ear to ear, revealing a row of sharp-edged teeth that seemed too small for his cavernous mouth. He also had a well-known reputation for "pressing the flesh"—as long as the flesh was fresh and fair skinned. He slid his plump hand down Sunny's shoulder, tightened it around her elbow, and tried pulling her into a hug. Sunny angled sideways to protect her breasts from squeezing against his chest, so that all he got was the defensive brush of hip against his groin, which he didn't seem to mind given the satisfied widening of his eyes.

"Sunny, we gotta talk. Quiet place." His drawl was deep and syrupy.

He steered Sunny into a corner, under an oil painting of President Hoover, which was appropriate because that's where Hoover had said prosperity was—just around the corner.

He whispered, "Sunny, I have some information that may be useful. It's about your momma."

Sunny had many choice names for Lois, and *momma* wasn't one of them.

"It's about to hit *Politico*. Sunny McCarthy . . . queen of the gun lobby . . . has a momma who wants to ban guns!"

Sunny glared at his fingers around her elbow, which quickly unclasped. "Gee, wonder who leaked that?"

"Wasn't me, Sunny. Swear. But you got bigger problems. Something else is coming."

Sunny folded her arms.

He lowered his head, exposing Sunny to an asphyxiating dose of whatever cologne he'd pumped through a fire hose that morning. "I was on a conference call today about your momma's election in Asatuck—"

"Asabogue," she sighed annoyedly.

"It's World War Three for the industry, Sunny. We can't let every piss-ass mayor of every piss-ass town start banning our products. Gotta stop her. We're organizing, Sunny. Raising money, sending in campaign operatives, making an example of her!"

Sunny mustered a dismissive shrug.

"The NRA just pledged over a million dollars to beat her. They got opposition researchers crawling all over."

"That's her business."

"Yeaaah. But seems her business might be your business."

"Meaning?"

"Did you know about your momma's little . . . tax problem?"

There were certain word combinations in Washington that got the old adrenaline racing, for example, "tax problem."

"Unpaid taxes. On the house where you grew up. Judgments, warrants, liens up the wahzoo. It's all gonna be public. You didn't know?"

Sunny McCarthy, whose favorite dress was hubris, felt it all suddenly yanked away, leaving her exposed and vulnerable, right there in the Republican Club, bested by an insufferable rival wearing gun suspenders and a gun tie and probably even "gunderwear."

No, she hadn't known. How exactly would that have come up? "*Sunshine, I have a meeting tonight so I left you a frozen dinner and I never paid my property taxes on our house?*"

"I just wanna help, Sunny. Keep you in the loop."

He looped his fingers around her elbow and squeezed lightly. "You wanna get a drink, Sunny? Talk more about what I know about your momma?"

"I have plans," she muttered.

"Well, you just lemme know how I can help in the future. Professional courtesy."

Sunny nodded, but she knew that in Washington when a rival offered help, it was with that final yank of a noose around one's neck.

Lois Liebowitz had planned to spend the next day handling routine matters in Village Hall. There was the unrepaired streetlight on Asabogue Bluff Lane; the rumbling intrusion of a new helicopter service that ferried $800-an-hour Manhattan hairstylists to the doorsteps of uncoiffed Hamptons clients after strenuous mornings of tennis; and a petition by the twelve-member Asabogue Village Merchants Association demanding the paving of a pothole on Main Street. Lois awoke punctually at seven. She dressed in a light blue running outfit, sipped coffee while skimming the newspaper, then pushed through the rickety screen door. Strong, hot gusts of wind blew in from the ocean. Lois wedged her bicycle helmet on her head, smoothed her ACLU tote bag against her hip, and pedaled slowly down the dirt driveway into the breeze. She opened her mouth to taste the warm salt air, knowing that both fall and a bitter election were just around the corner.

Just around the corner, Lois spotted a large sign tacked to a telephone pole. It featured a grainy, unflattering photograph of her, like a mug shot. Below her face, in big block letters, was the declaration:

TAX-LIEN LOIS
DUMP LOIS LIENOWITZ!

Then she saw identical signs nailed to every pole on both sides of the street, fluttering like pennants in the stiff ocean breeze.

Lois brought her bike to a rattling stop against a curb, dismounted, and squinted at the sign. She unfastened it from the

pole and folded it neatly into her ACLU bag, briefly considering
that she might be violating someone's free speech but refusing to
litter. She returned to her bike and began pedaling urgently toward
Village Hall. The posters rippled at her sides as she passed, like a
frothing gray wake. She panted against the wind, her heart pounding. There weren't many skeletons in Lois's closet. This one hung
from every telephone pole in town, haunting her as she rode. She
thought, *Sam will know what to do.*

She arrived at Village Hall, jammed her bike into the metal
rack, and rushed inside.

Sam sat at the conference table, fingers pressed against his
forehead. When he removed them, Lois saw that they'd left tiny
pale circles against the dark crevices in his skin.

He looked gloomily at Lois and sighed, "Well, that's that. We
just lost the election." He dropped his palms to the table with a
thud.

Lois plunked herself on a chair across from him, trying to catch
her breath, chest heaving in irritating pangs. "It's dirty politics,
Sam!"

"Is it true?"

Lois felt her lips moving, but the words seemed caught in the
back of her throat.

"You did pay your taxes, didn't you?"

Lois sighed. "It's a long story."

"Not according to what I've read on almost every telephone
pole in town."

"I paid back every penny. Plus penalties and interest—"

"Penalties? Interest?"

"Paid it all back. We just have to tell people. I'm not a tax cheat."

Sam nodded annoyedly. "Awww geez, Lois. That'll make a nice
campaign slogan. I'll ask Patsy Hardameyer to redo the lawn signs.
'Reelect Liebowitz. Not a Tax Cheat.' Maybe even make up some
bumper stickers. What with the six hundred dollars we have in our
treasury."

"I had no choice—"

"Funny thing about people, Mayor, they expect government officials who tax them to pay their own taxes."

Lois felt her lips pucker. The salt air she'd inhaled during her ride now tasted bitter. The only sound was the low drone of the television. She glanced at the screen and saw an interview with that congressman from Arkansas who'd lately been dominating the news. Trying to pass a law requiring gun ownership was madness, she thought. But she knew she had bigger problems. Closer to home problems. She blew a long breath, slumped her shoulders, and began her story.

Only a few months after Larry Liebowitz fell for the actress on the Bluff, he disappeared. Larry should have known that an A-list actress would quickly tire of a local real estate lawyer towing two children to her home on weekends. But men suffering midlife crises aren't in positions to grasp reality when their genitals are being grasped, particularly by a well-endowed starlet who was the masturbatory fantasy of countless Larry Leibowitzes around the world. Soon, Larry found himself pushed to the outside of the in-crowd that caroused at the actress's home. His feelings were particularly hurt at one such soiree when he discovered Caitlin in the affectionate embrace of not one but three men in the pool house. Upon finding this moaning, writhing, sweaty tangle of well-toned musculature and almost uncountable limbs, Larry decided to join the fun. His clumsy effort to angle his naked body between what appeared to be Caitlin Turner's thigh and the elbow of the actor Mark Van Pann was met by the sudden thrust of said elbow into Larry's groin, followed by the actress's suggestion that he "get lost," followed by an orgasmic moan that Larry had not heretofore heard in his own encounters with her. He staggered dejectedly from the pool house, a towel wrapped hastily around his waist. On the beach he spotted a group of bikini-clad women crouched around a small table spread with copious amounts of cocaine. Unlike his last interaction, Larry was heartily invited to participate by, he would always remember fondly, Stormy, Rainy, and Skye. Until that moment, his only infraction of controlled substance laws was smoking the occasional joint with Lois. He sampled, sampled some more, and that began a daily addiction to cocaine, which Caitlin kept in a kitchen cabinet next to the Keurig coffee pods. Turner, who'd built an immunity to the stuff, was less than impressed by a live-in boyfriend who, when high, howled at the moon and took to rolling his naked body back and forth across the beach. One morning, Larry was abruptly awakened in a sand dune by a gentleman named Vinny. Vinny, Larry recalled in his delirium, was the director of security at the Turner estate. He was best known for having discouraged a group of paparazzi from photographing Caitlin by barreling his armored Hummer at them in an uncompetitive game of chicken. Vinny "escorted"—dragged, more like it—Larry to his waiting luggage in the courtyard. Larry was taken to his law office in the village, where the driver, also named Vinny, told him that if he ever returned to Asabogue, he would lose his license to practice law as well as the ability to urinate, what with his "dick stuffed down his throat." Not surprisingly, Larry had not been seen since. Nor were his alimony and child support payments.

"I was stuck with the mortgage and all the bills," Lois told Sam. "I fell behind on some things. I knew I'd get back on my feet. Which I did. Repaid every penny of my taxes. Exactly $780. That's the whole story, Sam. But we can't get all that on a utility pole. Can we?"

Sam nodded slowly, soaking in Lois's confession. Then whispered, "Geez. Maybe people will understand. Maybe it'll blow over before the election."

But Lois wasn't listening. Her face was turned toward the TV, pain etched in her eyes. On the screen, she saw that ugly photo of her and heard: "Lois Liebowitz. She raised *your* taxes. She cheated on *hers*."

Lois's head slumped. It felt like fall.

23

Sunny McCarthy was in a foul mood. She awoke that morning to video clips of the attack ads on her mother, e-mailed by the infatuated lobbyist from GUN. Plus, she'd been summoned to Otis's home in New York, but denied the luxury of the Cogsworth Industries' corporate jet. Relegated to first class on the Delta Shuttle, she was seated next to a chatty passenger named Mel who didn't seem to grasp that Sunny's face, buried in a fully unfolded *New York Times*, meant that she didn't care to spend the entire flight discussing recent trends in the wholesale carpet business. As the plane descended to LaGuardia Airport, she looked at her watch and groaned. It was four o'clock on a late summer Friday. She'd spend hours in "Hamptons traffic"—ninety miles of gilded gridlock from Queens to the East End of Long Island. All this might have been tolerable if not for her destination: Asabogue.

Kill me, she thought.

Outside the terminal, in broiling gusts sharpened by jet fumes, she was met by a baggy-suited driver leaning against a black SUV. The only thing missing from his full-body scan of Sunny was a salivating tongue wagging from the side of his mouth. "Keep your eyes on the road," she snapped as she thrust her bag at his chest.

They crept onto the Long Island Expressway, jockeying for position among the most competitive drivers on earth: Hamptons weekenders, who were affluent enough to occupy fashionable East End retreats but too poor to commute by helicopter. And since their wealth was amassed in the Darwinian canyons of Manhattan hedge funds, investment houses, and law firms, they took their survival skills on the road, literally. This wasn't just a drive, this was a group ruthlessly driven to win. They cut each other off, swerved and tailgated, jutted middle fingers, hurled epithets, competed for every square foot of blacktop advantage en route to a weekend of serenity. The entire exercise seemed futile to Sunny, given the fact that traffic never exceeded the approximate speed of a sloth.

The ride made Sunny woozy. She sat in the backseat, dressed in white chinos and a black top, positioned to catch the crisp flow of air-conditioning from the vents. She poked at her smartphone, ignoring the gaudy storefronts and Soviet-style brick apartment buildings of Queens. She fidgeted through the suburbs, where all roads led to malls, mini mansions, and multiplex theaters. She tried, unsuccessfully, to nap through the exurbs, which yawned to stretches of green pine. Sunny lifted her eyes to the exit numbers on large overhead signs, like a countdown to her arrival in Asabogue. But there were other signs that they were getting close: her neck muscles tightened, her lips fell into a frozen frown, her fingers whipped at her hair like a high-speed kitchen mixer. And that queasiness grew worse. The road signs should have read WARNING: LOIS AHEAD.

It was twilight when they finally turned off the expressway and snaked through the tiny villages of the East End. Each was a flickering strip of luxury boutiques and elegant restaurants, like a line of tiki torches along the beach. Southampton, Bridgehampton, Sagaponack, Amagansett.

Then, ASABOGUE.

The sign was faded brown and curled at the corners, as if the weather had baked it over many years. For Sunny, it was like one of those impromptu highway memorials where a fatal accident had occurred. Asabogue. The scene of the crime.

"Fuck," she mumbled.

"Excuse me?" asked the driver. The lingering ache where Sunny's Louis Vuitton bag had impacted his ribs might have suggested that she wasn't exactly making an offer.

"Just drive."

No, don't. Hit the brakes, buddy. Abort! Abort! Abort!

They passed small farmstands, closed for the night, rickety roofs drooping against an azure sky. Hand-painted signs advertised apples, peaches, blueberries, and corn as well as homemade pies and fresh cut flowers. Weathered old farmhouses, embraced by wraparound porches, glowed from both sides of the road. Sunny saw the Presbyterian church. Once it was a towering landmark near Sunny's home. Now, it was a patchwork of missing shingles, topped by a precariously leaning wind vane.

They came to a crossroads. Main Street curved to the left, Village Hall in the distance, barely visible in the corner of Sunny's eye. Just past a flickering streetlight ahead, Asabogue Bluff Lane began its gradual ascent to the right, framed by high, thick hedgerows. As they climbed, a familiar taste settled on Sunny's tongue, warm and salty. The ocean humidity pressed against her skin and worked through her hair. She imagined her hair beginning to frizz, its permanent state when she lived in Asabogue. They passed the residence where Sunny had spent weekends with her father, until that day when Lois reported that dear old dad had left Asabogue, evidently, she said, to practice real estate law in Saudi Arabia. Sunny knew that Lois was lying, having witnessed Larry's not so gradual descent into a cocaine stupor. That was when Sunny Mc-Carthy determined she wouldn't let Asabogue trap her as it did her parents—mired in the quicksand of naïveté like her mother, or blinded by the glitz like her father. No, Sunny McCarthy would find any way out, and stay out.

Trigger Happy was up ahead.

Sunny tried to swallow against her nausea.

A sinewy blond assistant named Lars, snugly dressed in a yellow Trigger Happy polo shirt and black shorts, escorted Sunny to the terrace. Outside, a thin ribbon of pink separated dark ocean from sky, and the heavy salt air filled Sunny's mouth. One hundred of the Cogsworths' dearest friends, neighbors, and social allies had gathered in an ethereal, torchlit glow. They seemed dressed up to appear dressed down: sockless men in purposefully rumpled linen shirts, pastel sweaters draped across their backs; women wrapped in long floral dresses that barely cloaked their Jimmy Choo sandals. They swirled in accordance with the Hamptons laws of physics, like an undulating flock of birds, not colliding but colluding, calculating the minimum time necessary to see anyone worthy of being seen with, then flitting away. In a far corner, a classical guitarist strummed to the background of nearby waves lapping on the beach.

Sunny scanned the terrace until she found her target, standing alone in front of a bar: Congressman Roy Dirkey, the evening's honored guest. He wore crisp khakis, a solid blue shirt open at a stiff collar, and a blue blazer gleaming with the requisite American flag lapel pin. His hands were planted awkwardly in his pants pockets, and his eyes darted back and forth in search of any friendly face, relaxing only as Sunny approached.

"There you are!" he said in a heavily released breath.

"Welcome to paradise, Congressman. I need a drink!" Sunny grabbed a crystal glass of red wine from a row that had been neatly aligned on the bar. She sipped, sipped some more, and asked, "Recognize any Dirkey Chevy customers?"

Roy whistled. "So this is the top one percent the liberals keep whining about."

"Oh no, Roy. This is the top one percent of the top one percent. See that guy over there? With Otis?"

Otis was leaning against a rail, his back to the beach, nodding politely at someone a full head taller, with a long, tanned face and white sculpted hair that resisted the ocean breeze.

"That's the CEO of McDougal-Loop."

"The defense company?"

"Biggest arms exporter in the world. Had a bad year, though. He dropped from fourth-highest-paid CEO in America to fifth. Peace is hell."

"Poor guy."

"Relatively speaking."

She reached for a second glass. The wine and salt air percolated on her tongue. "Oh, and that woman over there? Recognize her?"

Fawning admirers encircled a short woman with close-cropped gray hair.

"Runs Celfex Pharmaceuticals. All the blue blood here is pumped full of her products."

"Do they make anxiety pills?" Roy laughed nervously.

"Relax, Roy. Everyone's here to show you some love. Big banks, big tobacco companies, big gun companies. All the merchants of death, taking a little break from their crimes against humanity. The crime of capitalism. The crime of success." She raised her glass. "To greed." She drained what was left and blew a long breath. She was starting to feel relaxed.

"You okay?" Roy asked.

"I'm getting there." She raised a third full glass of wine. "To Asabogue!"

Otis had broken away from his conversation and lumbered toward them. He wore a sky-blue Sagaponack Country Club polo shirt. Dark sweat stains had pooled under his armpits and across his belly. His cheeks were flushed and the sleeves of his sweater were tangled against his neck. He kissed Sunny, leaving a wet trail of sweat and the sharp stench of cigars on her cheek. She felt woozy. Then he patted Roy's shoulders, winked, and proclaimed, "Our man of the hour!" He pulled a thick, tattered envelope from his pants pocket and waved it excitedly. "Good news! We collected a hundred and fifty thousand in checks at the door. And I got commitments for another ninety grand!"

Sunny calculated that Otis's "man of the hour" had raked in a quarter of a million dollars in that hour. She wanted to ask if the haul exceeded his annual Coon Supper fund-raiser in West Bumfuck. But she held that in, which she considered a sign of lingering sobriety.

"I'm humbled," Roy stammered.

Sunny downed glass number three and smirked.

You should be humbled. You're nothing to these people. A rank-and-file congressman lumped in with all their other charity cases. You're a stray puppy, Roy. A rare disease. They're not here because they believe in you. They're here because you're a chit in their barter system. Otis asked them to fork over a few thousand bucks; now he owes them. "I'll trade a donation to your favorite Member of Congress for my favorite prostate cancer charity." Bend over, Roy.

She suggested that Otis introduce Roy to his guests.

"Good idea," Otis replied, then leaned toward Roy. "Didya bring it?"

Roy tapped knowingly at his blazer pocket.

Sunny stayed at the bar, watching Dirkey work the crowd while she worked through more wine. She watched them swoon as Roy fished that bullet-holed Constitution from his pocket and told his war story. They clasped his hands and patted his back. They dried their glistening eyes and thanked him for his service. Roy grew more comfortable, winning them over with that *awwww shucks* humility, the cocking of his head, and the hick grin. His shoulders seemed to rise, his voice grew stronger, his laugh exploded like fireworks over the beach. He produced that Constitution on demand. As lovable as, well, one of those adorable teddy-bear pups at the East End Animal Shelter gala. *Gimme paw, Roy! Attaboy! Good Congressman!*

By the time the guests began filing out, Sunny was steadying herself against the bar. She had to get to Otis's guesthouse, a five-minute walk on a slate path across grassy dunes. Once it was a stable for the Cogsworths' polo ponies. But Otis had no interest in the sport (and looked rather ridiculous bulging in an equestrian helmet and riding boots). So he sold the ponies and put Lucille in charge of renovations. Nearly two million dollars later, the only memory of its prior inhabitants was the valuable collection of equestrian art decorating the walls.

Sunny wondered where Roy would be sleeping that night. The aptly named Double Action had two bedrooms. A competent congressional staff would ensure he wasn't alone in the guesthouse with an attractive, half-drunk female lobbyist. They'd arrange for him to be driven to the Riverhead Holiday Inn Express—forty minutes away from temptation.

The good news, Sunny mused, was that Roy's staff wasn't that competent. The night had potential.

The bartender began removing glasses, leaving only one. Sunny took a few wobbly steps. Then a voice bellowed, "Carpe diem, everyone!"

Sunny swiped the last glass of wine.

Jack Steele made his grand entrance, trailed by young campaign aides plastered with red, white, and blue STEELE SUPPORTER stickers. His gravelly voice cut through Sunny like a buzz saw. "Sorry I'm late. Busy night on the old campaign trail!"

Jack embraced Congressman Dirkey like the old friends they weren't. "This is my boy," he proclaimed, dangling his arm over Roy's shoulder. "When are you running for president?"

Roy beamed as if he'd just been nominated.

Sunny thought, *What a performance! What range! From killing with his bare hands to glad-handing. And the Oscar goes to . . .*

Steele released his hold on Dirkey and approached Sunny with open arms. He proclaimed, "Sunny McCarthy! Good to see ya! How's Mom?"

You're an asshole, she thought. But it came out as an ambivalent, if slurred, "I haven't really seen her."

Jack put both hands on Sunny's shoulders and leaned toward her, the brim of his black cowboy hat nudging against her forehead. He lowered his voice. She smelled peppermint gum on his breath. "Look, Sunny. I know this is awkward. She's your mother. And blood runs thicker than water."

Let's experiment. Someone get me a knife.

"My campaign to defeat that woman isn't personal. It's politics. You understand, right Sunny?"

Over Jack Steele's shoulders, Sunny noticed Otis's eyes bulging.

In addition to the condescending "you understand," Sunny McCarthy despised the political pretense of "it's not personal." In fact, Sunny knew that politics was always personal. She viewed politicians with the cold clinical interest of an anthropologist. They were, she believed, a species of distended egos shrink-wrapped in diaphanous skin. When the skin was exposed to any form of insult, a chemical reaction occurred. The offended ego unleashed a mixture of volcanic adrenaline mixed with icy indignation, forming permanent landmarks in one's memory, impervious to erosion. Scores had to be settled, points proven. Before long, a slight became a skirmish, a skirmish a feud, a feud a war, and pretty soon entire continents were being invaded. All because of something that wasn't *personal*.

So when Jack said "it's not personal," Sunny knew that it was, well, very personal. And his delivery! That condescending tone, as if Sunny knew nothing about politics, compared to this political genius of, oh, about one week, who thought Sun Tzu was a Chinese restaurant franchise in Boca.

She narrowed her eyes through her inebriated fog. She studied Jack's sunken cheeks, pockmarked from half a century of caked-on makeup; the artificially whitened teeth shining through a snarl laced with spittle. Her prior thoughts of sleeping with Roy Dirkey were now overcome with the imperative to screw Jack Steele. She summoned the famous Sunny McCarthy comeback—words serrated to render Jack Steele a eunuch right on the terrace of Trigger Happy in the presence of eye-lifted witnesses.

Otis seemed frozen. Next to him, Lucille gave him a look that said *Do something!* An ugly scene was approaching, like the occasional squalls that formed on the horizon—dark, flashing, and speeding over Trigger Happy. Until now, the Cogsworths had successfully avoided the ugly scenes that had marred other Hamptons soirees. In fact, they had an unblemished record. But this! Not since that sordid item in the *New York Post* about the Asabogue billionaire who shed his third wife for a coed waitress at the Lobster Roll in Amagansett had such ugliness been portended on Billionaires Bluff.

Sunny opened her mouth, but her usually sharp tongue felt spongy. "Know . . . whaaat, Jack?"

Otis stepped helplessly forward. Lucille looked faint. Roy had a bemused smile.

"You're . . . a . . . a . . . ffffffffff—"

Sunny's sentence was cut off by a full-throttle puke.

Sunny awoke to a Gene Krupa drum solo crashing in her head, and the inside of her mouth tasted as if something had crawled in to hibernate. She was in bed, blankets pulled to her head, face smushed against a pillow. She groaned. It sounded like a death rattle.

Her eyes fluttered open to a sunlit room; she could hear the soft splashing of waves outside. She lifted her head from the pillow and a clump of tangled hair fell across her face. In the distance she saw horses charging toward her. Small horses, galloping from the walls.

Oh . . . my . . . God. I'm at Double Action.

Sunny kicked off the blankets and lifted herself from the bed. Her head throbbed and the room spun. Her belt was open and her pants unsnapped. The top buttons of her shirt were unfastened, revealing the upper ridge of her bra, and the shirt was damp with perspiration. She stumbled toward a dresser and looked in a mirror. She'd gone from "hot and sunny" to "help find a cure." Bloodshot eyes blinked from puffy rings of smudged mascara. Her left cheek sported a meandering crevice from a wrinkled pillow. A patch of dried saliva had formed on the side of her mouth. Sunny had no idea how long she'd slept, but from her own rank odor, it could have been days. In fact, she may have come back from the dead.

She thought, *Air. Coffee. Shower.*

Sunny shuffled barefoot into the living room and pulled open a sliding door with a grunt. She stepped out, gulping for fresh air.

"Well, good morning!"

Roy Dirkey sat back in a patio chair, clasping a coffee mug with the Trigger Happy logo, smiling mischievously.

Oh. My. God. Are you kidding?

Roy wore running shorts and no shirt. His skin sported various scars. Sunny assumed the injuries weren't sustained in the line of selling Chevys.

She quickly considered her options. The most sensible involved rushing toward the ocean, plunging in, and swimming for the horizon, never to return.

"Some fun last night, huh?" Roy smirked.

She pulled the top of her shirt closed. "Exactly . . . how much fun?" Her voice was scratchy, her mouth bone-dry.

Roy laughed. "I never saw someone go down for the count like you did. I wanted to call an ambulance, but Mrs. Cogsworth said, 'Absolutely no ambulances at a Cogsworth event.' Something about how ambulances attract the wrong kind of attention. I think if the choice was letting you die quietly or letting you live with some bad press, we'd all be getting dressed for your funeral today."

Probably true, Sunny thought. "How'd I get here?"

"Well, first they took you inside the main house and cleaned you up. We don't have main houses where I'm from, by the way. Then some doc showed up and said you were . . . 'overserved.' A couple of the household security staff—another amenity we seem to be missing back home—brought you down here and we put you to bed. I looked in on you a few times during the night. Don't worry, I stayed a respectable distance at all times. But I must say—girl, you can snore! Heard it a bedroom away!"

Really, kill me now.

Sunny reemerged an hour later, freshly scrubbed and dressed in denim shorts and a white tank top. She fell into a chaise lounge while Roy poured her coffee. She sipped slowly, letting the caffeine settle on her tongue and drift into her head, letting the warm sun bathe her skin.

"So this is your hometown, huh?" Roy asked.

Sunny squinted across the dunes to the waves lapping on the beach. "Here? Not exactly. I lived on the other side of town. Waaaay on the other side."

Roy was silent. Then he asked, "You going to visit your mother? I heard Steele talking last night. Seems like they're gonna get pretty rough with her."

Sunny focused on puffy clouds drifting high over the ocean and said, "Change the subject."

"Yeah, I know how you feel. Maybe that's why people like you and me do what we do. Always trying to prove we're not our parents."

Sunny set down her coffee and swiveled toward Roy, anger flashing across her face. "Hey! You wanna be the governor of Arkansas or an amateur shrink?"

"I just meant—"

"Here's the deal, Roy. I love my privacy. And I shoot trespass-
ers—"

"Whoah!"

"You're here to collect two hundred fifty grand, go back to
DC, and pass AFFFA. You worry about that. I'll worry about my
mother . . ."

Sometimes, critical secrets slip out of the most carefully
guarded minds. Take Sunny that morning. Maybe all those drinks
had weakened her defenses. Or maybe when Roy saw her stum-
ble onto the patio with her blouse open and her breath putrid, or
heard her wake-the-dead snore, that area of her psyche that protected her image just surrendered, figuring there was no longer
any point to guarding secrets. Whatever the cause, the words left
her lips before she could tug them back.

"I'll worry about my mother . . ."

24

S peaker of the House Frank Piermont loved being third in line to the presidency. He hated being near President Henry G. Piper, especially while news photographers jostled to record the moment. Their monthly Oval Office meetings were staged to show the party faithful that two of the most powerful Republicans in America were working hand in hand. The truth was that it was hand-to-hand combat.

They'd served briefly together in Congress. Piermont was known as the "Member's Member"—tucking earmarks into bills for his colleagues, advancing their amendments, traveling to far-flung congressional districts to speak at their fund-raisers. He'd laboriously paved his path to Speaker with the concrete mixture of chits and favors over twenty years. President Henry G. Piper, on the other hand, treated the floor of the House as a spring-board to a better gig. He charmed the Republican national donor network; he was a darling of the Sunday morning news shows; he had a golden tongue that operated deftly from both sides of his mouth.

His good fortune soured quickly upon taking the oath of office. The Republican base thought he'd become a weak-kneed moderate. The moderates thought he'd veered, sharp-elbowed, to the base.

Now, President Piper sat in his chair at one end of the Oval Office, rubbing his forehead with index finger and thumb. The nervous habit, triggered with every world crisis and bad headline, had, by now, produced a distinct pink blemish. Piermont sat in an adjacent chair, staring icily ahead. Staff sat on two couches separated by a coffee table, like two opposing teams glowering at each other. The Oval Office was decorated in accordance with the preferences of various focus groups commissioned by the president. The walls were a peachy yellow. The paintings looked as if they'd been swiped from a Motel 6. (The First Lady drew the line at replacing a portrait of Thomas Jefferson with one of the paintings from the *Dogs Playing Poker* series.)

The president's press secretary bellowed, "Thank you," a signal for the press corps to beat it. Shutters clicked, feet shuffled. When the last photographer exited, Piper slumped in his chair. He'd been slumping a lot lately. Chicago was a war zone. The Dow was plummeting. China and Germany were nudging the United States toward nine in the G8. The Middle East was one big nuclear arms bazaar. Climate change was pushing Jews out of an inexorably sinking South Florida for higher ground in the Poconos.

And the list of Republicans vying to primary Piper resembled an NCAA bracket grid.

Plus there was the matter of his schedule that evening—another tedious black-tie affair, this by the Association of American Gun Associations. They were the last bastion of support for the president, all his former loyalists having melted away like ice cream in the sweltering Washington summer. He couldn't afford to lose them, but there were grumblings within AAGA that Piper was, as quoted by an anonymous source in the *Washington Post*, getting "gummy on guns." This, despite the president's hundred percent NRA rating, his executive order allowing same-day pistol permits (registering to vote, on the other hand, now took approximately six to eight weeks), and his decision to light up the White House facade one night a month in gunsmoke gray. The dinner, days before a House vote on AFFFA, seemed timed to put the president in the political crosshairs.

So to speak.

Piper cleared his throat. "Frank, you can't pass this bill. It's just—"

"It's nutso," the Speaker interrupted. He enjoyed interrupting the president.

Piper scowled his disapproval, then continued. "I mean, the United States government cannot compel every American to—"

"Own a gun!"

"It just goes—"

"Way too far."

"So we agree?" asked the president.

"We don't disagree."

"So you'll bottle it up?"

"Can't. My Members are pushing. Hard."

"Push back."

Piermont thought, *This coming from a president whose last foreign trip was called the White Flag Tour.* He nodded defiantly. "Congress is taking its August recess soon. When we come back in September, I want my Members focused on passing a gun bill, not gunning for me."

"Well, then Binslap will just have to kill it in the Senate when you return."

"Not with a third of his caucus running against you, Hank."

25

The Association of American Gun Associations annual dinner was the hottest invitation in Washington, and a "must show" for any presidential aspirant. Candidates posed for photo ops waving their favorite firearm high above their heads in a display of presidential phallus worship that would roll Freud's eyes. It was a blend of gun rights rally, Hollywood awards ceremony, and New York fashion show. Guests traversed a red carpet, bearing arms in bare arms, strapless gowns, and rippled cummerbunds. Ivory glinted from gun grips and Victoria's secret was a concealed bra holster.

Hundreds of tables were spread across the massive banquet hall of the Washington Marriott, bathed in the soft glow of chandeliers. The white-draped dais was long enough to land a small jet. There sat Speaker Piermont, looking, as usual, glum. There was also a woman who might have been the correct response to

"Obscure Cabinet Secretaries for $200, Alex," and all seventeen announced Republican candidates for president, eyeing each other warily. They were the only ones who were required to check their guns at the door. At the microphone, the master of ceremonies implored his unruly audience to pay attention to the program, punctuating every few words with "shhhhhhh." But his words were whimpers against the oblivious roar of the crowd. He had no chance of being heard in a room filled with talking heads. Pundits pontificated, congressmen bloviated, celebrities chattered, all to the clanking of silverware and the soft thuds of dinner plates plopped on tables.

The buzz that night was the American Freedom from Fear Act. There was hyperventilating that the administration would issue a veto threat! That the Senate would filibuster! *Politico* had posted a grainy image of the leaders of the Senate secretly conspiring to kill the bill. SludgePost.net tweeted of similar plots at the White House.

Veto threat! Filibuster! Statement of principles of administration! These were the words that stimulated glands, pumped blood, released pheromones inside the Beltway. Outside the Beltway, people remained mostly nauseous.

In a far corner, there was a sudden surge of bodies, like a rolling wave. Cameras snapped and flashed. Heads turned and necks craned to glimpse the arrival of the new Elvis of American politics. He was barely able to move against the crowd as it closed in on him. Kate Kass of CNN maneuvered to his side. She was diminutive, but the woman could poke holes through any cluster of reporters.

Kass shouted, "How do you respond to reports that you're thinking of entering the Republican race for president?"

A rather overwhelmed Roy Dirkey insisted, "I haven't thought of that. I—"

Kass interrupted, "Planning any trips to Iowa? New Hampshire?"

"Just Arkansas. Third district—"

"So you're denying an interest in running for president?"

"Yes! No. I mean, right now I'm running for reelection!"

"Right now?"

Earlier in the day, someone had leaked the latest poll in the Republican presidential campaign. Until then, all seventeen candidates had been tied for seventeenth place. In fact, the highest vote getter was a guy named "Never Heard Of." Now, however, a new name had streaked brilliantly across the dense Republican field, like a meteor burning in red, white, and blue. The previously unknown Roy Dirkey was winning every head-to-head even though he hadn't dipped a toe into the Republican race. It didn't matter that the poll was conducted by an outfit known as Fudge & Bluster Associates (motto: "Where 2 + 2 Equals Whatever You Want"). This was news! Okay, maybe not news, exactly. More like a morsel that would temporarily feed the omnivorous appetite of the twenty-four-hour live-streaming news cycle. It would be chewed on, digested, and then regurgitated into the mouths of other pundits, like birds feeding an incessantly chirping flock.

Roy's sudden popularity was fabricated by the grease-oiled machinery of this manufacturing town. That day almost every news outlet in America featured a photo of Roy, cradling his favorite military assault weapon, flashing that boyish grin. Television network bookers were in mortal combat to land him for the following Sunday morning shows. CNN begged. Fox pleaded. MSNBC cajoled. And even though Roy Dirkey had only wanted to be governor of Arkansas, the words "President Dirkey" had a certain ring to them. The fact was that Roy's thoughts had recently been wandering up Pennsylvania Avenue and loitering at 1600.

Finally, Roy found his table. It was hosted by the NRA and accorded appropriate prestige, at the footsteps of the high dais. It was populated by the brightest stars in politics, entertainment, and sports. He wrestled his chair from the tangle of chairs next to him. He struggled to figure out which of the four separate wineglasses was his and which of the many forks splayed before him he should use. He was wedged between a breast-enhanced actress and steroid-enhanced NFL quarterback. At one point, both slinked off, returning later in various states of apparel malfunction, having obviously engaged in passionate debate over the Omnibus Appropriations for the Department of the Interior and Related Agencies Act. Over a wilted brown salad, Roy found himself in a one-sided conversation with the heavily accented French ambassador. Roy didn't understand a word. He did, however, make a pre-presidential decision to terminate diplomatic relations with France.

Sunny remained at the back of his mind. He called her that morning and asked her to attend the dinner. Her rejection left a stinger deep in his skin. It went something like "I'd rather be dead."

The dinner droned on. President Piper's speech had all the conviction of a plate of shimmering Jell-O. On the issue of gun rights, the seventeen presidential candidates struggled to, well, outgun each other. The undercooked beef left red rivulets on plates, the coffee was weak, and the featured comedian bombed. Through all of it, the center of attention was the gentleman from Arkansas. Yet despite the assemblage of journalists, tweeters, bloggers, analysts, and commentators, right there in the very capital of the punditocracy, no one thought to ask the most important question: Who leaked the poll showing Congressman Roy Dirkey closing in on the presidency? And why?

Toward the merciful end of the program, the emcee again attempted to shush the crowd, announcing, "A special greeting from a beloved hero to us all." The lights lowered to near black and the audience brought itself to a dull roar. Towering video screens flickered on. Then a voice thundered across the expansive hall. "Hi ya'll. This is Billy Bedford Forrest."

Everyone cheered.

In 1978, in the middle of a typically riotous concert at the Clarksville Speedway & Fairgrounds in Tennessee, the artist formerly known as Billy Dumphee called a judge onstage and legally changed his name to honor his boyhood hero, Nathan Bedford Forrest. The original Forrest was a lion of the Confederacy and first Grand Wizard of the Ku Klux Klan. The newly minted Billy Bedford Forrest was a heavy metal rocker wanting to make a statement, with an exclamation point in the shape of a burning cross.

Billy Bedford Forrest became a cult phenomenon. His songs were skull-cleaving anthems to political incorrectness. "Domestic Untranquilities" simultaneously rose to the top of *Billboard*'s Hard Rock and the Secret Service "Persons of Interest" lists. His cover of the Knack's "My Sharona"—renamed "My Sharia"—was received in various Middle East countries with the burning of American flags and stationing of grim-faced marines around U.S. consulates. To ignite sales, Billy spewed noxious diatribes at his favorite targets: liberals, vegetarians, and, especially, gun control activists. Billy had it figured out: the more loaded his sound bites, the more his fans downloaded his songs.

And now, here he was, in prerecorded grandeur.

He sat in a recording studio, cradling a Gibson Byrdland electric guitar. Now in his late sixties, he looked like an assisted living resident dressed as a rocker for the Halloween party. A Confederate flag bandana was stretched across a gaping bald spot; a stringy gray ponytail fell to his shoulders; and his chin sported a narrow clump of gray-flecked stubble. He wore a black tank top that advertised, in bright spangle, his current concert tour: Stun Gun Love.

He began. "Friends, I'm here to talk to ya'll about Jack Steele. Jack's running for mayor of a town called Asabogue. Maybe ya'll never heard of it. But, hey, who the—" (*bleep*) "ever heard of Lexington and Concord till the shot heard round the world?"

Eyes misted and heads nodded.

In the next two minutes and fifty-five seconds, Billy Bedford Forrest's fund-raising pitch for Jack Steele's campaign managed to include, among other phrases, liberal maggots, Constitution-shredding goons, jihadists, Jews, vegan scum, suck my Glock, fat feminist bitches, Lois Liebowitz, Barack Hussein Obama, anti-gun

26

In Washington, egos and libidos are naturally swollen. Exposed to certain influences—for example, press clippings that include the phrase "presidential contender"—they inflame grotesquely. It was in this euphoric state that Congressman Roy Dirkey met Sunny McCarthy for dinner a few nights before the August congressional recess. His delusions of grandeur alternated between sitting in the Oval Office in two years and seeing Sunny naked that night.

Sunny McCarthy was an expert at managing congressional libidos. There was a thin line between persuasion and seduction. It was a tricky business, requiring constant calibration and sufficient encouragement to keep a congressman engaged but not engorged. But she felt Roy lowering her resistance with gentle cranks of homespun charm and glimmers of naïveté settling under her skin and making it tingle. So, on the issue of sleeping with him that night, she was, in congressional jargon, firmly undecided. Roy, on the other hand, was quite firm.

They met at Vincenzo in Georgetown. It was Sunny's favorite restaurant, because it was miles from Capitol Hill and too expensive for most Members of Congress. Plus, Mario, the doting and obsequious maître d', knew her name, her wine preferences, and, telepathically, when to present the check to end an unpleasant date. Candles at each table cast the room in a moody flicker. Black-tie waiters glided efficiently through the room and patrons held themselves to a civilized murmur. Roy arrived in his pre-presidential off-the-rack suit and presidential red-striped tie. Sensitive to her last appearance with him, Sunny McCarthy upgraded from disheveled to de la Renta: sleek gray pencil skirt and clingy white silk blouse.

After ordering, Sunny immediately sensed that Roy was distracted. First, he skipped thanking Jesus for the overpriced meal they were about to receive. Second, his dark eyes shifted constantly over her shoulders, as if seeking signs of recognition: the excited pointing of fingers and dropping of jaws over a real live presidential candidate. If anyone noticed, they didn't seem to care. Here, presidential candidates were a dime a dozen. Or, this year, a dime a dozen and a half.

Mario poured a Bordeaux. There was a businesslike clink of crystal. Sunny sipped. Roy slurped. Then, with feigned casualness, he asked, "You hear the news?"

"I did! Exciting! I never thought I'd live to see Congress pass the reauthorization of the Export-Import Bank."

Roy grinned, revealing that sliver of space between his teeth. "You know that's not what I meant." He clasped his hands, leaned forward, and said, "Lots of chatter about me running for president."

"Oh, that." Sunny smiled politely.

"So, what do you think?"

"Roy. I—"

"There's a real groundswell out there."

"The thing is—"

"Of course, if I do run, I won't be able to sponsor AFFFA."

Sunny raised her eyebrows. "Excuse me?"

"If I'm running for president, that bill could be a problem. Got to appeal to the soccer-mom vote."

"If by that you mean the Armed Soccer Moms of America, Cogsworth Charities funds them. Besides—"

"Got to cut to the center, Sunny. Win moderate voters in battleground states."

"You may be getting ahead of yourself, there, Congressman."

He shrugged. "Introducing AFFFA made sense when I was thinking of running for governor. But the dynamic's changed."

"The . . . dynamic?"

"Mmmm-hmmm."

Mario slid dinner plates on the table, his eyes glued on Sunny, who stared incredulously at Roy. "You made a commitment, Congressman," she said icily.

"Just need some tactical flexibility is all."

Sunny McCarthy swallowed the remainder of her wine without taking her eyes off Roy. *Tactical flexibility? That's my line. Oh. My. God. I almost fell for it. He's no hick, he's a huckster. Like all the rest. Willing to throw me under a bus fueled with his own burning ambition. Well, fasten your seat belt, buddy. I'm taking the wheel.*

She leaned forward. "Want some advice?"

"Shoot."

"That groundswell of support for your presidential campaign? You're looking at her."

Sunny noticed a slight furrowing of Roy's brows. Something between worry and confusion. *Good.*

"Not only did I see the news about you running for president. I planted it."

"I don't get it," Roy stammered.

"You were an anonymous freshman congressman who happened to be sponsoring AFFFA. One: I had to get the media to take you seriously. Two: I had to put some pressure on the president to support the bill. So I leaked a bullshit poll about you, which got a ton of press, which got all the other candidates juiced up about AFFFA, which pushed the president further into a box. That groundswell is a tactic, Congressman. Cheers." She tipped her now-empty wineglass.

Roy's determined jaw seemed to unhinge. "You used me?"

Sunny giggled. "C'mon, Congressman Dirkey, spare me the Pine Bluff bluff. You've been around the block. In fact, you had a Constitution strapped against your not so bleeding heart."

Roy seemed frozen.

"So congratulations. You've made it to the major leagues. As one professional cynic to another: enjoy the presidential ride, because it's a short-term rental. Just long enough to pass AFFFA and get it to Piper's desk in September. Then back to plan A: Arkansas. I might even come to your inauguration in . . . what's the capital of Arkansas?"

"Little Rock," Roy mumbled.

"Sounds lovely."

Sunny watched Roy's cold eyes narrowing on her, and the slight twitching of his temples. She sensed Mario hovering protectively nearby. She wondered if she'd gone too far. Playing with fiery egos often created a backdraft. Roy could storm out, drop AFFFA. *No,* she thought, *he's too smart for that. And ambitious. He needs that bill. We need each other.*

Finally, Roy said, "Did it work? The tactic?"

"You were at that dinner. Every presidential candidate was gushing about AFFFA. It could have been a Rose Garden bill signing. Piper has nowhere to go. Now he has to support it. That bill's about to become law. And you're about to become governor. If you don't screw it up."

Roy mulled this over for a few moments, slowly nodding his head. Then he said, "So . . . I guess we're a good team."

"In the most brutal game on earth. Politics. More wine?"

"Careful. Last time I saw you drink, it didn't work out too well."

Now Sunny froze. *Touché*, she thought.

"Been thinking a lot about that night," Roy continued. "Coulda been a good team in that little guesthouse."

"Timing is everything, Congressman. That night was just bad timing."

"How about tonight? Or are you going to destroy my presidency and my fantasy at the same time?"

Out of nowhere Mario deposited a check in front of Sunny.

Sunny smiled. "Let's get AFFFA passed. Then we'll have a team celebration."

It was a commitment. With some flexibility.

27

In 1863 two armies—one Union, the other Confederate—stumbled on a largely unknown town in Pennsylvania where one thing led to another and that other thing led to something else and the whole thing became the Battle of Gettysburg. That's pretty much how the Battle of Asabogue erupted: the convergence of opposing armies and an accidental bumping of shoulders, in this instance, over a Morning Glory muffin at Joan's Main Street Bakery.

The armies that converged on Asabogue that August would change it forever. There was the pro-Steele army: a collection of gun defenders, militiamen, and biker gangs; hunters and recreational shooters; armed opponents of the IRS and Bureau of Land Management; and a handful of Obamacare combatants, like Japanese soldiers emerging from caves years after World War II. At the invitation of Billy Bedford Forrest, they deployed to a town they'd never heard of—this new beachhead against the left wing's march on their Constitution, their homes, and their guns. They arrived heavily armed, waving above their heads their assault weapons, rifles, shotguns, and pistols, as well as their brass knuckles and military knives. They were dressed to kill, girded for battle in tactical boots and vests, concealed carry jackets and fatigue pants. They carried American flags, DON'T TREAD ON ME flags, and the flag of Bundyville, Nevada, whose board of supervisors had just passed a resolution to secede from the Union over a dispute involving grazing rights for cows. They arrived in pickup trucks, flatbeds, and 4x4s with gun racks. They called themselves the We the People Army.

The other army carried oak tag and Sharpies and was armed with indignation and noses elevated at the sophistry of their opponents. They looked like a field trip from an adult education class on social activism. They were "silkscreen liberals," displaying their allegiance to world peace, animal rights, and alternative dispute resolution on designer T-shirts. They arrived in minivans equipped with Wi-Fi, child seats, and bike racks. Ironically, they were also called the We the People Army. However, in a couple dozen conference calls preceding their arrival, the word *army* was debated as overly aggressive and off message. So they became the We the People Coalition of Peace for All Americans Working Hard to Get Ahead if That's What They Want, We Don't Judge. They never had a chance.

There was a third army—the army of media that rumbled through Asabogue in caravans of TV network satellite trucks. They deployed makeup artists, engineers, producers, and production assistants. They pitched tents on Veterans Park and broadcast live reports with Village Hall as a backdrop. The more they reported from Asabogue, the more Americans rushed to Asabogue. They rose from the sidelines to the front line in America's culture war. They engaged in the great battle of the time: the campaign between Jack Steele and Lois Liebowitz, which, as Chris Matthews said on camera, "isn't a local election, it is defining who we are as a nation." And when you're defining who we are as a nation, you can expect emotions to flare. Elbows to fly. Even over a Morning Glory muffin.

Guarding the door of Village Hall, hands on hips and feet spread wide, Chief Ryan realized that his police force of four men and three driveble cars might not be able to keep the peace in this tinderbox. So he called the Suffolk County Police Department for reinforcements and soon another fleet of vehicles rumbled in, blue and red lights swirling.

All of this to the mocking squawks of seagulls on the beach.

The Riverhead Holiday Inn Express had filled up quickly. So the armies began quartering in the village's tiny homes and summer cottages. Vera Butane was first to rent her modest Cape Cod to a CNN news crew for ten grand a month (plus a security deposit, which Vera would have waived if it were from a different network, say, the Food Channel). Then the Wickhams rented their place for fifteen grand. When Claudia and Theodore Brady sold out for twenty thousand, a new war erupted—over real estate. Money flowed in and natives temporarily moved out. And with a new population came new demands. The old wooden floor at the Wick & Whim groaned under the shuffling feet of strangers aimlessly shopping for supplies and knickknacks. Veterans Park was now moonscaped—trampled under the crush of boots, portable stages, tent posts, and klieg lights. Long lines snaked out of Joan's, which was selling out of its Morning Glory muffins like, well, hot cakes.

The invasion had claimed another feature of Asabogue: its middle ground. You were either with Jack or with Lois; pro-freedom or pro-safety. Loyalties were plastered on bumpers and pinned to lapels. Lawn signs sprouted everywhere. Campaign money from across America flooded the village, like waves breaking on the beach. Asabogue found itself awash with Jack Steele pens and Lois Liebowitz potholders. Televisions glowed day and night with gray grainy images of Jack and Lois. Against the din of protestors and the press, you could hear the constant shrill ringing of phones in every home in the village—phone bank canvassers asking voters who they were for and who they were against, reminding them to vote, exhorting and cajoling. The phones rang ceaselessly, drowning out the old Presbyterian church bell when it clanged on the hour. Streets teemed with volunteers knocking on doors and handing out literature, eyeing each other angrily across demilitarized zones established on each block. Volunteers pleaded their cases in alien accents from the Midwest and Deep South and places faraway from Asabogue.

Mayor Michael Rodriguez arrived in mid-August with three burly Chicago Police officers, two pretty staffers, and a gaggle of reporters covering his nascent presidential campaign. He was there to endorse his fellow mayor for reelection. And since he was in the neighborhood anyway, he figured he'd sample some Hamptons restaurants, get in some beach time, and rub elbows in order to shake loose some campaign contributions.

Aaaah, the sacrifices one endures for a noble cause.

His retinue walked on crowded Main Street, Rodriguez assuming the gait of a politician desperate to be recognized: neck craned, eyes sweeping, face set in a self-important clench. But the crowd was so thick and self-absorbed they didn't realize that the author of the Chicago Compact was walking right under their noses, and at five feet four inches, quite literally.

They reached Village Hall.

"This it?" the mayor asked, his foot tapping against a chipped brick walkway. *No high school marching band, no bunting, no key to the city?*

The door swung open and Lois Liebowitz emerged, arms outstretched, Sam Gergala and Chief Ryan lagging behind her. She greeted him for the prearranged photo op and they assumed their positions behind a rickety podium cluttered with microphones.

His Honor endorsed Her Honor with some heartfelt talking points. They gripped and grinned, then executed a fumbling thumbs-up for the cameras. After a final handshake, Rodriguez turned to leave. But Lois wasn't finished. She pulled him back and began asking questions about the Chicago Compact—as if the politician who conceived of and announced it had any idea of its specifics. Rodriguez resumed his foot thumping, only now heavier and more rapid. An aide interceded, urgently reminding him of "that important meeting in Chicago," which required him to leave Asabogue forthwith. Reluctantly, or so it appeared, he left Village Hall with a final wave of his arms and returned home, but not before wrangling a coveted table at the famous Nick & Toni's in East Hampton, followed by being honored at a five thousand per person fund-raiser at the summer rental of a Chicago hedge fund executive.

The day after the "Meeting of the Mayors" (as the *Asabogue Bugle* called it), Ralph sat in his basement, reflecting on the transformation of his hometown. He was calling it the "Asabogue Armageddon": the gathering of armies in a cosmic battle that would consume his village in flood and fire.

Ralph was never happier.

For weeks he'd wore a satisfied smile across those voluminous cheeks. He felt vindicated. In fact, he felt like renting a plane and skywriting I TOLD YOU SO!!!!! over the village. Not that he was thrilled about the Islamex invasion, or all those Jews and jihadists pushing their way around town. But for a guy who'd been universally mocked for his paranoia, validation was some consolation to the end of times.

Ralph had been monitoring events from his windowless basement, which he renamed "the Bunker." Maps of Long Island were taped to walls and splayed across Mrs. Kellogg's laundry appliances. Mrs. Kellogg had foraged provisions from every convenience store between Asabogue and Montauk. Steel shelves were crammed with a survivalist's buffet: junk food, crackers, canned fruit, and beer. There were aluminum packets of freeze-dried meals and meals ready-to-eat. A locked cabinet—only Ralph had the key—contained a tattered box of pre-owned Yugoslavian gas masks, a tangle of two-way radios, and, hidden at the back, one biochemical personal protection suit, extra large, which was reserved for Ralph. On a rickety coffee table sat an English-Arabic translation guide (just in case) and mood lighting from Sterno emergency candles.

There was also enough firepower to defend the village. Guns of every shape, caliber, and gauge. Handguns, shotguns, rifles. Sawed off and modified. Automatic and semiautomatic. Uzis, AR-15s, M16s, AK-47s. Colts, Magnums, Glocks. Grenades and grenade launchers. And hundreds of thousands of rounds of ammunition, including armor-piercing bullets. All delivered in the past few months by an increasingly nervous UPS driver, who figured that when Ralph Kellogg went deer hunting, he really meant business.

The latest rumor involved various federal agencies deploying to Asabogue to "monitor events." This was a clear act of aggression by Washington, or the United Nations, which Ralph believed was actually running things. Soon shiny-badged bureaucrats would be snooping around town. He imagined the FBI, the Bureau of Alcohol, Tobacco, and Firearms, even the CIA poking their noses where they didn't belong, like Village Hall, where they might learn of certain favors that Ralph bestowed on his friends. Or the local bank, where Ralph collected generous kickbacks for such favors. (Gunrunning wasn't a cheap proposition, after all.) They'd issue search warrants, question neighbors, knock on doors, kick in the doors, then set the place ablaze. Like they did in Ruby Ridge. And Waco.

Game on, Ralph sneered.

Ralph summoned reinforcements. They arrived at the Bunker

from across Long Island's Twin Forks, which pointed like the tips of two bayonets, ready to defend against the invading hordes. They left their farms and subdivisions. They crowded into Ralph's house and spilled onto his yard. They pitched tents and draped their camos on Mrs. Kellogg's tilting clothesline. They hoisted flags that said MAKE AMERICA EVEN GREATER and REMEMBER BENGHAZI! They burned campfires and sang songs about taxes and tyranny late into the night. They propped their rocket launchers on Ralph's picket fence, a particular annoyance to his neighbor, George Kilmner. George was a zealous defender of the Kilmner-Kellogg property line, and three-time winner of the Asabogue rhododendron competition. But this time he didn't complain. Picking a fight with people capable of firing short-range missiles at his herb garden didn't seem advisable.

There was also the stench. The Kellogg house had only one tiny bathroom for its forty guests. It featured its original pink tile and very finicky plumbing. So the entire property was enveloped in thick vapors of backed-up sewage and unwashed bodies, farts and belches, junk food and beer.

The original members of Ralph's Organization—Louie Delmarco and Bobby Reilly—didn't particularly care for the newcomers; how they sprawled their air mattresses in the basement so that no one could move without tangling their feet; how their heavy metal music blared from their earphones; how they pushed their way around and ate Louie's junk food and guzzled his beer. Even the chain-smoking Bobby Reilly objected to the asphyxiating haze of cigarette smoke. In such close and unventilated quarters, the combination of high-fructose diets, combustible testosterone, and excessive paranoia strained already jittery nerves.

One day, Louie opened a supply cabinet for his midmorning snack of Cheez-Its. He plunged his thick fingers into the red box. They probed deeper and deeper until hitting bottom and emerged with nothing but orange crumbs clinging to the tips. Louie grabbed the box, turned it over, and watched a few orange flakes waft onto the cement floor.

Louie blinked back his rage. Then he asked, "Who finished my Cheez-Its?"

When no one answered, Louie Delmarco asked again, only louder. "Who finished my Cheez-Its? And left the empty box?" His plump hand closed against the box, crushing it.

No one paid attention. Ralph was leaning against the washing machine, studying a map of Connecticut, wondering if Islamex terrorists could dig a tunnel under the Long Island Sound and pop up in Veterans Park.

Louie yelled: "Hey assholes! You finish my Cheez-Its, it's common courtesy to go out and replace them!"

There was a deep growl in a corner, like an engine revving. A newcomer who went by the name Levi ("short for Leviathan," he liked to tell people in a husky voice) stepped forward. He was tall and powerfully built. A Mohawk sprouted from an otherwise clean scalp. His biceps were plastered with American eagle tattoos and a handlebar mustache plunged like a frothy waterfall down his jaw. On that jaw were small traces of Cheez-Its. "Dude, calm down. It's not the end of the world."

Ralph looked up from his maps. He saw Bobby Reilly move protectively next to Louie. Bobby said, "There's manners, is all."

Levi hooted: "Manners! La-dee-fucking-da!" His comrades giggled. He stepped closer to Louie, his biceps flexing in excited anticipation. "Who are you, the Martha fuckin' Stewart of the militia?"

Louie had no clue who Martha Stewart was. But he took this as an insult, likely aimed at his manhood. He dropped the Cheez-Its box. Clenched both fists. Stepped toward Levi. A circle formed around the two, ready for action. Meanwhile, Bobby Reilly moved toward one of the weapons cabinets.

Ralph thought, *Crap.*

Louie Delmarco was built to idle, not to fight, especially opponents who could bench-press his rotund body. Louie's eyes leveled on Levi's wide chest as it heaved against an American flag tank top. Levi's arm muscles rippled so that the eagle tattoos looked like they were trying to flutter away. Louie craned his neck and rolled back his head, then suddenly gulped a full blast of Cheez-It–flavored breath expelled from Levi's cheeks.

Bobby reached toward a metal shelf, grabbing the first weapon he touched. It was small, round, and fit in his palm. It was an M67 hand grenade, which from everyone's perspective, including Bobby's, may have been overkill for not replacing an empty box of Cheez-Its.

"Stand back!" Bobby yelled, waving the grenade wildly above his head for effect.

A rapid tangle of fetid bodies suddenly pressed against the wall, under the now-drooping Jack Steele movie poster.

Ralph sighed resignedly. As a student of the Military History Channel, Ralph knew that all great warrior leaders reached crises like this, when low morale and privation turned men on each other. George Washington at Valley Forge. John Wayne at *The Alamo*. Mel Gibson in *Braveheart*. He had to diffuse the live grenade who was clutching a live grenade, then deal with the issue of low morale in the Bunker. He stiffened his back, jutted his chin like George C. Scott in *Patton*, and strode toward Bobby. He put out his hands. "Gimme," he grunted.

Bobby fidgeted. Ralph leaned toward Bobby and said, "Gimme. I got a mission for you. Special."

Bobby's eyes darted. They were bloodshot and yellow from nicotine. They rested on Louie, who nodded, relieved not to be strangled by Levi but anxious about being blown up by Bobby. Bobby handed the grenade to Ralph. There was a chorus of sighs, punctuated with some *Holy fucks!*

Ralph said, "Bobby, Louie. Report to me. Upstairs. Now."

They sat at a wobbly table in the kitchen. Heaps of crusted plates overflowed from the sink. Outside the window, a plume of smoke coiled from a campfire. The refrigerator buzzed and thumped and generated an eye-watering odor.

"Boys," said Ralph, "you've been good and loyal soldiers. You deserve some time off."

One of Louie's favorite phrases was "time off." He pumped his fists.

Ralph continued: "I want you to go into town. Get some fresh air, stretch your legs. Conduct reconnaissance on enemy positions. And pick up some more Cheez-Its while you're out."

He slid a stolen AmEx card across the table, which Louie grabbed.

"Take your weapons, boys. But don't shoot till you see the whites of their eyes." Ralph chuckled. He thought it seemed like an appropriate cliché.

Ralph was wrong.

They took their weapons, walked through the dark hall and out to the front porch, where the screen door squealed closed.

They went to town.

In Village Hall, Lois Liebowitz and Sam Gergala shuffled through piles of papers on the conference table to the din of protestors outside. Lois signed a letter to the local congressman about helicopter noise and yet another requisition for the installation of a brand-new streetlight at Asabogue Bluff Lane. Then said to Sam, "Coffee?"

"Sounds good. I'll pick some up from Joan's."

Lois pushed back her chair. "Let me go, Sam. I need a walk."

Sam glanced out the window and warned, "Be careful."

"It's Joan's. Things aren't that dangerous."

She pushed open the door with a chuckle.

Louie and Bobby turned a corner onto Main Street. Deprived of his morning snack in the Bunker, Louie lagged behind, massaging his growling stomach and whining, "Let's eat." He'd been whining since they'd left.

Bobby asked, "Eat where? Everywhere's a crowd. Look at this place. Don't look nothing like Asabogue!"

They stood still in the late-morning heat. Long lines meandered out of every storefront. Main Street was gridlocked with hundreds of vehicles and motorcycles bearing out-of-state plates. The sidewalks teemed with visitors, guns slung over their shoulders and stuffed into holsters. On Veterans Park, a bank of news cameras were trained on anti-gun demonstrators in pink shirts, swaying and singing "Kumbaya."

Louie grimaced. The grinding in his belly felt like knives and he was growing more agitated. Streams of sweat ran down his puffing cheeks. Bobby stared at him and reached a diagnosis: Cheez-Its withdrawal.

"This is our town!" Louie shouted above the din. "Shouldn't have to wait on line to get something to eat. I'm going to Joan's!" Louie stomped off indignantly, melting into the sidewalk congestion. Bobby scrambled to catch up.

A crowd was gathered at Joan's Main Street Bakery for yet another celebrity sighting. There, in tanning-parlor flesh at a small Formica table, sat ABC's Harry Holt. Harry had a knack for close proximity to war, genocide, typhoon, tornado, plane crash, mass destruction, starvation, or near apocalypse. Which is why he wasn't invited to many parties. He was the new young face of the network, having replaced the old new young face a few months earlier. And what a face! A hawk-like intensity, crystal-blue eyes, a faded scar meandering across his forehead ("Somalia" was his one-word explanation to the curious), thick brown hair carefully styled to look carefree. And a swarthy Australian accent that made every word sound exotic. He was with his cameraman, swiping at his iPad while sipping the fresh organic tea the network was contractually required to import from London. For a newsman, Harry seemed completely oblivious to the crowd that had formed to catch a glimpse of him. They stretched cameras high in the air to snap his picture and shoved each other out of the way for a better view. They crowded deeper into Joan's, scuffing the black-and-white tiled floor, pressing against the glass counter, bumping against the small tables.

By the time Louie arrived, his stomach was like the heaving waves and crackling flashes of an ocean storm. The warm smell of the bakery didn't help. It swept through the room, propelled by ceiling fans spinning lazily. It wafted into his nostrils, watering his eyes and flooding his mouth with saliva. It drew him through the crowd, elbows flailing as he barked, "Official village business!" His blue Parks Department T-shirt gave him an air of authority. Louie knew that people respected uniforms, even if, as in his case, the uniform was ripped, mud-stained, and revealed the lower third of a hairy and undulating belly. Finally, Louie made it to the counter and breathlessly plunked his arms down on the glass. A group of Joan's employees greeted him numbly. They were dressed in black JOAN's aprons with smudges of various colored frosting streaked across their sweaty faces. The counter looked as if locusts had buzzed through, leaving empty dishes and crinkled cellophane. The ticket number display high on the wall had lost count hundreds of customers ago. It blinked helplessly at Louie.

"Gimme a cheese danish! Quick!" Louie panted.

The staff stared back. "All out," one said.

"Prune, then. One prune danish."

"Sorry. No prune. No cherry. No danish."

Louie felt light-headed. He wrung his hands on the glass. "Then what kinda pie you got?"

"Sold outta pie. All we have are these . . ."

A single dish of brown muffins was displayed in the showcase, fresh from an overworked oven, moist and glistening.

"I'll take them. All." Louie fished for the stolen AmEx card.

The plate was set on the counter. Louie reached for it. And then—

"Hold it. I was here first!"

Louie turned. Next to him was a man dressed like Darth Vader, in urban tactical gear from black tactical helmet to black jackboots.

"Who are you?" Louie asked angrily. He could taste the Morning Glory on his tongue.

"Brigadier General Jeb O'Malley. Indiana Militia of Jesus. Greene County Brigade."

"Louie Delmarco. Asabogue Parks Department Maintenance Assistant III. Nice to meet ya. Now, get lost." He tugged at the dish.

The general tugged back. "Maybe you don't understand. I'm a brigadier general. I outrank you."

Out of the corner of his eye, Louie caught Bobby cutting through the crowd, moving toward him. "Maybe in Cowturd, Indiana, you outrank me. But not here. Not in Asabogue!" Louie turned to the bakery staff. "Am I right?"

Since the Joan's Bakery employee manual was silent on the order of precedence in various civilian militias, the staff stared back, slack-jawed and exhausted.

Louie tugged the plate to the right. The general tugged to the left. The Morning Glory muffins jiggled. Louie tightened his thick fingers on the rim of the plate. The general grunted. Behind him, four soldiers from the Indiana Militia of Jesus stepped forward, Ruger Mini-14s drawn.

For the second time that morning, Bobby Reilly sensed threat closing in on his friend. This time, however, there was no Ralph Kellogg to disarm Bobby. Just a group of lanky Indianans in urban gear with their guns pointed at Louie Delmarco, whose reddened fingers were now clamped around the plate of muffins. *Fair's fair*, thought Bobby.

He drew his Sig Subcompact. Pointed it in the air. Pulled the trigger.

The Battle of Morning Glory commenced.

A thick stream of blood ran across Harry Holt's forehead, meandering down toward his eyes. He was about to wipe it with his sleeve, then stopped suddenly. ABC had interrupted its regular

programming and was about to go live to Asabogue. Blondes were
a dependable ratings booster at Fox News, but ABC now had blood.
Real, hot blood. So Holt dropped his arm and stared defiantly at
the camera, worrying that his cameraman's shaking hands would
ruin the shot. "You okay?" he asked without moving his eyes from
the lens.

"Think so."

"Nice and steady, mate. This may be our Emmy."

Behind him, tables were overturned, plates and mugs were
smashed, and the bakery counter was a pile of broken glass and
bent steel. The black-and-white tiled floor was scattered with
guns, brass knuckles, and military knives. One of the ceiling fans
was hanging by its wire, the blades wobbling through a thick, acrid
haze.

In his earpiece, he could hear the urgent voices of technicians
and producers scrambling to turn the world's attention to Harry
Holt. Or was it buzzing from the gunshots? He felt numb, his ears
were ringing, and the deep gash across his head was starting to
burn. He listened to the ABC "bad shit is happening somewhere"
theme music. Then he heard the sonorous voice of Chad Atlas:
"dramatic footage" ... "our own Harry Holt" ... "actually caught in
the crossfire."

His cameraman pointed a trembling index finger, indicating
they were live. Not just live, Holt thought, alive!

He took a deep breath, tried relaxing his jaw. "That's right,
Chad. I was right here at Joan's Main Street Bakery in Asabogue
when it all happened." His voice was scratchy. Not nervous sounding, he hoped. He lowered his pitch. "Senseless gun violence between rival militias over what seems to have been a dispute over ...
muffins."

"Harry, we can't help but notice what appears to be a pretty
nasty wound on your head."

I'm glad you noticed. Holt wiped the blood away with the back of
his hand, leaving a Jackson Pollock streak above his eyebrows as he

tried to convey the proper amount of pain. "I'm okay. Just grazed. I think."

The truth was that Harry wasn't grazed by a bullet. When the shots were fired, he dove, hitting his forehead against the rim of the table. Now he'd have two scars: one from Somalia and another from Formica.

"Harry, can you tell us exactly what happened?"

"Chad, my cameraman is the real hero here. When the violence erupted, he kept shooting. Take a look . . ."

ABC viewers watched the grainy, careening footage. People screaming. Bodies diving. Morning Glory muffins splattering. Glass shards flying. A seemingly brave but pudgy village employee wrestling a militiaman clad in black. Soldiers from countless militias converging. More shots. Bodies diving. The picture suddenly flipping upside down as the cameraman hit the ground, then turning right side up. The voice of Harry Holt, yelling against gunfire and screams: "Are you getting this? Keep filming! Keep filming, mate!"

Chad asked, "Do we know how many casualties?"

"No word yet, Chad. Although I can confirm at least one official of the Village of Asabogue."

28

Sunny McCarthy was at her best when things seemed their worst. When crisis erupted, when a wind shear in public opinion pitched Cogsworth International Arms into free fall, when Otis and his idiot nephew Bruce huffed in breathless panic, that's when Sunny took control. She'd calmly direct the reverse thrust of the fan when the shit hit: pressing buttons, shifting speeds, pushing, pulling, spinning, and steering until things went her way, as they always did.

Sunny McCarthy was the CEO of crisis management.

But not now. Now she was slumped back in her chair in a self-diagnosed panic attack. A cold sheen of sweat covered her body. She frantically twirled her hair into spidery clumps. Her neck muscles closed around her throat, slackening her jaw. Her fingers stumbled over the television remote as she numbingly clicked from network to network, searching for one image.

Lois.

She watched the impromptu news conferences from Asabogue featuring grim-faced officials in government-issued Windbreakers. She vaguely recognized old neighbors, like ghosts from the past, haunting her as they nodded their heads, clucked their tongues, and described the carnage. The last time Sunny saw so many twirling lights on Main Street was Christmas, many years before.

She'd tried calling Lois, bracing herself for the inevitable lecture about gun violence in Asabogue sprinkled with a few *Didn't I tell you*s? But there was no answer. Just the sound of her mother jangling the phone and declaiming: "Hullo. This is Lois. Leave a message." *Beep*.

Sunny hung up before recording anything. Because *Hi, Mother. Just checking to see if you're alive. Call me back if you are* didn't seem appropriate.

Don't panic.

I'd have heard if something horrible happened to her.

Why doesn't she call me to tell me she's okay?

When her phone rang, she lunged for it.

It was her brother, Jeffrey, his voice quivering from Vermont. He'd tried reaching Lois ever since hearing about the shooting on National Socialist Radio, or whatever he listened to. Now he was racing somewhere through the Green Mountains to Asabogue.

"Lemme know as soon as you hear anything," Sunny ordered. She stood, rendered a nervous breath, and walked toward the sun-filled windows overlooking Penn Quarter. Far below, workers plodded back from their lunch hours. They clutched supersized receptacles of iced caffeine. Their earbuds were firmly in place, sealing them off to events in Asabogue.

The Capitol dome rose against a cloudless sky, topped by the Statue of Freedom. She'd been perched there since 1863, in a gaze of eternal indifference, staring frozenly through war and peace, depression and prosperity, protests and pageantry; staring past the homeless living on sidewalks in the shadows of Capitol Hill, the crime scenes in nearby neighborhoods and in the marbled building below. Sunny had a theory on why her nineteenth-century handlers had positioned her facing eastward, her back turned on the entire continent. She was a national monument to looking the other way.

The cell phone chirped again. Sunny's heart pounded, then sank. It was Bruce.

"Otis wants a conference call. Hold on. I'll put us through."

Sunny paced while the theme song from *The Guns of Navarone* warbled through the phone. She imagined the explosions on Main Street carrying to Otis's high sanctuary on the Bluff. She wondered whether the *pop-pop-pop* of the bullets interrupt the soft slapping of waves on his beach, prompting him to cock his head, wondering what was happening downtown.

Would he even ask about Lois?

"Hullo? Who's on?" Otis's voice sounded an octave higher than normal.

Bruce answered, "Me. And Sunny."

Otis squawked: "Good Lord! This shooting! Right in my neighborhood!"

Well, not exactly your neighborhood. We lobbied the post office to give the Bluff its own zip code, remember?

"What's our response?" Otis demanded.

Silence.

Otis blurted impatiently, "Hullo? Hullo? Anyone alive out there?"

Sunny tried to swallow Otis's ill-timed choice of words. They left behind a burning trace.

Bruce said, "Uhhhhh. Same as always? Let it blow over?"

"Except this time it's blowing right over Asabogue, Bruce! What do you think, Sunny?"

I think you should ask me about my mother.

"Sunny!"

"Bruce is right."

Someone gasped. Probably Bruce, she thought. "He's right," she repeated. "It'll blow over."

"Exactly!" Bruce's voice rang with renewed confidence.

"Do you both understand that the entire national press corps is in Asabogue? They're probably heading my way right now! I can just imagine the headlines: 'Mass shooting near gunmaker's home.' We need a statement!"

"How about this," Bruce ventured. "'If everyone in that bakery had a gun, it would've been safer.'"

"Ummmm. Almost everyone did have a gun," Sunny reminded him.

"C'mon, people! I can practically hear the reporters banging on my gates!"

"Don't answer!" Bruce yelped. "Pretend you're not home!"

Sunny heard Otis's frustrated groan. "So my only option is to sit tight. Behind closed doors. In the dark. With Lucille."

"Just for a few days," Bruce said assuringly. "By then no one will remember what happened in Asabogue."

The words stung at Sunny.

"You agree, Sunny? Just lay low?"

Or fuck off.

"Sunny?"

"I'm here."

"You're awfully quiet."

"Bruce said it all."

"Hmmmm. You all right?"

My mother is missing, my hometown is a shooting gallery, and I may be in the middle of a serious breakdown. Other than that, I'm peachy.

"When does Congress come back from its taxpayer-funded August vacation?" Otis asked.

"That would be in September. A few weeks."

"Will this delay the vote on the Dirkey bill?"

Bruce chortled. "If Congress delayed gun votes every time there was a violent shooting, there wouldn't be any votes. Right?"

Oh. My.—

Otis grumbled, "Sunny, call the Speaker's office. Make sure AFFFA's on track. This shooting's bad enough. We can't let it kill our bill."

God.

Then, "Have you heard from your mother?"

Wait. Is this the faint sign of a heartbeat? "Not yet. I'm a little—"

"I mean, if she hadn't tried banning guns, we wouldn't be in this mess. This is her fault!"

For Sunny McCarthy, that was the heaping of insult to possible injury. Or worse.

"Get back to me when you hear from Speaker Piermont!" Otis commanded, then hung up.

Sunny stared at the television. It was all so familiar, this American ritual. The BREAKING NEWS banners crawling across the screen. The steely glare of the news anchors trying to summon a fresh urgency to lines repeated from the last episode. The montage of images: the swirling lights and yellow tape, the shadowy movements from crime scene surveillance cameras, the faces contorted with grief and swollen cheeks flooded with tears, the eyes widened in monstrous horror, the fusing of bodies into quaking hugs. Sunny knew what was coming. The ragged nest of microphones sprouting from a podium; the officials huddled around the podium. The obligatory references to "thoughts and prayers" going out to the victims and their families, the platitudes about "pulling together." The gnashing of teeth, wringing of hands, and beating of hearts. The governor. The sheriff. The police chief.

The mayor?

The fade to black.

"We'll be back," the anchor would promise.

Yes, they would, thought Sunny. After all, this was America's longest television rerun.

She grabbed her cell phone but didn't dial Speaker Frank Piermont.

Jack Steele kicked back in a plush recliner in the media room at Villa di Acciaio. It was designed to replicate a vintage Hollywood theater, complete with heavy red velvet wall panels, ornate chandeliers, and the piped-in scent of popcorn. The room was dark, except for the glow of SOSNews on a wall-sized flat-screen, like a cozy fire in winter. One of his housekeepers—Maria, or Rosa or whatever her name was—stood dutifully at the door. Jack had publicly ranted against the illegal immigrants who he believed swarmed America's borders, broke its laws, took its jobs, coveted its women, stole its guns, and decimated its language. But for as long as he had gardens to be manicured and his favorite sangria to be mixed, he could demonstrate a quiet pragmatism on the issue.

SOSNews had assembled a panel of experts to diagnose the prospects for AFFFA in light of the "Muffin Massacre." There was Megan Slattery, Robert Thomas, and Ashley Barnes.

And the sultry pundit Cailee Cox. Even at his advanced age, Jack felt a pleasant sensation in the vicinity of his prostate surgery whenever Cailee Cox appeared on-screen. She was called "the Insultress." Sleek thighs spilling from tight black-lace skirts; beautiful cleavage; shimmering blond hair that fell almost to her hips. But it was mostly her sumptuous, pouty lips that aroused Jack. When opened, they released incinerating flames at her many targets, her top two being godless Democrats and gutless Republicans.

Cox groused: "Nineteen people get shot at one bakery and the liberals want to take everybody's guns away. Yesterday ninety people were killed in car accidents and I haven't heard a single liberal demanding the confiscation of their Saabs, have you?"

The SOSNews anchors nodded righteously.

"Congress reconvenes in less than two weeks. If Speaker Piermont delays this vote by so much as one day, it will reveal to his caucus what a spineless wonder he is. And trigger the coup that will remove him from the Capitol and put him where he belongs: on display at the Invertebrate Exhibit at the National Zoo!"

Cailee Cox could take or leave Frank Piermont.

"Stay with SOS!" Megan Slattery commanded.

As Speaker of the House, Frank Piermont enjoyed many privileges. High on the list was not having to return home when Congress was on recess. His district was electorally safe, which meant he could remain a safe distance from those pesky constituents who reliably elected him every two years. Now he was slumped on a broad red-striped couch in his Capitol office. The walls were a satiny yellow and exhibited mementos from happier times. There were the family portraits with his wife, Francine, and daughters Faith, Fawn, and Felicity, and his prized *Golf Illustrated* montage of the most beautiful courses in America (he'd played them all). The room was dominated by a massive mahogany cabinet housing six televisions, all set to a low drone. His eyes meandered from screen to screen, then landed on Cailee Cox.

"Turn it up," he instructed a staffer through lips clamped on a cigarette.

He began puffing angrily, leathery cheeks expanding and contracting, his mouth spewing smoke like an overworked furnace, agitated wheezing accompanying each gust.

His staff lined the walls, shifting on their feet, eyes darting nervously from Cailee Cox to their mobile devices to the Speaker. They waited for him to react, but the Speaker was speechless. His shoulders heaved as he puffed. His bloodshot eyes narrowed against the thick haze. His cigarette had burned to a tiny stub between his nicotine-stained fingers. A stream of sunlight fell through a window, turning the cigarette smoke into soft bluish wisps hovering flatly in the air. Outside the window stretched the entire National Mall, from Capitol Hill to the Washington Monument and behind that, the Lincoln Memorial. All the majesty and power of Washington was at the very feet of the Speaker. Who was now being compared on national television to a species without a skeletal system.

The communications director, a wiry young man who had taken up chain-smoking in order to acclimate his lungs to the job, muttered under his breath.

"She's fomenting a caucus rebellion!"

The Speaker crushed the cigarette stub in an overflowing ashtray. Then he said, "Get the bill on the floor. First thing we vote on when the Members get back."

He lit another cigarette.

President Henry G. Piper sat in the White House Situation Room, which was actually several rooms of different sizes, depending on, well, the situation. Mass shootings were generally "mediums," requiring enough space for the president, attorney general, and the heads of various agencies, bureaus, divisions, and departments. At the front of the room were rows of red digital clocks blinking DC time, Zulu time, and the times in Kabul, Paris, Oman, and now a place called Asabogue. Television screens were mounted on every wall. On one screen, a network was airing its slickly packaged "Muffin Massacre" complete with foreboding music and a still image of a blood-streaked Harry Holt. A mahogany conference table was cluttered with water bottles and styrofoam cups imprinted with the gold presidential seal.

An aide sought the president's approval of the usual statement offering the deepest condolences of a heartbroken nation. Piper approved it with a sullen grunt.

Across the table sat the attorney general, strangely overdressed for the Situation Room, in black tie and cummerbund. He tapped his forefingers on the table, obviously annoyed about being late to a campaign fund-raiser. "Mr. President, now is not the time to consider a law mandating gun ownership for every citizen. You must issue a veto threat. You must stop Congress. Immediately."

The attorney general spoke with great moral certitude. And no moral certitude was greater than his political survival. The administration's approval of AFFFA, he calculated, would sink his campaign for governor of left-leaning California.

The president sighed. "We don't have the votes to sustain a veto."

"Use your bully pulpit . . . sir!" That last word dripped mordantly.

Piper thought, *There is no bully pulpit anymore. Just a thin sheet of ice melted by the hot air of blowhards like you. Where presidents slip and slide before falling on our asses.*

The president pressed his thumb and index finger against his forehead. By now that blemish looked like an overripe black cherry.

At the back of her mind—an organized place where she stored rarely utilized thoughts as if on the high shelf of a closet—Sunny always considered the possibility of a situation requiring contact with someone in Asabogue. Her "in case of emergency, break glass" scenarios included, and were generally limited to, Lois falling off her bike, a mild heart attack, a broken hip. Getting shot was never contemplated. Now she searched her phone for the number she'd stored long ago. She pressed Call, heard several rings, and pleaded, "Pick up!"

"Hullo?" Sam Gergala's voice was barely audible through crackling static.

"It's Sunny McCarthy."

"Sunshine?"

"I tried calling my mother. She didn't answer. I—"

"She broke a wrist in the panic," Sam reported, matter-of-factly. "I'm at her place now."

Relief washed over Sunny. "Can you put her on?"

"She's sleeping."

"But she's okay?"

Several seconds passed. "You really wanna know?"

Sunny's eyes squeezed closed. "Tell me."

"No, she's not okay. Nothing in this town is okay. Your friends at Cogsworth—they don't just want to beat your mother, they want to destroy her. And Asabogue. We need help, Sunshine."

"Sam—"

"Come home."

"I can't. I have work to do in Washington."

"Just for a few days. Tell us what to do, so we have a fighting chance. Give your mother that, at least."

Sunny gazed out her window, at the statue above the Capitol dome. "Two days, Sam. Tops."

She figured the statue would still be there when she returned.

29

For the occasion of Louie Delmarco's interment, Ralph Kellogg skimmed Pericles's Funeral Oration and some Shakespeare. He quickly realized that they hovered well above the grasp of the newly consolidated Louis Delmarco Division of Defiance. It was Ralph's idea to merge the various militias that had converged on Asabogue and rename them in Louie's memory. After all, the man had died for his principles (and, an autopsy revealed, indirectly from plunging blood sugar levels). So Ralph arrived at the funeral with a eulogy befitting Louie: short, simple, and undernourished.

They gathered under a slate-gray sky at Asabogue Rural Cemetery, just next to a shabby brick building with a warped tin roof that housed the village animal shelter. The wailing of dogs added to the sense of despair. In addition to the representatives of various militias, several of Louie's coworkers from the Parks Department showed up in their dress blues, which were the same as their ordinary uniforms, only laundered for the eternal adieu to their comrade in shovels. Flags fluttered at half-mast in a gentle breeze, like the lineup outside the United Nations. American flags, Confederate flags, skull and crossbones flags, and the flags of various county and state militias. A single television cameraman was there, leaning against his tripod. SOSNews was devoting a full twenty seconds to the ceremony in a package poignantly called "Louie." A bugler from the former Rio Grande Border Militia played "Taps," with a slight hint of Herb Alpert's "Tijuana Taxi." The farewells were fond; bloodshot eyes glistened as Louie was lowered into the Asabogue dirt he'd spent an entire career trying to avoid digging.

Ralph was angry.

There were no official dignitaries at the funeral, despite the placement of an entire row of gray metal folding chairs stenciled with VILL. OF ASABOGUE in white. Lois Liebowitz didn't show up. Or Jack Steele. The chair with a placard that said GOVERNOR was empty. So were the chairs reserved for the Suffolk County executive, and the neighboring village mayors. No town fathers or mothers. Ralph never expected a state funeral, but, Christ, could they at least have sent the deputy assistant director of the Parks Department? Show a little respect?

Respect. It had eluded Ralph his entire life. And now, it eluded Louie Delmarco, even in death.

He stared at the grave of Louis Alfonso Delmarco, his fingers reflexively shredding the text of the eulogy. His prepared words were overtaken by a frothing indignation that reddened his cheeks. Through a clenched jaw, in a voice deep and bitter, Ralph said, "I won't let you die in vain, Louie. The whole world is watching Asabogue. Now we're really gonna give 'em a show."

The mourners harrumphed righteously.

Ralph flexed his big fists.

In his own grave, Pericles would be spinning.

30

Sunny McCarthy wondered, *What do you get for a mother you've tried ignoring for years? Will a nice blueberry pie do?*

On the outskirts of Asabogue, she brought her rented car to a rumbling stop in the gray gravel parking lot of Marion's Famous Farmstand. It was a landmark for weary travelers to the Hamptons. They loved its rustic charm; the wooden lean-to that slouched over crates of freshly picked produce, and the satisfaction of supporting a local farm whose cheap migrant labor worked the soil so close to, but safely out of view, of the resident's tennis courts. Marion's offered bountiful selections of corn on the cob, cherry tomatoes, cucumbers, cauliflower, and nearly two dozen varieties of pie. Plus, to satisfy recent consumer demand, there were piles of the *New York Times*, the *Wall Street Journal*, and *American Resistance* magazine, and a rack of cell phone chargers.

Sunny headed to the counter. Behind it stood a woman with

a contented gaze, plump arms folded. She wore a ragged black T-shirt that said: MARION'S! BEST FORK OF PIE IN THE SOUTH FORK. Soft wrinkles spread across a puffy face. Her thin brown hair was pulled back, revealing gray roots.

Sunny ordered a blueberry pie and slid cash across the dirt-encrusted counter.

The woman chirped, "Howya doin'?"

Sunny nodded politely.

"Ohhhh, you don't remember me, do ya?"

"I'm sorry. I—"

"It's Kay!"

"Kaaaaay . . ."

"Kay Hardameyer! Patsy's daughter! We were in school together. You lived at Twenty-Eight Love Lane. I'm at Twenty-Three."

"You're still—"

"You bet! Hey, the rent's cheap!" Kay Hardameyer's laugh was a languorous wheeze, gulped back with a loud snort. "My mom told me you were coming back. Welcome home, Sunshine!"

Sunny smiled weakly. "I'm just visiting. Two days."

"Oh. Too bad." Kay placed a white pie box in a crinkled plastic grocery bag and leaned toward Sunny. "I'm real sorry about your mother. Can't wait for this election to be done with. Get our town back, ya know?"

Sunny resumed her ride. The car radio droned about a new poll that affixed President Piper's favorability somewhere between root canal and head lice. Plus, there'd be a vote in Congress on much-needed legislation declaring National Cancer Awareness Day, which, Sunny thought, deserved congressional attention for more than one day.

Then—"Jesus!"

Sunny knew that Asabogue traffic was particularly heavy just before Labor Day weekend. But this had the feel of Times Square on New Year's Eve. Red blinking brake lights stretched endlessly ahead. Blue-uniformed police and olive-green–clad members of the National Guard lined the curbs. Her car radio was drowned out by the honking of horns and spuming of protestors.

Sunny inched her car toward Love Lane, the pie at her side.

The years hadn't been kind to 28 Love Lane. Red shingles dangled loosely from the front of the house. The roof sprouted unworldly clumps of thick green moss. The yard was a jungle of overgrown grass and gangly weeds, barely revealing a crumbling slate path that meandered to the front porch.

Sunny gave her hair a few twirls. Since leaving Washington on the noon flight, she'd been anxious about her reunion with Lois—the tearful embrace, the weepy remonstrations about years wasted. But this was a business trip. Her plan was to analyze Lois's most recent tracking polls, review the campaign budget, tweak the media buy, overhaul the voter turnout operation, save her reelection, and then quickly return to Washington to get AFFFA back on track.

All in a day's work.

She grabbed the pie and exited the car, then walked up the path and opened the squeaky front door.

She smelled pizza.

Nothing in the kitchen had changed. Not the yellow Formica cabinets or the yellow-orange linoleum floor; not the boxy burnt-orange refrigerator-freezer humming in the corner; not even the shaft of late-afternoon sunlight peaking through the yellow sunflower curtains. Lois was hunched over the kitchen table, just as Sunny remembered, except for that bulky cast around her wrist. She was lost in piles of tattered folders. Oblivious.

"Hello, Mother."

Lois looked up, blinked several times, and smiled. "Welcome home, Sunshine. Sam told me you were coming, so I ordered a pizza. You must have missed Gino's!"

On the subject of missing things—say, for example, a neglectful mother missing her estranged daughter—Gino's Pizzeria wasn't high on Sunny's list. Her stomach tightened.

That's it? That's the dramatic reconciliation between neglectful mother and victimized daughter? Have a slice of pizza?

Lois continued, "I'm researching for my debate with Jack Steele. Sam thinks we should cancel it because of the shooting. But I think that'd be a victory for our opponents. What do you think?"

I think I shouldn't have come, Sunny wanted to say.

"It's not till October. But you know me. I like to be prepared. How long are you staying?"

"I have to be back in DC. I just wanted to see how you were doing."

Lois blinked and said, matter-of-factly, "Let's eat."

Sunny thought, *One slice*.

They cleared Lois's files from the table and opened the white pizza box. Sunny watched plumes of steam rise high above the table. They grabbed slices straight from the box, resting them on flimsy paper plates.

"Patsy Hardameyer called just before you got here," Lois said. "She said you ran into Kay."

"Mmmm-hmmmm," Sunny chewed. Spices exploded on her tongue, putting Washington pizza to shame, she had to admit.

"I never understood why Kay never got married. She's so lovely. And such a beautiful disposition."

"Cheap rent, from what I'm told," Sunny snarked.

"And you heard about Ethel Fisher's sister? Such a pity."

"I don't know who that is, Mother."

"Violet! Ethel Fisher's sister."

"Mother, I don't know Ethel Fisher. Or her sister."

"Yes, you do, Sunshine. You met them at one of our block parties. In tenth grade, I think."

"Of course."

"Anyway, she died."

"Oh."

"I left you a message about it. Maybe you didn't get it. You're so busy."

"Very."

Lois chewed hurriedly, then asked, "Did you hear about the Dosemart Drugs application?"

"Guess that slipped by as well."

"Another one of those chain drugstores. They're applying to re-zone the old Tuthill farm. Can you imagine? They want to go from R1 zoning to C4! Well, that just won't fly."

On she went, prattling about zoning applications, the disease states of various neighbors, the mighty challenges of the artisanal chocolate industry in Vermont, the wars in the Middle East. Sunny nibbled on one pizza slice, then two, nodding politely and venturing an occasional "uh-huh." She recognized exactly what her mother was doing because it sounded so familiar.

Sunny McCarthy knew a good filibuster when she heard one.

After that early dinner, Sunny climbed the creaky wooden stairs to her old bedroom. She opened the door and walked in. It smelled strangely familiar, even comforting. Pink floral wallpaper peeled at the seams. Tangled blinds covered a small rectangular window. A pink blanket was rumpled over a small bed. Two stuffed animals were perched on a pillow, plastic eyes frozen on Sunny, as if pleading to be liberated. She walked aimlessly around the room, her feet crunching against a ragged shag carpet. She absently ran her fingers across layers of dust on the furniture—a white pine dresser, a teetering nightstand. Then she pulled on a closet door, which refused to budge. She tugged harder, until it opened with a bark of protest and a stinging whiff of dust and age. Her eyes wandered across a childhood locked away for years, like an archaeological dig: tangles of flannel shirts and frayed jeans, shelves of dolls, toys, and games. Sunny reached for an item on a high shelf, a bicycle helmet, pink and purple; she cradled it against her chest and carried it to the bed, which groaned as she sat.

She thought back to her fifth birthday. Lois was at the kitchen counter, absorbed in the act of scrambling eggs. Her father sat at the table, arms resting on a newspaper opened to the sports pages. A smile broke across his unshaven face. "Sun's up!" he liked to pronounce, acknowledging the light and warmth that she brought to his day.

They took her outside. The yard was modest but manicured by a weekly landscaping service. Cattails rocked in a gentle breeze, and Lois's wind chimes tinkled. Sunny crinkled her nose at the salt air. Her gifts were in the driveway: a pink and purple bicycle and matching helmet, sparkling in the early-morning sun. Even now—sitting on her old bed—Sunny could feel her father's hands at her sides as she mounted the bike, holding her steady and safe. She could hear his soft voice, encouraging her to pedal. She remembered the feel of the pedals against her feet, resistant at first, then lighter as she gained speed. Her father was still beside her, one hand pressed against her back, the other clutching the bike seat, breathing heavily as he ran. She could hear Lois's voice. "Let her go, Larry. Let go." Finally her father gave a last long grunt. She felt his hands slipping away from her as she pushed against the pedals. She remembered the fear of falling mixed with the pride of letting go, of racing ahead, breaking free.

And how she lost control of the bike and it toppled when she turned her head back.

Her thoughts were interrupted by soft knocking on the door. Lois stepped in tentatively. Her eyes scanned the room, falling on Sunny. "I never cleaned up in here. I wasn't sure what to do with everything."

"It's fine, Mother."

Lois sighed. "Maybe after the election. Sam thinks I'll have plenty of spare time."

"That sounds like a concession speech," said Sunny.

Lois shrugged. "Everyone in town thinks I'm losing. You can see it in their eyes. Like I have some kind of horrible disease or something."

"Do you think you'll lose?"

Lois's eyes widened incredulously. "Oh, darling, we don't think like that in this family. Do we?"

Sunny nodded softly.

"We're having a campaign meeting tomorrow. Vera Butane's bringing blueberry cobbler."

"I'll be there," Sunny promised.

"Well, I'd better get back to debate prep. I bet Jack will criticize me for the Peace Pole. Can you imagine? Who could be against peace?"

The door closed behind her.

Sunny realized that her father may have taught her how to ride a bike, but Lois had taught her how to pedal. Always forward. Back turned defiantly on the past.

31

The next day, Sunny sat in Lois's kitchen with the senior staff of the Liebowitz reelection campaign and thought, *I'm assisting a political suicide*. Crowding the table were Lois, Sam, Vera Butane, and Patsy Hardameyer, of lawn sign fame. Vera's blueberry cobbler was surgically sliced onto chipped plates with daisy patterns. An ancient coffee maker gurgled, its glass pot coated with brown crust.

Sunny had just asked for the most recent polling.

"We didn't do a poll," Sam said.

"How do you know if you're ahead or behind?"

"We're winning," Lois said assuredly.

"What's your cash on hand?"

Patsy Hardameyer reported: "Three hundred fifty-six."

"Please tell me that's three hundred fifty-six thousand."

"No. Three hundred fifty-six dollars."

"Do you have a voter turnout model?"

Silence.

"Television budget?"

Stares.

"Mail plan?"

Shrugs.

"We don't have a chance," Sunny pronounced.

"We have you," Sam said.

"And Vera's pie!" chirped Patsy as she slid a plate toward Sunny.

"Which would help if this were a pie competition. But it's not. It's an election." Sunny felt stinging remorse and put her hand on Vera's, which felt like a brittle old leaf. "But keep baking. We need all the firepower we can get." Vera smiled vacantly.

Sunny scanned the table. This was the war council that would defeat the combined might of the national gun lobby, the conservative media, Sidney Schwartzman, a network of think-tank academics who thought mostly with the far right side of their brains, and a group of Super PACs with treasuries dwarfing the operating budgets of several states.

We can't win. Steele has to lose. But how?

"I need a walk," she announced. Her chair screeched against the linoleum floor. She pushed against the front screen door; it rattled closed behind her. A line of heavy dark clouds was drifting in from the ocean. Sunny folded her arms against a morning breeze that hinted at the last days of summer and ambled down Love Lane. She could hear the din of protestors on the village square blocks away and the cawing of birds. Old trees leaned toward the street, forming a canopy of green leaves. She passed cottages squatting on measly plots of sandy soil—a dingy, paint-peeled landscape of brown, gray, white, and yellow facades, with one identical feature: a front porch. Sunny remembered the summer cacophony of screen doors squeaking open and clacking closed; the rhythmic groaning of metal rockers; the eruptions of laughter up and down the block. That was when neighbors gathered on porches. Before neighborhoods became communities and communities became gated; when the biggest threat to Asabogue wasn't a mass shooting but a chain drugstore.

A line of traffic was stalled at the intersection of Main Street. Billionaires Bluff rose in the distance. She remembered that its foliage was first to turn a lush orange each fall. The powerful were first in everything, Sunny thought, even seasons. They progressed while the rest of the village clung to the past, like those summer leaves above her, clinging stubbornly against the breeze. She imagined the forces gathered at Villa di Acciaio. The high command of campaign consultants, pollsters, press assistants, fund-raisers, researchers, targeting analysts, and field organizers. All huddled in a high-tech war room, planning and budgeting, mobilizing and organizing, summoning allies large and small to the great national cause of defeating this seventy-two-year-old liberal woman with a lisp. Up there. On the Bluff. Once it was Sunny's weekend home. Now it was enemy territory.

Enemy territory.

She whispered: "To know your enemy, you must become your enemy."

Not Sunny, but Sun Tzu.

Who also had a few good strategies in his day.

She turned back. For the first time since returning to Asabogue, she felt a twinge of hope.

32

I n the course of her career, Sunny McCarthy had dined at Michelin-rated restaurants and attended several state dinners (including one with the president of France and another with Their Royal Highnesses the King and Queen of Some Tiny but Opulent Emirate Sitting on an Ocean of Oil). She was proficient in the State Department's *Protocol for the Modern Diplomat*. Plus she could, with a sharp sniff and gentle swirl, identify the appellation of the finest wines.

At the moment, however, these skills offered limited utility. She was in Ralph Kellogg's basement, trying to ignore the over-powering stench of sweat, farts, and fast food as Ralph devoured a Big Mac. She watched as his jaw thumped up and down, like a hydraulic machine. A dozen of his men sat tensely on couches around the room, clutching their weapons, their eyes fixed on Sunny, who wore tight jeans and a revealing camisole top for the occasion. (When she left DC, she didn't pack an appropriate out-fit for militia-visiting.) Had she the courage to sniff, she thought she'd pick up the distinct scent of raging testosterone.

The room was dim. Guns and explosives had been heaped carelessly in piles around the room. The dryer clonked loudly. Sunny noticed a framed photo of Louie Delmarco propped on the washing machine, with a homemade sign: IN MEMORIUM.

She didn't think it made sense to point out that *memoriam* was spelled incorrectly. Latin probably wasn't a prerequisite for admission to the newly minted Delmarco Division of Defiance.

Ralph took a final chomp of his burger and crumpled the wrapper into a ball. Then he narrowed his eyes on Sunny and said, while still chewing, "The enemy of my enemy is my friend. That it?"

The man knows his proverbs, thought Sunny.

Ralph washed down his food with a voluminous chug of his vanilla shake, which left a glob of white frost on his mustache. His thick pink tongue washed it away, like a windshield wiper. He released a satisfied belch and said, "Still don't make sense to me. Helping you beat Steele." He began picking at his teeth with a plastic straw.

Sunny had anticipated Kellogg's reservations. She was going to say, "It's for the betterment of Asabogue," but she knew that civic virtue was never really Ralph's strong suit. So she got right to the point. "Revenge."

Ralph's lips curled.

"Let's face it, Ralph. Turns out we're not so different after all. I was always the lonely kid with the cheap clothing and weird mother. And you. You've always been . . ." Sunny began stammering. "Well . . . you."

Ralph grunted.

"Remember how people laughed at us? Behind our backs?"

"I got laughed at to my face."

"How they mocked us?"

"I wanted to kill 'em. Coulda, too!"

This wasn't where Sunny wanted to go. She watched Ralph's fists pump and crimson flush into his cheeks. "Yes, you could have, Ralph. But you didn't. You did what I did. Tried to become one of them. Right? Doing their dirty work. Giving them our total loyalty and getting squat in return."

Ralph nodded slowly, then said, "Mr. Fixit."

"Huh?"

"That's what Jack Steele calls me. Mr. Fixit. 'Fix this building permit, Ralph.' 'Fix that zoning application.' 'Pay off this guy.' I coulda lost my seat on the Village Board. Maybe even gone to jail. And for what? The man didn't even show up to Louie's funeral."

Everyone lowered their heads, so Sunny lowered hers.

Ralph continued. "Ever hear of Stockholm syndrome?"

Somewhere in Sunny's head, an alarm pinged.

"I read about it once. It's psychology," he said. "It's when a hostage thinks the guy who's gonna behead him is a friend. That's us. We're like hostages to those people on the Bluff."

The words *hostages* and *behead*, pronounced in the underground headquarters of a militia committed to the violent overthrow of the U.S. government, in a basement cluttered with heavy weapons and thick with seething resentment, concerned Sunny. She quickly changed the subject. "You and my mother don't agree on much, Ralph. But she has always respected you. Always will. That's more than you can say for Jack Steele. Let's join forces, Ralph. Let's take him down."

She watched as Ralph scanned the room. Ever since Louie's demise, retention of fighters had suffered. Evidently, there was something about that loss that suggested to some that a safer method of overthrowing the government might be posting anonymous rants on Facebook from the comfort of their parents' basements. Bobby Reilly remained, and about a dozen others. They were outcasts and castoffs, convinced of conspiracies because life had ruthlessly conspired against them.

He raised his half-crushed McDonald's cup and proclaimed, "For Louie."

"Louie!" they responded.

Ralph returned his focus to Sunny, nodding slowly. "One condition. I got my own plan. So I do my thing. You do yours. We stay outta each other's way. Where we can cooperate, we will. Deal?"

Sunny smiled. "Deal. Now tell me, Mr. Fixit. Exactly what did Jack Steele ask you to fix?"

33

Wayne Bright's finely calibrated political radar was on high alert. This was new terrain: a dimly lit, stuffy living room frozen somewhere in the 1990s. It featured tan leather couches, frayed Berber carpet, a large glass and mahogany coffee table, and a vintage television coiled to a blinking VCR. He sat on a broken recliner that kept reclining. Wayne struggled to sit upright, but the chair stubbornly pulled him to a half sprawl. Sunny McCarthy was eyeing him with the glint of a sadistic torturer about to commence waterboarding.

Hardly a befitting position for the president of the Chicken Liberation United Committee, known as CLUC. Wayne was the mastermind behind a multimillion-dollar enterprise dedicated to the humane treatment of chickens, which, to many, seemed at least a rhetorical contradiction since chickens weren't human. Still, Wayne was a maestro of mobilizing, money-raising, and marketing on fowl issues. It was Wayne's brainchild to do that heart-wrenching Super Bowl commercial featuring the pigtailed little girl and her Easter present, an adorable baby chick she named Mr. Peepers (which she pronounced "Mithta Peepeth" as a result of an endearing and well-coached lisp). In the spot, little Mr. Peepers wandered off. He found himself crammed into an industrial poultry processing facility where he was pumped with arsenic, grotesquely fattened with hormones, then, to mournful piano notes, shackled upside down, stunned in an electrified bath, slashed at the neck, bled, defeathered, deboned, and delivered fresh to the grocer's freezer. "Poor Mithta Peepeth," the disconsolate girl sniffled straight at the camera, a tear falling from one eye. That halftime, there wasn't a dry eye in America, as millions of chicken wing platters were slid far forward by sauce-stained fingers. The threat of a sequel—involving some little girl's unwitting consumption of Mr. Peepers at a family dinner—compelled the National Poultry Processors Association to sign a pledge—a Magna Carta of sorts—on chicken rights.

Now, from the discomfort of that reclining chair, Wayne scanned Lois's living room. A dozen people occupied a couch, love seat, and some metal folding chairs brought in for the occasion. They'd trickled in from Washington in the past week. There was the finance director of the Chromosome-X PAC, the largest bundler of campaign donations to female candidates; the national president of the League of Arctic Voters; the pollster for the League of Liberals; the national political director of the United Pizza Delivery Workers Union International, AFL-CIO; and the aging alumni of the campaigns of various losing and left-leaning candidates for president of the United States, dating all the way back to McGovern.

In the "politics makes strange bedfellows" department, this

was Sunny's liberal orgy. She'd thought of playing some of Lois's old folk music to pump everyone's adrenaline.

These were the grassroots generals of the armies of idealism. The hard-bitten veterans of soft causes. Also, they were Sunny's last resort. No one else would heed her call for reinforcements, or even return her e-mails. Sunny McCarthy, the conservatives' Queen of K Street, was now banished. All the consultants and lobbyists that she'd favored, fed, and fattened had abandoned her. She should have known: in Washington, IOUs are the most deflationary currency on earth.

Sunny was left with, well, what was Left. They'd relished her defection. Now they had an obligation to close their thinning but well-organized ranks around her. From saving the whales, saving the glaciers, saving the planet, saving the poor to saving poor Lois Liebowitz. Game on! Of course, these were the same operatives Sunny had mocked and disdained for most of her career, who, prior to sticking a fork in an almost-defeated opponent would pause to argue among themselves about the size of the fork, whether everyone had a fork, what the fork was made of, and whether there should be a fork research and development tax credit. All while a knife was being thrust in their backs.

Now they had Lois's life in their hands.

Things looked bleak, which was their typical starting point. The pollster for the League of Liberals began his briefing with the usual overture: a long despairing moan. Then, "Liebowitz is twenty-four points down. I see no path to victory. It's simply hopeless."

Music to their ears.

Wayne Bright committed to having his media consultants produce some commercials not involving the eviscerating of chickens.

The leader of Chromosome-X PAC pledged $500,000 for one week of television ads attacking Jack Steele.

"I can have fifty of my members knocking on doors!" whooped

the political director from the United Pizza Delivery Workers Union International.

Phone banks were organized. Canvassers galvanized. Opposition researchers mobilized. Money raised.

They celebrated with a nice Long Island chardonnay.

Only a few days later, Jack Steele sat comfortably in his plush media room, fingers around a glass of wine, salivating over a television cooking show of sorts. There was Megan Slattery, butter-flying and bringing to a pink broil a Democratic congressman from California. The issue was immigration. Under Megan's withering interrogation, the congressman now seemed ready to self-deport.

Jack heard the jingling of the phone in another room. Then the tentative footsteps of Conchita. Or Rosita. Whoever.

"Mr. Jack, it's Mr. Carl."

Carl Schmidt was Steele's campaign manager. He was calling from his temporary residence: the guest cottage at Villa di Acciaio.

"Crap," Carl began.

Jack hated conversations that began with *crap*. Conversations that started with *crap* usually ended with Jack spending craploads of more money.

Carl reported: "Liebowitz went up on TV. Dunno how she can afford it. But I'm not worried. Their money'll dry up. They'll go dark soon."

Then, through the magic of television, the ad appeared.

There was an aerial image—captured by drone—of the luxuriant expanse of Villa di Acciaio: stone turrets, high gates, infinity pool, then the red-roofed guest cottage and slate walkway meandering around a koi pond.

Jack smiled. Home sweet home. Right?

The camera zoomed in on the guest cottage. The four-bedroom

structure jutted into a ribbon of woods that marked the border between Jack and the billionaire next door. There was a massive earthen gash where Jack's crew had bulldozed trees and buried a piping plover, a federally designated threatened species whose inconvenient choice of habitat should have blocked the project. A project, viewers learned, that lacked the requisite zoning variances and building permits and therefore skirted any increase in Jack's tax assessment. Which was a violation of multiple subsections, sections, and entire chapters of the Asabogue Village Code. A document that Jack Steele would take an oath to enforce, so help him God.

"Crap," Jack Steele hiccuped.

The narrator's voice dripped with snark: "Hollywood actor Jack Steele. The only thing he hasn't played is BY . . . THE . . . RULES!" Then, rapidly: "Paid for and authorized by Asabogue Neighbors for Fair Play."

There was a time when Jack's plan for the guest cottage at Villa di Acciaio seemed reasonable. That was before he decided he needed extra space for four bedrooms and a koi pond; before a real estate survey showed a property line crimping said koi pond; before the nesting of that damned piping plover. "The real endangered species in this country are capitalists!" Jack bellowed to Ralph Kellogg one morning. "Can you fix this?" At which point Mr. Fixit eagerly wielded the tools of his trade. Necks were turned, palms greased, arms twisted, papers shuffled, eyes diverted, and a Caterpillar bulldozer did the rest. *Piccolo Acciaio*, as it was called, rose from the grave of an ignominiously buried piping plover.

Who would know? Even the billionaire next door wouldn't notice the loss of a few dozen wispy pines and one less family of piping plovers on Jack's side of the tree line.

Now everyone knew.

And Jack Steele knew this: small towns like Asabogue weren't consumed by the weighty issues of war and peace, pestilence and poverty. Big problems in small towns were more parochial: a storage shed one thin blade of grass over the statutory setback; an illegal accessory structure; an overflowing trash can in flagrant violation of the directions clearly printed in the annual Village of Asabogue Trash Pickup & Recycling Calendar. These issues were quality of life . . . and death.

Jack snapped, "Double our television buy."

That night, for dinner, Sam Gergala enjoyed a cold-cut sandwich, a generous heaping of potato chips, a warm beer, and the savory taste of justice. He sat in front of his television, on an upholstered rocker that had been passed down through multiple generations of Gergalas. His dinner plate teetered precariously on his lap as he clicked through channels, mesmerized by what he saw. The commercial was everywhere: the news channels, the old movie channels, the sitcom channels, the reality TV channels, the history channels, the sports channels. Whatever one chose to watch on television, they were forced to view the illegal guest cottage at Villa di Acciaio. That night, there were piping plover prayers across Asabogue.

Sam chewed contentedly.

One week and hundreds of television commercials later, Sunny and the campaign pollster met in Lois's kitchen. He was accustomed to spitting out data with speed and authority. He never had to do so with Vera Butane's blueberry cobbler sloshing between his cheeks. Every statistic was accompanied by soft blue pellets of saliva from blue-stained lips. The news was good. And bad. Pollsters hedge their bets.

The good news was that Jack Steele's lead was nudging downward. Lois was now eighteen points behind.

The bad news, the pollster despaired, was that there wasn't enough time to close the gap. The election was seven weeks away.

"Seven weeks," Sunny scoffed. "That's an eternity in politics."

Lois Liebowitz generally disdained personal attacks in campaigns. Negative advertising corroded democracy and soiled governance. Lois preferred principled discourse: a virtuous exchange of high ideas.

The new ad kicked Jack Steele right in the balls. Lois loved it.

She sat in the living room, which was now a war room. Cell phones rang constantly. Consultants sprawled on couches and chairs, squinting at laptops. Wayne Bright was now comfortably ensconced in the broken recliner. Thick reams of voter files were piled on bookshelves. Sunny sat behind a cheap folding table in a corner, cradling phones and snapping orders. Her hair was twisted in a loose bun and she wore her new uniform: jeans and a bulky blue sweatshirt with ASABOGUE PARKS DEPT stenciled in yellow across her chest. Streams of volunteers picked up stacks of campaign literature. Their knuckles were raw from door-knocking, their ears like cauliflower from phone banking.

Lois focused on the television.

There was another aerial image of Villa di Acciaio. Then a voice: "Hollywood actor Jack Steele. He wants to be our mayor. But how can Jack Steele fight for Asabogue when he really lives here . . ."

A new image, high above an ultra-modern beachfront home in Malibu, sleek and sharply angled.

"And here . . ."

A sprawling lodge in the Adirondacks Nestled between evergreen hills.

"And here . . ."

A pink stucco villa on the eighteenth hole in Bermuda, palm trees swaying.

"And here . . ."

Trump Tower, Manhattan, black glass and gold trim.

"Jack Steele. How can he fight for your quality of life . . . when he's not sure *where* he lives? Paid for by Asabogue Neighbors for Asabogue Values."

By the middle of September, Lois had come to within twelve points of Jack Steele.

Everything now hinged on the Asabogue League of Women Voters debate.

It would be explosive.

34

Congress had returned to Capitol Hill from its August slumber. Roy Dirkey found himself slumped in a chair in the conference room of Republican Whip Fred Stinson. He should have been happy—ecstatic, even. The House Republican Leadership was fast-tracking a vote on AFFFA, and he'd been called to the Whip meeting to discuss rounding up the two hundred eighteen votes necessary for passage. In a Congress known for breaking all legislative records for doing nothing, Dirkey's bill seemed to be hurtling to a vote.

But Roy felt unsettled. Since the Muffin Massacre in Asabogue, Sunny had disappeared. No e-mails. No phone calls. No cackles. A vice president at Cogsworth International had stepped in for Sunny (tripped in was more like it). Bruce Cogsworth seemed cluelessly pleasant. No matter how many times Roy asked about Sunny, he'd giggle nervously and say, "Hey, what am I, chopped liver?"

The night he returned to Washington, after completing the fund-raising circuit, Roy ditched his aide and went to Sunny's condo in Penn Quarter. A desk attendant with the name HECTOR stitched into his cream blazer greeted Roy with an apathetic grunt. Roy could hear a Nationals game from a radio in a back room.

"I'm here for Sunny McCarthy," Roy said.

"She's gone."

"Where?"

Hector shrugged.

Roy flipped on the charm switch. "Hey . . . Hector. Just between us, I'm a Member of Congress and I just gotta know where she is. It's a national security deal, so don't tell anyone. You can trust me, Hector. I have top secret clearance. Can you help me out, bud?"

Hector smiled, then giggled, then, after an eruption of spasmodic laughs, wiped his flowing eyes and said, "Dude, if I had a buck for every congressman whose girlfriend dumped them and used that line, I wouldn't be workin' this desk. I'd be watchin' the Nats in my penthouse upstairs! Jeez, maybe I'd own the team!"

So here Roy was, flying blind. Or, flying with a novice pilot whose uncle just happened to own the airline, which seemed a risky proposition.

The Whip's office was imperiously decorated in red. Red walls, carpet, drapes, and red-striped chairs. Two chandeliers hung above both ends of a long conference table, glowing against the polished mahogany. Historic oil paintings from Stinson's home state of Texas dominated the walls in garish gold-leaf frames. The largest was positioned prominently above Stinson's chair at the head of the table: Robert Jenkins Onderdonk's *Fall of the Alamo*. There was Davy Crockett, desperately swinging his flintlock like a club; dead and dying sprawled on the ground amid shrouds of gunsmoke. Roy knew that Fred Stinson was obsessed with the Alamo. He solemnly invoked its memory in every legislative battle, no matter how inconsequential. Once, when passing a resolution proclaiming National Sinus Tachycardia Awareness Week, Stinson barricaded himself in his office, sleeplessly working the phones until assured unanimous passage, proving that the legislative fort would not fall as long as Whip Fred Stinson guarded it.

Stinson entered, his staff in tow. He was short and plump and barreled into rooms like one of those cartoon bombs with a lit fuse. He wore a rumpled suit tautly stretched around a protruding belly, and a wrinkled tie speckled with remnants of his last meal. A mop of black curls sat above a puffy, crimson face. His brown eyes had a militant glare, as if set for the next Alamo.

But his arms! They were abnormally long arms built perfectly for a Whip—able to swing around his prey, pat their backs while probing their spines, and pull them in close. His title was Whip, but he was better known as "Knife," for two reasons. First, there was that dagger he constantly held against Speaker Piermont's back, waiting to be plunged at the first sign of weakness by Piermont, who simultaneously had a knife to Stinson's jugular. The two men and their factions despised each other. The power struggle between them had reduced Congress to a gang rumble using *Robert's Rules of Order*. Second, Stinson deftly used that knife to butter his colleagues with favors thick and sweet. The path to Members' votes went straight through their egos with a sharp turn toward their campaign treasuries. In pursuit of those votes, Whip Stinson dispensed pork, privilege, and PAC checks. Stinson was a father confessor and political advisor. Therapist. Marriage counselor. Fund-raiser. Concierge.

And what did he expect in return for this enduring solicitude? Undying loyalty on legislative matters large and small. He deployed his lieutenants across the House floor, armed with index cards and blue markers. They had officious titles: chief deputy whip, deputy assistant whip, chief deputy assistant regional whip. They'd nuzzle against a Member, inquiring about their position on a particular bill, mark their tally cards *Yes, No, Lean Yes, Lean No*, or *Undecided*. Then they'd scurry back to Stinson, where the cards were tabulated. If a congressman showed signs of straying on a vote, Stinson went on reconnaissance. He'd find the congressman on the House floor, unfold those long arms, and pull him in, subjecting them to an uncomfortable proximity and the effluvia of cheap aftershave and an earlier meal. Then he'd whisper, in a soft drawl, about how "we really need yaaaaaa'll on this vote," followed by syrupy praise and the inevitable historical references to "sticking together, just like my boys at the Aaaaalamo." Who could resist? Those boys sacrificed their very lives for principle. This was just one vote that any politician with minimal proficiency could spin to advantage back home; one uncomfortable vote that could be soothed with, say, an appointment as an ex officio member of the Kennedy Center Board of Trustees, complete with cocktail party and decent seats to certain performances. And if the congressman still couldn't toe the line, the line wasn't completely severed. Stinson knew there'd be another battle, another bill ahead. In the gospel of the Whip, today's rupture was tomorrow's rapture. Stinson would release his prey from his grip with an affectionate pat on the back and a soft but clear message: you'll be with us next time. There was always a next time.

This time it was AFFFA. In a Congress with more than three hundred pro-gun Members, passing the bill should have been a cinch. But as the Whip liked to say: "Remember the Alamo!" No victory was guaranteed and nothing could be taken for granted in his unruly caucus. There was always that last-minute snag, a done deal about to be undone. Then, of course, there was the matter of commitment, which had a rather loose translation in his caucus. A promise to vote "yes" could mean anything up to and including "no." "No" embraced a full range of possibilities, including "yes."

Sure enough, AFFFA had hit an unforeseen circumstance in Washington, the world capital of unforeseen circumstances.

It was sex.

Specifically, a militant pro-choice group called Uterus United had organized a nationwide movement urging women not to have sex unless their partner signed a "precoital agreement." The agreement acknowledged the woman's ultimate right to decide what she would do if sperm and egg happened to, well, caucus. In the heat of passion, signing a legal agreement to consummate the act was a slight inconvenience, but no greater than a rushed and fumbling search for a condom. In certain areas—namely large liberal cities—the agreements were signed, sealed, and delivered with gusto. In socially conservative areas, the agreements were causing a national backlog of fluid in the testicles of already angry Republican white men. Red states reported epidemic levels of blue balls. You could identify a pro-life male by his delicate steps, the wince upon standing and sitting, and the protective grasping of his groin. This concerned Republican leaders. At some point—mostly in bedrooms, backseats, or cheap motels—ideology would be surrendered for a good shtup. Millions would whip out pens to sign precoital agreements before whipping out other instruments. Suddenly the party would lose one of its galvanizing issues. Elections would be lost to erections.

Uterus United had to be eliminated.

Opportunity arose in northern New Jersey.

At a Uterus United clinic in Newark, a poor and pregnant teen entered the building for a health screening. During the session, a Uterus United professional used the A-word, violating a federal law that women's health centers could not perform abortions, refer to abortions, use the word *abortion*, or, for that matter, utter any word sounding like *abortion* (with the exception of *abhor*, *abhorrence*, or *abhorrent*). It turned out the young girl was an undercover intern for an outfit whose mission it was to infiltrate liberal organizations with tiny video cameras and reveal the truth about them with heavily doctored footage.

This proof of Uterus United's depravity quickly became a maleficent threat to America's survival. It required immediate action from Congress. Select investigative committees were formed and gavels were clacked. Lawyers were hired, subpoenas issued, hearings held. The Congressional Caucus on Life (known as "the

Lifers") had its own plan. Its members drafted a new law to shut down Uterus United's clinics and deport its executive director to Saudi Arabia, not exactly known for its warm embrace of family planning clinics. (The latter provision was removed after strenuous objections by, among others, the Saudi Embassy.) The caucus attempted to hitch the amendment to every passing legislative vehicle, annually threatening to shut down the entire federal government unless Uterus United was shut down first.

Dirkey sat across the table from the chairwoman of the pro-life caucus, Sarah Backfury. He'd always been intrigued by the gentlewoman from Virginia. She was alluring, with shoulder-length blond hair and striking blue eyes. But her most prominent feature were her razor-thin lips, frozen in a viperous smile that conveyed the sheer, cold-blooded joy of snaring her opponents.

Whip Stinson rapped his fists on the table and began the meeting. "We're voting on AFFFA this week. Problem is the president is squishy on it. May even veeeeeto it."

Dirkey was encircled by soft grumbling about the gutless, godless, feckless, spineless president.

"We need every vote on this. Pass it biiiiigggg. Send the president a message. You veeeeto this bill, we'll override you. Override you biiiiigggg."

Backfury cleared her throat. "Mr. Whip?"

"Saaaaaarah."

"You have my commitment that every member of the Lifers will vote for AFFFA!"

Stinson nodded silently. Waiting for the "however." There was always a "however."

"However . . . we want to attach a little amendment."

"Just hooow little?" asked Stinson.

"Well, AFFFA is about the right to bear arms. What about the right to bear babies? AFFFA protects the lives of the born. We want to save the lives of the unborn. By eliminating the single greatest threat to life: Uterus United."

She described her amendment. Dirkey noticed that her lips never loosened. Like a ventriloquist, the words just slithered out, clipped and sparse.

"We can't support anything of the sort!" huffed Congressman Leonard Landover. Landover represented that tiny group of moderate Republicans called the Main Street Caucus, which wasn't so much of a Main Street as a dark and lonely corner. They were known as "the Streeters." "Attaching an antiabortion rider will anger female voters in our districts."

"Well," hissed Backfury, "I thank the *gentleman* for educating me about *women*."

Dirkey felt queasy. Where was Sunny when he needed her?

Stinson puffed his reddened cheeks like a blowfish and exhaled hard enough to be felt at the far end of the table. Backfury locked onto him, her lips clenched. Dirkey thought he detected a tiny pellet of foam at both corners of her mouth and a low snarl.

Stinson said, "Saaaarah."

"Frrrrreeeeed."

"Give me a few hours. To see what I can do."

"Of course. Take your time, Mr. Whip."

Truce.

In a venerable old room with a concave ceiling, tucked a floor above the House chamber, hidden from the flashing cameras and the plodding feet of tourists, was the most obscure but powerful committee in Congress.

The Committee on Rules.

Here a handful of Members of Congress labored in Talmudic fashion over the most arcane verses in parliamentary procedure. They decided if, how, and when a bill became a law; which amendments lived and which died; how many would pass and how many would perish.

The chairman of the rules committee, Ernest F. Chandler of

Kentucky, was known as "Maestro." His job was to orchestrate every motion and minute on the floor. This required Chandler to have an unusual expertise in the minutiae of House procedure. The man was an idiot savant. Ask him who won the Nationals game the previous night and his eyes would fall into a catatonic glaze under bushy white eyebrows. Ask him what to do when "a Member moved the previous question and whether that question should be put" and his eyes would sharpen, his eyebrows would dance, and he'd belt out Section XXXIV of the Rules of the House of Representatives, as adopted. Chairman Chandler wasn't a whole lot of fun at parties. Which is why he spent most nights at his Watergate condo overlooking the Potomac.

That night, Chandler wrapped himself in a satin robe and settled into his favorite Queen Anne chair with his favorite Kentucky bourbon and James H. Billington's classic *Who Was Robert, Anyway? The Man Behind "Robert's Rules of Order."* It was a thick and musty edition procured from the Library of Congress. His phone rang. It was the Whip.

"Mr. Chairman, I have a little situaaation."

"Proceed."

"I must have a unanimous vote on AFFFA and can't get one."

Chandler felt his parliamentary juices begin to flow.

"The Lifer caucus is just insiiiiiisting on attaching its damned Uterus United amendment. If I give it to them we lose the Main Street Caucus. If I satisfy the Main Streeters, I lose the Lifers."

"Why is this a problem?" asked Chandler.

"Well, I don't see how we can saaaatisfy both."

Chandler thought, *My dear Whip. We can do anything. We are the Rules Committee.*

That night, Roy Dirkey sulked alone in his Capitol Hill apartment. As congressional residences went, this was more shack than swank. It was a tiny basement studio furnished in modern garage sale decor. A kitchenette featured a slow-dripping faucet. Bare walls were pocked with holes where previous tenants had hung decorations. In Roy's case, there was a single picture of his army unit in Afghanistan. They stood in their fatigues, combat boots planted on a rocky field of hard caked mud and withered weeds, pointing their M4 rifles toward a harsh, overcast sky, mugging for the camera from behind Oakley sunglasses. Now, Roy was sprawled on a sleeper sofa he was too tired to unfold. His shirt spilled out of his pants and his tie had been slung across the couch. Outside a narrow window it was dark—the long days of summer were over.

A television sat on a wobbly metal stand. Fox News was reporting on the latest yapping of the Chicago mayor—something about a trade by the Chicago Cubs. Basically, the team had traded . . . itself. It was headed to safer pastures in a suburb near the Iowa border, well out of the line of gunfire. The mayor had tried desperately to keep them in his city. Lighting Wrigley Field was one thing. But a bulletproof domed stadium was entirely out of the question.

Dirkey fumbled for the remote. Clicked onto SOSNews.

There was Megan Slattery and the latest panel of experts on the Asabogue election, writhing in orgasmic punditry.

"The Quinnipiac poll has this in a dead heat!" whooped pundit number one.

"Siena shows undecided voters breaking almost evenly!" howled pundit number two.

"It's a horse race!" bellowed pundit number three.

Oh, and there was drought in California and famine in Africa and Russia was opening a tropical waterfront resort where some Arctic glacier used to be. But these developments tended to annoy SOS viewers. They didn't like liberal preaching about bad science.

Roy watched B-roll from the campaign trail. There was Jack Steele strolling down Main Street, greeting voters, signing autographs, drawing people like a magnet. Then, Lois walking door-to-door with a small band of volunteers.

Roy sprang up.

There was Sunny, just behind her mother. She disappeared when she realized she was on camera. Still, there was that split second of eye contact.

His cell phone rang.

A young voice croaked, "Hold on for the Whip."

Then, "Roy, it's aaaall worked out. AFFFA will pass tomorrow. Our caucus is unaaaanimous!"

"What about the Uterus United amendment?" Dirkey asked.

"It's in."

"But won't the moderates vote against us?"

"We took it out."

Dirkey was confused. "So . . . It's not in the bill? Or it is?"

"Correct."

"It's not?"

"Not if you ask the Main Streeters."

"And if you ask the Lifers?"

"It's right there. In black and white." Stinson chuckled.

"So there'll be a vote on Uterus United—"

"And there won't. Got it?"

"No."

"Look. Chandler's calling it a self-executing motion on the previous question deemed as having passed without requiring an actual vote on the base bill. Or some such gobbledygook. That clear it up?"

"Ummm. Yes."

"Good. Me too!"

But from the sound of his voice, Fred Stinson seemed as befuddled as Roy Dirkey. That was the thing about this Congress. It seemed to get the most done when no one knew what they were doing.

Asabogue High School was built in the early 1900s, when Theodore Roosevelt was president. It was a quaint brick affair featuring a cupola and a clock with rusted green Roman numerals that hadn't been accurate since, well, Theodore Roosevelt was president. Weather-beaten shutters framed the windows of the twenty classrooms inside. A large white marquee on the front lawn said GO ASABOGUE CHIEFS!!! in black magnetic letters. It also advertised upcoming meetings of the PTA, Board of Education, school plays, and various student bake sales and car washes. Behind the school was a modest though well-tended football field, with slightly drooping bleachers and a massive scoreboard. The scoreboard was dominated by a glowering Indian chief in full headdress and war paint. In fact, the Asabogues, historically speaking, were a docile tribe known for their love of trading (which may explain the concentration of retail strip malls on Long Island). Sadly, they were around only long enough to name their little village before their own tribal name was changed by the federal bureaucracy. During the Coolidge administration, the Bureau of Indian Affairs decided to consolidate minor tribes. On Long Island, the Asabogues were merged with the better known Shinnecocks. The new name—the Asacocks—caused some squeamishness in an administration not known for its ribald humor. So the Asabogues simply became the Shinnecocks, leaving their former name for the village, the high school, and the football team.

All major community events in Asabogue were held at the high school. During the Battle of the Bluff, the citizenry of Asabogue assembled there, in the Rockwellian spirit of the American town meeting, to shriek, froth, spit, jeer, throw punches, and announce lawsuits against each other. This is where Sidney Schwartzman announced that, in exchange for permission to erect Taj Too, he would replace the high school football field with a climate-controlled domed stadium. His offer might have tempted the citizenry had it not not included a small print provision requiring that the Asabogue Chiefs would henceforth be called the Asabogue Schwartzmans.

The largest room in the high school was the "Cafetorium." On one side was a kitchen, outfitted with stainless-steel ovens and a sliding rack for school lunch trays heaped with the usual school lunch fare: pizza, deli sandwiches, chicken nuggets, and watery mac and cheese. On the other was an elevated stage behind heavy red curtains for student plays. The stage smelled like thick varnish; the kitchen smelled of a century of spaghetti sauce and stale milk. The blend was pungent.

The Asabogue League of Women Voters held its annual Meet the Candidates Debate in the Cafetorium. Once a thriving organization, the Asabogue LWV had shrunk to a few frail survivors. Its mayoral debates were respectful, even genteel. Residents wrote their questions on index cards. The president—Patsy Hardameyer for the past twenty years—carefully read the questions into a microphone with the soothing enunciation of a host on National Public Radio. Candidates sat at a folding table on the stage, offering somnolent orations on the weighty matters of state, mainly helicopter noise and stop signs. A few partisans from either side clapped politely, and everyone celebrated by going to the other side of the Cafetorium for coffee and cake.

This year was different. Given the national obsession with the Asabogue mayoral campaign, the debate between Jack Steele and Lois Liebowitz promised to be a television blockbuster. The cable news networks hyped it as if it were an ESPN boxing match, with split-screen graphics of Jack and Lois glaring at each other. Actually, Jack glared and Lois looked bemused. The networks deployed to Asabogue High School rigs, technicians, news correspondents, pundits, and spools of black cable that snaked through the building like overgrown vines.

Debate negotiations were intense. Sam Gergala represented the Liebowitz camp. The Steele campaign retained a woman whose business card read DEBATE CONSULTANT. She was very short and very round; her black hair sprouted harshly from her scalp, and her voice sounded like the low rumbling of thunder on the beach and, when she was angry, the crackle of lightning. The negotiations commenced a week before the debate in a neutral spot demanded by the debate consultant: the Cafetorium. Patsy Hardameyer presided. The first order of business by the consultant was announcing the suspension of all negotiations because Patsy was not an "impartial adjudicator." Her fingerprints were on every Liebowitz lawn sign. Literally.

"But I'll be fair," insisted Patsy, who looked genuinely wounded at the assault on her integrity.

The consultant, who had represented four Republican presidential candidates in debate negotiations, was unmoved. The meeting was adjourned. An emergency call was made to the LWV New York State headquarters. They called the LWV national headquarters. There it was decided to send to Asabogue the national president, Shelly Pettigrew, to moderate both the debate over the debate and the actual debate.

A week later President Pettigrew convened a new round of negotiations in the Cafetorium. She instantly established how she rose to the zenith of LWV power. The woman was no pushover. Decades of moderating LWV debates at every level of government had thickened her skin, dried out of her any sap of favoritism, and instilled a zealous adherence to fairness, impartiality, and punctuality. She commandeered a twelve-foot-long Cafetorium table. She placed in front of her a yellow legal pad, four freshly sharpened No. 2 pencils, a copy of *Face-to-Face: The League of Women Voters Guide to Candidate Debates*, and a four-inch brushed nickel call bell. She wore an austere black suit and pinned her hair in a bun, adopting the visage of a Supreme Court justice. She ordered Sam and the debate consultant to sit opposite her.

The consultant began by proposing that both podiums be exactly four and a half feet high. Sam chewed on this and said, "That doesn't seem fair. Jack's over six feet. Lois is barely five. All you'll see of her is the top of her head."

President Pettigrew ruled that the podiums would be of equal height at four and six inches, but Lois would have a four-inch platform. The debate consultant's vociferous protest was met by a sharp ding of the call bell.

Next was the matter of Q&A. The debate consultant knew that Jack was a disciplined script reader, but fairly weak on the ad lib. So she insisted on written questions, preapproved by representatives of both campaigns.

"Preapproved questions?" Sam huffed. "Geez, this is Asabogue. People oughta be able to ask what they want."

With a clever grin, the debate consultant said, "So you want anyone to be able to stand up and shout out whatever the hell they want?"

"I didn't say that—"

"Sure you did. We want a debate. You want some kind of . . . chaos!"

President Pettigrew seemed troubled. The prospect of a democracy where anyone could just ask anything without prescribed time limits or three-by-five index cards was, in her view, a brief layover in anarchy en route to a barbarian state. "Questions will be submitted in writing on preapproved LWV cards. Each campaign will be able to disqualify a maximum of two questions."

Ding!

They argued over who would call heads or tails in the coin toss to establish speaking orders; they dickered over opening statements, closing statements, response times, rebuttals, stage positioning, debate attire. Each decision was punctuated by Mrs. Pettigrew's long and well-practiced index finger landing precisely on the call bell and a ding that echoed symphonically in the vast Cafetorium. When there was nothing left to negotiate, President Pettigrew adjourned the session with a final ding. The exhausted parties shook hands. Sam and the debate consultant exchanged polite small talk as they exited through the dark halls of Asabogue High into a cool evening.

The debate was scheduled for the first week in October. Shelly Pettigrew was satisfied. She had brought decorum to chaos, order to anarchy.

She was overly confident.

36

Megan Slattery crossed her supple legs and focused on the camera, trying to ignore the frantic swirl of annoyance around her. There was Robert Thomas, hacking phlegm, grinding his jaw, and clicking his teeth; and Ashley Barnes, smoothing the hem of her very short skirt. Nearby was the haughty crew from CNBC, pancaked noses jutting in the thin air of their rarified ratings; the teen idols from the Marxist-Socialist National Broadcasting System (also known as MSNBC); and an acronymic assemblage of other news networks jammed into a confined space brought to a boil by blazing klieg lights. Plus the Spanish-speaking team from Univision, which really galled Megan. Bad enough you couldn't call customer service without opting into the native tongue. Now those people had their own television network!

What's happened to America? she thought.

Megan Slattery, who dreamed of reporting from mountain caves and desert battlefields, was now suppressing waves of nausea brought on by the rancid odor of food residue at a high school Cafetorium. Megan Slattery, the ice-queen moderator of presidential debates, whose withering questions and dismissive laugh were like a trapdoor through which candidates' aspirations plunged, was now covering a local debate for mayor of a place whose name had become a national punch line, rolling hilariously from the chapped lips of high school dorks across America: "Asssss-abogue!" All because some senior vice president of programming, perched high in glittering Schwartzman Tower on East 57th Street, saw this event as ratings rocket fuel. Once SOS decided on "Live Coverage of the Asabogue Mayoral Debate," all the other networks chimed "us too!" It had become a well-coiffed gang rumble, jostling for turf on a soiled linoleum Cafetorium floor, pointing cameras at a varnished stage where *Oklahoma* and *Fiddler on the Roof* had been mauled by student drama clubs for decades.

Baronial music streamed through Megan's earpiece, followed by: "Stand by!"

Megan swallowed hard, imagining the nausea away, and switched on that beguiling smile. "Aaaaaaand welcome back to SOSNews live coverage of the Asabogue mayoral debate. I'm Megan Slattery, joined by my colleagues Robert Thomas and Ashley Barnes. Robert, what do both candidates have to accomplish tonight?"

Robert Thomas droned. Megan drifted.

An empty stool stood nearby, soon to be filled with a guest. The original plan was to bring on one of SOS's resident experts— Cailee Cox or Karl Rove or George Will or any of the SOS propagandists dressed up as pundits. But the senior vice president insisted that a local election needed local color.

The guy standing off camera had all the color of a ghost.

Petey Scrafel.

He rocked back and forth nervously, despite a technician's attempt to steady him with a firm hand on his shoulder. He fidgeted with an earpiece, pushing it so far into his ear canal that the technician winced. His curly blond hair was slicked back and a thick coat of makeup covered some kind of breakout on his face. He wore a blue blazer with sleeves dangling at his knuckles, khaki pants freshly ironed by his mother, and a crinkled black tie that leaned stubbornly to one side.

"Go to break," a voice directed in Megan's ear. She was pleased to cut off Robert's soliloquy. Something about how "this is truly what democracy is all about in our town halls, from sea to shining sea with amber waves of grain." All to the ratifying purrs of Ashley Barnes.

"Thank you, Robert! After the break, we'll be joined by an expert who has covered local politics here in Asabogue his whole life. Stay with SOS."

Megan thought, *Once I made Bob Woodward cry. Now I'm about to interview the editor of the high school yearbook.*

She scanned the Cafetorium.

The television lights glinted off rows of folding metal chairs that stretched all the way to the stage. Locals—a preproduction debate about whether to call them Asabogites or Asabogians was settled in favor of the less tongue-challenging "locals"—streamed in, creating a rolling thunder of metal chairs scraping against linoleum and bodies plopping onto the chairs. This was the hottest ticket in Asabogue, almost as exciting as the night Vice President Agnew visited. (The Nixon administration had a full-time staffer whose job it was to find the most remote venues for Agnew's speeches. It was unofficially called "Project Tree Falls in the Forest.") All of Asabogue was here! They came from Joan's Bakery and the Wick & Whim, from the fruit and vegetable stands that lined the roads. They wore light jackets and sweaters against an early fall chill, festooned with buttons and stickers proclaiming allegiances: I LOVE LOIS!, STEELE SUPPORTER!, PRO-GUN, STOP GUNS, SAVE ASABOGUE, SAFE ASABOGUE, and red circles with back slashes slapped over crude caricatures of the candidates. Patsy Hardameyer sat in the front row, a quivering smile barely masking her crushing disappointment about being replaced as moderator. Vera Butane sat beside her; one seat over was Coach McHenry, nervously looping his whistle lanyard around his pudgy index finger, turning it a pallid pink. Sam Gergala paced near the stage, arms folded across his chest, eyes riveted to the floor. The leaders of Stop Helicopter Abuse in Asabogue filled a few chairs in the third row, hoping to ask a question about helicopter noise. Their representation was sparse, though. Most had returned to Manhattan for winter. In their helicopters.

There were town fathers and town mothers and sons and daughters of Asabogue. There were militia members with pistols strapped against hips and rifles slung over shoulders and assault weapons cradled against chests. Megan thought it all looked like a mobilization center for an invasion of Southampton.

She noticed some familiar faces. There was the boss himself, Sidney Schwartzman! His elfin body was perched in the front row, next to his stunning new wife, Mrs. Stormy Schwartzman née Divine, who towered over him. This was Schwartzman's triumphant return to the little town that spurned him. His head, draped with a toupee that seemed a shade too orange in the harsh lights, turned in slow robotic movements, scanning enemies of the past, scores settled and unsettled. The entire row behind him had been commandeered by the cast of *Steele Shudder III*, including the diminutive Harry Haddad and Sid "Sidekick" D'Amico. Otis Cogsworth sat on an aisle seat, next to Lucille, his thighs spilling over the narrow metal chair, which seemed to sag under him.

Plus—

Oh! My! God! Sunny McCarthy!

In Washington, Sunny McCarthy and Megan Slattery traveled in the same high-velocity circles. They dined at the same Georgetown restaurants, shopped at the same boutiques, attracted lustful frothing by the same men. They shared secrets. Actually, Sunny shared the secrets and Megan broke them to a prime-time viewing audience of millions. That was their bond. Sunny leaked to Megan,

Megan flooded the airwaves, reputations sank. Sure, the subjects were guilty before proven innocent in the gladiatorial arena of SOS viewers. But public service was, well, public. Americans had a right to know! It was all there in the First Amendment, which Sunny used to protect the Second.

Now, Megan's reliable source was leaning against a wall, under a handmade poster for an upcoming meeting of the Asabogue Student Senate. She wore a tent-sized blue sweatshirt and jeans. Her arms were folded across stenciled yellow letters that read ASABOGUE PARKS DEPT.

Ewwww. She's gone . . . native!

Megan had heard the rumors about Sunny's abrupt departure from Washington to be at her mother's side and subsequent resignation from Cogsworth International. How very principled! How mother-daughter! How mawkishly boring. Megan could hear the piercing whistle of ratings in free fall. What really intrigued her were the gathering whispers about Sunny's relationship with Congressman Roy Dirkey. Now, that had potential. Broken hearts were always breaking news.

She made a mental note to do some digging. Yes, they were friends. But what was Truman's line? If you want a friend in Washington, get a dog.

Just make sure it doesn't bite.

"Coming out of break in ten seconds!" Megan heard.

She relaxed her shoulders. Snapped on that smile.

She began: "Welcome back . . ."

Across the room, Sunny ignored Megan Slattery's undisguised stares. Otis's were more intriguing—amusing, actually, in the way he kept turning his head awkwardly toward her, catching her eye, then jerking it forward in sheer panic.

Time for some fun, she thought.

She walked toward him, eyeing the sweat streaming down his cheeks.

"Hey Otis!"

He smiled weakly, offering a trembling hand instead of the usual sloppy kiss. Sunny tried to ignore the wet spongy feel of his palm. She nodded to Lucille, who nodded back.

Otis's cheeks shuddered, as if grinding over words he couldn't get out. Then, "How's your mother?"

"Not bad for a tax-cheating, gun-confiscating, left-wing lunatic who's trying to make Asabogue the capital of the new Islamic caliphate. At least according to your commercials. And I thought she was just a bad cook."

"C'mon, Sunny. Your side has been pretty negative as well. Good Lord, you're making a damned guest cottage the end of our way of life."

"Well, it was. For those piping plovers."

Otis scowled. "We're doing what we have to do and you're doing what you have to do. Isn't that how politics works? Didn't you teach me that?"

Sunny thought, *I've created a monster. With an excessive sweating condition.*

"Look, Sunny, when this is over, I want you to come back to Cogsworth. Put this mess behind us. We need you to get AFFFA passed. We're almost there."

"I dunno, Otis. I'm told there's an opening here in the Parks Department. If I pass the civil service test."

Otis seemed insulted, and Sunny wondered whether she'd gone too far.

"C'mon," Otis continued, "I'm trying to do the right thing here. Maybe your mother wins this election. Then what? You gonna leave Washington and move back to Love Lane? Give up all that power?"

She looked around, at the reflections of her power. Megan Slattery and the crowd of reporters were speaking breathlessly to their national audiences. Consultants from both campaigns were milling about, patting each other's backs where they'd left puncture wounds. They'd come to Asabogue because it was the place to be seen and heard. But they were tethered to the Beltway and couldn't go long without its supply of thick oxygen and burning ambition. They'd leave as soon as they could. And just then, Sunny McCarthy couldn't imagine being left behind. Maybe Otis was right.

"We'll talk after the election," she said, turning away from Otis. Then turned back and said, "Meanwhile, may the best woman win, Otis."

"You always do, Sunny. Call me after the election."

Petey Scrafel's most notable reportage had been his exposé on incorrect fund balances in the Asabogue-Southampton school budget. Now he was under the harsh glare of television lights, Megan Slattery, and approximately two and a half million SOS-News viewers. This, he calculated, was a particularly inopportune time to lose consciousness. He was experiencing a sense of ghostly detachment. The entire Cafetorium seemed to spin in slow motion. Everything was closing in on him.

He heard a distant voice say: "We're joined by Peter Scrafel, editor in chief of the *Asabogue Bugle*. Peter, welcome."

Petey blinked at Megan Slattery. He noticed her high gloss red lips and shimmering green eyes. And those legs! Megan Slattery's legs pulled him from a cold swoon on national television. He was revived.

"Thank you, Megan." He gulped.

"Now, you've been covering Asabogue for a few years. Any predictions on who wins this election?"

Petey leaned forward. "Well, Megan, I think every vote will count."

Interview with Elmer P. Sepp, candidate for Asabogue-Southampton School Board.

Robert Thomas affirmed his judgment with an emphatic, "You betcha!" Ashley Barnes underscored it with a long "uuhhhh-huuuuuuh."

Megan pushed on. "The polls have this race too close to call. Has Asabogue ever had such a close election?"

"Megan, the only poll that counts is the one on Election Day."
Frank Weznofsky, losing candidate for Asabogue Tax Receiver.

"Which means tonight's debate is critical. So what's the strategic objective by both candidates? What constitutes a win tonight?"

Petey didn't quite grasp the question. He nodded slowly, put two fingers under his chin, and began: "My sources tell me, Megan, that this is a must-win for both candidates. They have to come out swinging. Get momentum. Put their opponent away in the early rounds."

Boxing night on HBO.

"Fascinating!" Robert Thomas intoned. "But lemme ask: Is this the biggest thing ever to happen here in Asabogue?"

"Ummmm, this and the annual Fall Pumpkin Festival. Cars line up for miles."

Robert, Ashley, and Megan erupted in a group giggle.

Petey wasn't sure exactly why that was funny but felt relieved when Megan flashed him an alluring smile and, eyes twinkling, invited him to "stick around, after this break. Stay with SOS . . ."

37

For what would be the final mission of the Delmarco Division of Defiance, Ralph Kellogg dressed in black tactical pants, matching urban tactical shirt, urban body armor, urban helmet, and urban tactical gloves. It didn't matter that Asabogue wasn't urban. When the SWAT shoe fits, wear it.

Ralph stood alone in his basement. It had been stripped to its bare concrete walls of almost everything: the steel gun racks and metal cabinets, the folding snack food trays and mismatched couches, the air mattresses and coffee table, the old RCA TV, the maps of Asabogue, and the remembrances of Louie Delmarco. Only the laundry appliances remained, standing like silent relics in the dim light. Ralph Kellogg wasn't sentimental, but bidding farewell to the Bunker brought tears to his eyes. Or maybe it was the lingering odor of explosives.

He planted his hands on his wide hips and blew a long, anxious breath. Then glanced at his watch. Six minutes to launch. He was approaching the culmination of his planning, procuring, and paranoia; of long nights sitting at that wobbly desk upstairs. He'd run and rerun every intricate detail in his head to the recordings of his favorite war movie theme songs and Mrs. Kellogg's thunderous snoring down the hall. He'd reviewed all those entries in what was now a two-volume spiral-bound list of enemies. Some nights the details overwhelmed him. He'd sink his throbbing head into his ample palms, massage the pressure in his eyes and temples, start drifting to sleep. Then he'd remember Jack Steele and Lois Liebowitz. They'd come to him like a nightmare, joined by the countless others who angered, annoyed, or aggrieved him. Jolting him back to the plan, until sunrise.

Ralph perused the room one last time. Grunted softly. Then marched up the wooden steps, which groaned under the weight of his armor.

He entered the kitchen. Mrs. Kellogg sat at the table, wrapped in a fuzzy pink robe, oblivious to her warrior husband. She was reading *People* while methodically ladling great gobs of strawberry ice cream from the carton into her mouth. A wall clock ticked loudly. Seven forty. If everything went as Ralph planned, he'd return by midnight. If not . . . He bent toward her and planted a good-bye kiss on her plump, abrasive cheek.

"Going out?" she mumbled, eyes fixed on the magazine, spoon on fast approach to the ice cream.

"I shall return!" Ralph proclaimed, like MacArthur.

"Pick up more ice cream on the way home," Mrs. Kellogg replied, like Mrs. Kellogg.

He closed the door behind him with a thud. Heavy clouds were rolling across Long Island. No moon or stars. A chilly breeze blew in from the ocean, but he felt clammy under layers of body armor.

A large white Department of Public Works cargo van sat in the driveway, guarded by a handful of militia dressed in their own urban tactical attire. For two days, they'd loaded the vehicle with items from the basement: cabinets, shelving, tools, multiple cartons filled with Jack's little memo pads. Also, several cans of M-80 fireworks and propane tanks; a dozen containers of gasoline; heavy-duty leaf bags filled with fertilizer purloined from the Asabogue Parks Department; a pressure cooker from Mrs. Kellogg's kitchen cabinet; two cheap plastic alarm clocks; and various wires, fuses, and tubes.

Bobby Reilly leaned against the van, an unlit cigarette dangling from his lips. He was about to strike a match.

Ralph rushed toward him. "Put that away! You'll blow us to kingdom come!"

"Calms me down," Bobby whined.

"Later!"

Bobby annoyedly shoved the cigarette in a shirt pocket.

"You pack the flags?" Ralph asked.

Bobby giggled. In the truck was a box filled with an arts and crafts project: dozens of small Mexican flags stitched by Mrs. Kellogg with an Islamic crescent. It was Ralph Kellogg's homage to the Islamex invasion.

"Get in the truck," Ralph ordered Bobby.

Ralph wedged himself behind the steering wheel. The odor of fertilizer, gas, and gunpowder was dizzying. His eyes watered and he felt a burning at the back of his throat. He inhaled nervously. Held his breath. Turned the key in the ignition. The van rattled and wheezed to a start without blowing up Ralph, his house, or his block. So far, the plan was a resounding success. He yanked on the gearshift. The van beeped loudly as he backed down the driveway— a rather frivolous safety feature under the circumstances. The rest of the militia scurried to their cars. Engines roared. Headlights flickered. The Delmarco Division of Defiance rolled toward its target.

"Operation Back to School Night" was under way.

Since Jack Steele loved dramatic entrances, he took his time preparing for his arrival at the League of Women Voters debate, as he would for any starring role—in a dressing room fit for a king, specifically, Louis XIV at Versailles. This was one of his favorite rooms in Villa di Acciaio—carved woodwork, gilded walls, parquet floors, and crystal chandeliers. A floor-to-ceiling shoe rack was stocked with polished boots in every conceivable color, style, and hide. Jack draped himself in a burgundy velvet robe and sat at a vanity with a towering illuminated mirror.

He looked into the mirror and sighed. Eighty-two-year-old Jacob Stoll, born in the Flatbush section of Brooklyn, stared back, sadly. He had an ashen, pockmarked face that looked like the surface of the moon. His thin hair was in a disorderly retreat, leaving brown splotches across his scalp. His neck had withered like a dried-out vine. His head shook slightly. Without makeup, Jacob Stoll looked like he should be shuffling through the early-bird buffet in Boca rather than kicking in doors in Baghdad.

He began the transformation—not a makeover as much as a reconstruction project. He pasted his scalp with a concoction that smelled like curdled milk and covered it with a shiny gray toupee. To his face he applied various white lotions squeezed from small gray tubes as well as dabs of anti-wrinkle cream and drops of age-defying eye ointment. Plus, forehead rejuvenator, lip fortifier, chin restorer, cheek toner, blemish remover, neck revitalizer. All polished off with something called Hollywood Secret Bronzing Formula Pigment #42, which had the smell and sheen of varnish. Then he leaned in the mirror. Flashed a smile. And exhaled a satisfied "That's better."

He curled two fifteen-pound weights five times. It was getting harder. He felt his chest heave, his lungs wheeze, and he imagined all the new parts of his heart rattling around. He sat to catch his breath.

After a few minutes, he muttered, "Wardrobe."

Jack selected a pair of sharply pressed black jeans and a checkered shirt that could have been folded by a marine honor guard. He found a blue blazer from an endless rainbow display of blazers, and carefully inserted an American flag pin through the lapel. Then he slipped on a pair of crocodile-skin cowboy boots and perched a black cowboy hat on his head. He straightened his back. Snapped his spine into place. Projected his chin. Just the way George C. Scott had taught him.

Next, he rehearsed the lines written by the campaign consultants, flicking his tongue and regulating his breath to ensure that perfect Jack Steele delivery: the recognizable clip of syllables and somber gray gravel of his voice.

"The Constitution does not end at the village line."

"The Mayor of Mayhem."

"Lefty Lois."

He stole a final glance at the mirror. Issued a crisp "Carpe diem!"

Showtime!

Jack found Amber in her bedroom, which she'd occupied in recent years when his snoring became insufferable and the sex became barely sufferable. She was sprawled on a plush red divan, dressed in black spandex shorts and a gym halter, lazily flipping through a glossy East End real estate magazine, previewing her options when Jack finally carped his last diem. He kissed her goodbye. She squeezed his hand in a sign of affection or, perhaps, a check of his pulse.

A small elevator whisked Jack from his living quarters to a garage glittering with high gloss metal and redolent of fresh leather. Jack thought he'd look good in black that evening. He pressed a button, a massive platform rotated silently, and a vintage black Ferrari 328 GTS presented itself. He pressed another button and the garage door hummed open. He rumbled down the long gravel driveway, the flood-lit towers of Villa di Acciaio receding in the rearview mirror. Jack made a sharp left onto Asabogue Bluff Lane and accelerated, the Ferrari roaring. He sped past the Cogsworths' place and then Caitlyn Turner's, ignoring the stop sign near her gates. He felt just a little jealous that the mediocre actress with collagen-swelled lips was vying for an Oscar nomination. The closest he ever came was appearing at a Golden Globe tribute with Sylvester Stallone, Steven Seagal, and Chuck Norris. He comforted himself by thinking, *In my day you didn't have to show your tits to get an Oscar. Not on camera, at least.*

The DPW van bounced, squeaked, and rattled with every pothole that the DPW hadn't paved. Ralph winced whenever he heard jostling in the rear compartment. One tiny splatter of fuel, one errant spark, would bring Operation Back to School Night to a premature and inglorious end. He tightened his beefy hands around the jiggering steering wheel.

Bobby Reilly sat next to Ralph, nervously tapping his fingers against his knees. "Really could use a cigarette," he whimpered.

"Later." Ralph looked at his watch. Almost eight. He calculated another couple of minutes to the intersection of Asabogue Bluff Lane and Main, then a straight dash to the high school. He narrowed his eyes on the dark road ahead.

Jack raced along the winding descent toward town. It was so dark he couldn't make out the high hedgerows against the night sky. There were no other cars on Asabogue Bluff Lane, which made sense because famous actresses and fugitive Russian tycoons probably didn't have the time or inclination to drive to the Meet the Candidates Debate at Asabogue High School. Not everyone on the Bluff was as civic-minded as Jack Steele.

He rehearsed additional lines to the shifting of gears and the accompanying humming of the Ferrari.

"My gun permit is the Second Amendment."

"It's not gun control. It's freedom control."

"Lefty Lois." Jack really liked that one.

He took the final curve with a growling downshift and squealing tires. Then accelerated toward the intersection of Asabogue Bluff Lane and Main Street, and that streetlamp that had been broken forever. He promised his first act as mayor would be to fix the damned thing.

Ralph Kellogg checked the rearview mirror to make sure his men were maintaining pace. Headlights bounced behind him. He returned his eyes to the unlit intersection ahead.

"Oh shiiiiiittt!" screamed Ralph Kellogg.

"Oh shiiiiiittt!" shrieked Jack Steele.

It was, as Ralph would say shortly after the conjoining of a cargo van packed with thousands of pounds of explosives and a Ferrari packed with one hundred and seventy pounds of explosive ego, "a fuckin' miracle" that they weren't consumed in a massive fireball. The front end of the van T-boned Jack's car as it sped through the intersection. Both vehicles came to a rest against the streetlight, which, in a moment of taunting irony, flickered back on.

Jack Steele staggered out of his car, dazed and tottering, blood trickling from under his toupee.

The convoy behind Ralph screeched to a stop. He could hear the urgent steps of his men approaching, accompanied by a chorus of breathless profanities. Next to him, Bobby Reilly moaned and rubbed his head. Ralph pushed open his door and stepped out. His legs wobbled.

"Ralph Kellogg?" slurred Jack.

"Mr. Steele?" asked Ralph.

They stared at each other.

Ralph recommended the customary exchange of licenses and insurance cards. Actually, he remained silent while considering whether to shoot Steele or just beat him to death. The question would have to wait. Ralph had a bigger problem. He left Steele standing in delirium and hurried toward the rear of the van. The doors had opened and were creaking back and forth. Ralph peered carefully inside. Everything was packed so tightly that the impact hadn't done much damage, as evidenced by the fact that Ralph was peering inside the van and Ralph's insides weren't splattered outside the van.

There was, however, the distinct odor of gasoline leaking from the van's undercarriage.

Bobby Reilly had plunked himself on the side of the road, near Jack Steele, who was babbling incoherently about needing his "next line." Bobby held his bleeding head in one hand and a lit cigarette in the other.

"Bobby!"

Bobby blew a heavy gust of smoke. "Okay, okay," Bobby said groggily. "Just one puff. Geez!"

He flicked the cigarette into the air.

Ralph watched in horror as the burning projectile floated toward the van. It seemed to travel in slow motion, straight out of a Jack Steele movie, the bright orange ember twirling as it approached.

Ralph thought, *This isn't gonna be good.*

His final order of the evening, and, he considered, possibly for the rest of his life, was "Duck!!!"

38

Petey Scrafel was regaling Megan Slattery and a couple of million viewers with a brief political history of Asabogue when the entire Cafetorium shuddered to the dull thud of a distant explosion. There was a collective gasp from the audience, accompanied by the spontaneous howling of car alarms outside and a rush to the exits. Petey Scrafel was among the first out, sniffing for a local news story. His nose quickly filled with fumes.

A fireball illuminated the high school from a mile away. Petey quickly realized this wasn't the usual Village of Asabogue Annual July 4th Fireworks Extravaganza. This was more like the Village of Asabogue First Annual Reenactment of the *Hindenburg*.

Oh, the humanity.

Petey raced toward the scene, nearly leaping over cars in the school parking lot.

"Wait for me!" a voice pleaded. He stopped and turned. Megan

Slattery was rushing toward him, hobbled by her Christian Louboutin Pigalle pumps. Coming on fast was Harry Holt, cheeks puffing, preparing a vicious hip check against Megan. A furlong behind were the networks' camera crews, equipment banging against their heaving shoulders. They all charged forward in the luminous night.

The *Asabogue Bugle* would not be scooped. Petey ran faster. Sprinting across the school grounds, across Main Street, down one block, then another, toward the Bluff. He sensed someone gaining on him and turned his head sideways. Sam Gergala leaped past him.

A wall of heat at the intersection forced them all to a sudden stop. The fireball had sunk to a roaring flame. The crowd caught up, then reared back, retching on searing air thick with smoke. Sirens wailed in the distance. Petey could make out the burning wreckage of a vehicle. Then saw the twisted remains of another. It looked like it used to be a sports car. Now it was rocking on its side, its alarm system futilely warbling for help.

Someone screamed, "Heads up!"

A chunk of metal temporarily wedged in a tangle of tree limbs suddenly crashed to the ground. It was from an old RCA television set. Then, the ashen remains of notepads fluttered on the crowd, like light gray snow. Plus the burnt remains of homemade flags from either Mexico or Saudi Arabia—Petey couldn't figure out which.

The intersection was sheer carnage, except for a streetlamp that glowed resiliently overhead. (It was later designated as the official village memorial to the evening's events: "the Eternal Light.")

Petey heard soft moans coming from the side of the road. He could see several figures sprawled in various contortions. One sat against a tree, cradling his knees. His clothing was singed and shredded. He looked like a minstrel—face blackened from smoke, except for large white circles around wide eyes mesmerized by the flames.

"That was awesome!" said Bobby Reilly.

39

L ois Liebowitz called Sunny and Sam to an emergency meeting at midnight. Sunny's Parks Department sweatshirt reeked of smoke and her pinned-back hair was flecked with gray cinders. Sam stared catatonically at Lois's kitchen table.

"I want to discuss where we go from here," Lois began.

Sunny found her mother's voice surprisingly steady, and suggested that in view of the tragedy, state officials would likely postpone the election. "Someone'll need to check the state law on that. Review our options."

"None of that matters anymore," Lois declared.

"Meaning?"

"I'm withdrawing from the race. I don't want to be mayor."

"Mother—"

"I've been thinking about it since the shooting. I mean, what difference does being mayor of Asabogue really make?"

"You've been through a lot, Mother. Let's talk about it in the morning. After we all get some sleep."

"We can't sleep. We have work to do."

Sam mumbled, "You just said you're quitting the campaign."

"I said I won't run for mayor. I have a better idea. But we only have a few hours."

40

Asabogue's representative in the U.S. Congress was Otis J. Pickerling. A man of pleasing visage and perfect coif, the twenty-year incumbent hadn't faced a competitive election in, oh, about twenty years. He dressed daily in a crisp blue suit, red-striped tie, and American flag pin glimmering from his lapel. In Washington, he'd compiled a voting record which, depending on the audience, he described as "fiercely conservative," "moderately progressive," "proudly partisan," or "pragmatically bipartisan." What was indisputable was his lifetime NRA Political Victory Fund rating of one hundred percent, for which he received from the fund the maximum contribution of ten thousand dollars in thanks every two years. Of course, there was no quid pro quo, though the congressman was quite the pro. Pickerling's legislative gymnastics were exceeded only by his exceptional ability to angle his body into any assemblage of constituents and cameras.

It wasn't that he was a press hound, it was that he was a rabid one, foaming at the sight of any audience.

So, when he received an early-morning call inviting him to a press conference with Mayor Liebowitz to discuss the tragic events of the prior night, he defied the usual congressional gridlock and moved swiftly. He never stopped to ask why Sunny McCarthy, who was always too important to return his fund-raising calls, would personally summon him.

The national press corps herded into Asabogue Village Hall for the usual post-random-act-of-violence media availability. The Old Sitting Parlor was packed. Dozens of tripods were splayed, cameras pointed, pads unfolded, and recorders activated. The wooden floor groaned and the single air conditioner hissed at having to labor in the off-season. From their oil-painted perch high on the walls, the village fathers glowered. Or maybe those were nineteenth-century guffaws. Life was harder back then.

Lois Liebowitz stood behind a podium, the brim of her straw beach hat hovering just above a thicket of outstretched microphones. She was flanked by Chief Ryan and Sam Gergala. The chief assumed his customary stance, feet spread, hands on hips, braced for incoming. Sam Gergala stared absently ahead. Behind them were politicians from every level of government, down to and including the deputy commissioner of the Town of Southampton Sewer & Water District. Plus the many representatives of local, state, and federal law enforcement. And Congressman Pickerling, who plastered himself next to Lois. So broad the bureaucracies, so narrow the camera apertures.

Sunny strategically positioned herself within eyesight of Lois. They'd worked most of the night; she'd had just enough time to shower and change into a fresh Parks Department sweatshirt. Lois fumbled for her reading glasses, then fidgeted with the pages of her statement. She nervously cleared her throat, producing a guttural noise unprecedented in the headsets of the network audio engineers. She glanced at Sunny, who returned an encouraging nod. Sunny thought back to that day in Chicago, when it was Roy Dirkey seeking her support from offstage. She chased him out of her mind.

Lois narrowed her eyes through her reading glasses and began: "At approximately eight o'clock last evening, a terrorist plot to attack and murder hundreds of Asabogue residents was disrupted by one of our neighbors, Jack Steele. Mr. Steele was en route to the Meet the Candidates Debate when he apparently encountered a stolen van belonging to the village. The van carried thousands of pounds of explosives. Its destination was Asabogue High School, where the debate was to be held."

The officials behind Lois commenced their officially grim nods.

"It's still unclear how Mr. Steele foiled the plot. We do know that had it not been for him, the perpetrators would have arrived at the crowded school. Their intent was to detonate the vehicle. The fatalities would have been"—Lois bit her lip—"catastrophic." She paused, drew in a deep breath, and returned a trembling sigh. Sunny wrapped her baggy-sleeved arms around her chest. *Steady*, she silently coached her mother.

"Sadly, Mr. Steele did not survive. In this case, life has imitated art. Jack Steele's final act was an act of heroism."

Sunny didn't like that part. Too schmaltzy, she thought. But Lois insisted; and given everything her mother had been through—a brutal campaign, the Muffin Massacre, an attempted assassination—Sunny conceded. The fact that Jack had died of a heart attack seemed, well, anticlimactic.

"The perpetrators of this crime are all in custody and receiving medical attention. As mayor, I can tell you the Village of Asabogue is . . ."

Lois glanced at Sunny again. Sunny nodded back. Lois removed her glasses, glared straight into the phalanx of cameras, and proclaimed, ". . . dangerous."

The officials behind her fell out of rhythm. Some nodded

robotically; some froze noncommittally; some darted their eyes nervously. This wasn't how it was supposed to go. Where was the part about being stronger than ever; evil never wins; hearts and prayers; all that stuff?

The reporters stirred from their "same story, different details" torpor.

"We used to be a safe place. No one even knew we existed unless they were driving somewhere bigger and better. When we saw violence in other places, like Chicago, we thought it could never happen here."

Chief Ryan nodded indignantly, his ruddy cheeks now inflamed.

"Now we know better. It's happening everywhere. There are three hundred twenty-five million Americans and about three hundred million guns. So guess what? Law of averages, people. Random violence is coming to a theater near you. Or a mall, a school, maybe where you work. You're all on the losing end of a national game of Russian roulette!"

Lois waved an index finger in the air, to lightning bursts of flashbulbs.

"But don't worry. The good news is that Congress is about to pass a law giving everyone a gun . . . The bad news is that they're not giving out bulletproof vests."

The congressman suddenly appeared as if his earlier breakfast was fermenting. He forced a grin, which seemed pretty grim, like the paintings overhead.

"I mean, wouldn't that make sense? Bulletproof vests. In red, white, and blue. With little tags that say MADE IN AMERICA?

"And speaking of made in America, we're the world's leading manufacturer of gun violence. Countries and states with stronger gun laws have fewer gun deaths. But that's just a statistic. Which our government isn't allowed to study because Congress blocks important federal funding of gun violence research. They are, however, spending four hundred thousand analyzing the effects

of Swedish massages on rabbits. So, at least someone feels safe . . .
The rabbits, I mean. Right, Congressman?"

The congressman must have thought there was an urgent
phone call from the White House or the Post Office Subcommittee, or anyone. He tried nudging his way out of camera range. Chief
Ryan blocked him.

"Here's the other thing," Lois continued. "I get that law-abiding
citizens have the right to own guns. No argument. But the de-
ranged individuals in this very town, who methodically planned to
kill their own neighbors, they shouldn't have been able to get their
hands on assault weapons. Period."

The congressman silently planned the mass firing of his staff.
He definitely didn't recall reading on his schedule "Nine AM: Public
excoriation on national TV. Followed by light refreshments."

"The national media is here because Asabogue is today's violent news story," Lois said. "And everyone watching us? They'll just
shake their heads and shrug. Because they know that this story will
end like all the others. Nothing will change. Nothing will get done.
It's just going to go on and on and on.

"Well, not this time."

Lois seemed to hold her breath.

"Today I'm announcing my candidacy for United States Congress. Against you, Congressman. I can't take another moment of
silence. I've learned that silence never works. It's time to get loud.
Annoyingly, obnoxiously, uncompromisingly loud. Something,
I'm told, I'm very good at."

It was directly out of Jack Steele's script: announcing a candidacy on national television, giving new meaning to the phrase
"donor network." At that moment, Patsy Hardameyer was opening
a campaign account at the Bank of Southampton, proudly affixing
to the forms her signature and title: campaign treasurer.

The congressman glared at Sunny. She smiled back. Each
knew what the other was thinking: *ambush.*

Lois held up an index finger once more. "Oh, one more thing.

To all the press and the protestors who came here in the past few weeks. Thank you for visiting Asabogue. Now, please go home. Leave us alone. We were fine without you."

She looked at Sunny.

"We'll be fine again."

Sam Gergala's funereal eyes jumped in amusement, and the first smile in weeks deepened the spidery lines across his face. Chief Ryan's compact body seemed to expand in a threatening huff. The congressmen dried his pallid face with a hankie. Sunny thought, *Looks like another Liebowitz is going to Washington*. She watched Wayne Bright and the team of consultants she'd recently imported to Asabogue close ranks around Lois, and reporters swarm the hapless congressman.

Time to go, she thought. She pushed against a ravenous clamor of gaping mouths and rattling tongues starving for a deliciously dripping story. They bellowed questions. They bounced, bobbed, and waved frantically for attention. They shoved each other to scoop each other. She felt a painful smack against her face—a monstrous lens careening for a better angle. Her eyes watered as she rubbed her cheek. She zigzagged around tripods, ducked under outstretched microphones, wrestled against a tangle of bodies and equipment. She heaved her body against the front door. Slammed it behind her.

She felt the sting of autumn air, redolent with beach, ocean, and the first fallen leaves. She took a deep breath. Her nose tingled. She ran her fingers through tangled clumps of hair.

In the chilled gray morning, Veterans Park stretched desolately before her, more a trampled battlefield than town square. The Peace Pole leaned at a precarious angle; a clump of leaves tangled around its base. The lawn was brown and pocked and strewn with litter and leaves that tumbled in the wind. Dented blue ASABOGUE RECYCLES bins lay at odd angles. In the distance, she saw the first stirring of shopkeepers on Main Street. They swept the leaves in front of the Wick & Whim, and scrubbed the new plate-glass windows at Joan's Bakery. They prepared for a new day.

Sunny wondered what that day would look like; whether Asabogue could return to what it used to be. She knew that after the crowds left, a still winter would grip the town. Then spring would come, the farmstands would reopen and the beaches would crowd (just not the private ones on the Bluff). By then, Asabogue would return to what it had always been: nowhere. Which seemed fine to Sunny.

She leaned against the rickety metal rack where Lois had propped her bicycle that morning, without a lock. Because, as dangerous as Asabogue had become, that was one thing Lois wouldn't allow fear to change. Pedalling forward, into an uncertain future, unafraid.

Sunshine McCarthy got on the bike.

She rode home.

About thirty minutes from Asabogue was Southampton Hospital, an ordinary brick building well hidden from the unordinary sparkle of the Village of Southampton only blocks away. Here, the year-round Hampton residents were treated for the usual afflictions, accidents, and diseases. During the high season, however, the hospital did a brisk business treating humanity's lowest frailties: detox, drug overdoses, drunkenness, and the occasional injury caused when one luxury car plowed into another in a fit of inebriated rage. This is where Ralph Kellogg regained consciousness just as Lois was making her announcement. He found himself wrapped snugly in gauze and plaster and tangled in cables and tubes. Every part of his body either hurt, burned, or both; even his eyes, as he struggled to blink away a thick haze. He was comforted to see concerned visitors at his bedside. He became less comfortable when he realized they were from the Southampton police, Suffolk County police, New York State Office of Counter-terrorism, and the FBI. To name a few.

No one brought get-well cards.

Ralph's plan was to assume control of Asabogue as the surviving member of the Village Board after everyone else perished in an Islamex attack. He'd even rename Asabogue Bluff Lane as Steele Street, in memory of its dearly departed resident. Then declare martial law. Just like in that television show on the Reichstag.

He now concluded that his plan hadn't worked.

41

A week later, President Henry Piper pounded his fists in the Oval Office and pronounced that he could not in good conscience sign the American Freedom from Fear Act. The legislation had passed Congress in an anti-climactic landslide. Now it was on the president's desk, which dated back to his days as a Navy admiral. The desk was constructed of wooden beams from a nineteenth-century frigate.

His senior political advisors were wedged onto two couches facing one another, separated by a large oak coffee table. Their senior assistants stood behind them, lining the curved walls of the Oval Office. Everyone was bleary-eyed, frazzled. They awoke every morning to plunging poll numbers and an ever-expanding list of Republican primary opponents. Reelection looked bleak.

Still, the president had his principles. He was so hostile to signing AFFFA into law that when he banged his fists, the sculptures of his favorite naval heroes—Farragut, Jones, Dewey, and company—shuddered on the bookshelves.

His pollster winced at the heated veto threat. "Sir, you are losing the Republican primary in twelve must-win states. I've analyzed the crosstabs of undecided primary voters and applied a candidate support model. When we allocate predictive behavior to voters with high scores on gun rights, your head-to-head declines into single digits."

"Tell me what it means. In English," grumbled Piper.

"Sir, it means we're on a sinking ship."

The words hit the president hard, like a torpedo.

"Your only chance of winning this primary is to get to the right of everyone on guns. You must sign AFFFA. Enthusiastically."

The president rubbed his forehead. That blotch above his eyes was now distinct enough to have become a campaign issue. One of his primary opponents charged that it was a Muslim prayer mark.

"Actually, Mr. President, I wouldn't worry too much." This came from the White House legal counsel. She was ravishing—in a hair-in-a-bun, "I'll eat you alive in depositions" kind of way. The president liked having her around. She lifted his spirits and at least one other thing. To put it in presidential terms, the state of their union was strong (especially during the First Lady's Five Continent Goodwill Tour).

"Not worry?" the president asked.

"OMMMAG has already announced a legal challenge to AFFFA."

"OMMMAG?"

"One Million Mad Mothers Against Guns. They're getting injunctions, then going all the way to the Supreme Court. Which, by the way, will never allow AFFFA to stand. It's totally unconstitutional. So you can sign it."

"I can sign it?"

"Only because it's unconstitutional."

"And if it were constitutional?"

"Then you'd have to veto it. To prevent it from becoming law."

"Uuuh-huuuuuh."

"Bottom line, sir. You sign this unconstitutional act and let the court tear it up. We get the political upside. And no policy downside!"

The president felt a stirring to full mast. "So there's no way this law stands if I sign it?"

"I'll bet my law degree on it."

"It's a win-win!" his pollster chimed.

A sense of relief settled across the Oval Office. Shoulders rose, chests expanded in a collective presidential *pheeewww*.

"Anyone got a pen?" joked the president.

"Not yet," advised the pollster. "Let's do this right!"

His funk over Sunny McCarthy dissipated, Congressman Roy Dirkey practically skipped through a slowly opening White House gate while whistling that old country song, "I beg your pardon, I never promised you a rose garden." Then giggled as he headed toward the Rose Garden.

The day was cool and bright. In the distance, beyond a lush expanse of rolling green lawn, a formless gaggle of tourists peered through a high wrought-iron fence. The Washington Monument soared against a cloudless blue sky. Roy could hear the soft rumble of planes departing Reagan National Airport. He lifted his eyes to the Truman Balcony, which curved gracefully around the White House second-story residence. He imagined luxuriating there one day, when he wasn't saddled by the deprecating visitor's pass now slung around his neck. He marveled at what a First Lady Sarah Backfury would make! Their pending nuptials—sentimentally announced in a joint media advisory—would certainly lock in Virginia when Roy ran for president. It was a match made in electoral college heaven.

The White House press corps had assembled on a temporary platform. Roy watched a presidential aide methodically arrange a dozen pens on a mahogany table. Several rows of folding chairs encircled the table, each bearing a calligraphied placard. Dirkey's eyes scanned urgently for his name. There were reserved seats for Speaker Piermont, Senate Leader Binslap, William Overbay, the attorney general, Otis and Bruce Cogsworth, and others. There were a dozen seats for congressional chairpersons. Finally, near the back, Roy spotted the small white card that said HON. ROY DIRKEY.

No matter, he thought. Soon he'd be stretched on a chaise lounge—up on that balcony.

His thoughts were interrupted by a sharp whiff of tobacco. "Congratulations," said Frank Piermont.

"Never thought the president of the United States would be signing a law that I introduced."

The Speaker took a final draw of the cigarette, then blew a thick gust of smoke that was carried away on a gentle breeze. "Don't get too worked up. Soon as the president's signature is dry the Court's gonna strike down your law. But I like your strategy. AFFFA passes. The Supreme Court ultimately nullifies it. Then you run for president, railing against the left-wing judiciary. Probably win, too."

Roy stayed quiet, thinking, *Never argue with a man giving you more credit than you deserve.*

An officious voice boomed: "Ladies and gentlemen. The president of the United States."

Piermont flicked his cigarette stub on the lawn. "Don't forget your presidential pen, Roy. Make a nice souvenir one day. I've got a drawer full of 'em."

Roy said, "Maybe the court will uphold—"

Piermont smiled, yellow-stained teeth peeking through his leathery lips. "Fogettaboutit, son. You got your law passed. Now the court's gonna kill it. That's the beauty of this town. At the end of the day, everyone gets what they want. Everyone lives happily ever after."

42

Justice John A. Scallion was the swing vote on a badly divided Supreme Court. The swing he really cared about, however, wasn't on the court, but on the course. Justice Scallion loved golf, immensely. So when his old friend Sid Schwartzman invited him to play Long Island's venerable National Golf Links in Southampton, only a week after AFFFA was signed, Mr. Justice was swift. Off came the black robes and on went black pleated golf pants, a dotted burgundy golf shirt, and luxury Italian golf shoes. Scallion flew to Islip Airport, where he was met on the tarmac by a small convoy of Suffolk County police and U.S. marshals. He was whisked east, not far from Asabogue.

The National Golf Links was founded in 1911 for, among others, the Bacons, the Deerings, the Fricks, and the Vanderbilts. The O'Malleys, the DiNapolis, and the Epsteins were, well, underrepresented. The clubhouse was a brooding brown Tudor affair with gabled roofs and tall chimneys, surrounded by undulating lush greens edging to the sparkling Peconic Bay. A second security detail met Scallion at the entrance. This was unnecessary, since Supreme Court Justices were barely recognizable. It's not like they were daytime television judges, who were better known and better paid.

The foursome that day included Justice Scallion, Otis Cogsworth, Sid Schwartzman, and Mrs. Stormy Schwartzman. Mrs. Schwartzman instantly brought to Scallion's finely honed legal mind a prior court's decision in a well-known pornography case: "I know it when I see it." In this particular case he saw ample cleavage and skimpy shorts that clung just above the smooth curvature of her buttocks. It was hard for him to maintain judicial restraint in a specific area of his anatomy.

They set out in a convoy of golf carts. It was a magnificent day. The sky was a brilliant blue, a salty bay breeze blew gently, and the greens were radiant. Scallion steered the first cart and Schwartzman sat beside him. In the cart behind, Otis drove and Mrs. Schwartzman jiggled. Trailing them were several carts loaded with sufficient firepower to repel an attack on Justice Scallion, or an invasion of the Eastern seaboard.

Sidney had planned to raise a few issues: the weather, the Mets, the Jets. Oh, and the recently enacted gun ownership law that might one day land on His Honor's docket. The conversation would constitute a clear violation of judicial ethics and decorum. Scallion was cognizant of this. He was also cognizant of the fact that he had a lifetime term. Throughout American history, the total number of Supreme Court judges who'd been impeached was one. In 1805. He was acquitted. Scallion liked the odds.

They rode to the first hole. In the distance, the Links' famous windmill twirled lazily in the soft breeze.

Sidney skipped over the Mets and Jets and got right to the topic of the day: "Have you been reading about this American Freedom from Fear Act?"

"Mmmmm-hmmm."

"Looks like it's going to be challenged."

"Mmmmm-hmmm."

"Those anti-gun nuts and the liberal trial lawyers will try to block it. In court." Sid emphasized "in court." Just in case His Honor missed the point.

"Now Sidney," Scallion warned softly, "you know we're not supposed to discuss these matters."

Schwartzman nodded. "Yeah, yeah, yeah. We're just having a friendly conversation. As old friends. Very . . . old . . . friends."

Once upon a time, John Scallion was an underpaid and very junior associate at a Miami law firm. One of the firm's clients was a struggling new motel called Sid's Stay & Play. The owner of the motel—one Sidney Schwartzman—took a liking to John, lured him away, and installed him as his in-house counsel. As the empire grew into Schwartzman Global Properties, so did Scallion's prestige. During the Ford administration, Schwartzman called the White House chief of staff, Dick Cheney, and redeemed some campaign chits. Scallion was appointed to the U.S. District Court in Nevada, where he could, as Sid said, "watch over things for me." Several years later, he ascended to the U.S. Supreme Court. Where he also watched over things for Sid.

Scallion stopped the cart, stepped out, and hoisted his golf bag. His clubs rattled inside. "I dunno, Sid. Mandating weapons for every American. It's constitutionally challenging and unsafe."

They watched as Mrs. Schwartzman scurried toward them. Otis was far behind, leering at her.

Sid positioned himself between Scallion and the tee. "You know how much I pay for all those government regulations that supposedly keep people safe?"

"Actually, I do. I was your lawyer—"

"Labor regulations. Banking regulations. Environmental regulations. Hey, you know what a bog turtle is?"

"A . . . turtle?"

"Yeah. A few years ago I was developing an office complex in Hackensack. Schwartzman Plaza. Job was half-finished. Then some bureaucrat finds a bog turtle. Little baby bog turtle. They tell me it's an endangered species. I tell them: all the construction jobs I created are an endangered species."

"And?"

"One day I'll take you to Bog Turtle Tower. It's a masterpiece. My point is, where in the Constitution does it say the government must protect a bog turtle? And if we're gonna do that, why shouldn't we protect the American people?"

The logic was, of course, strained. But Justice Scallion hadn't come all this way to a hear a pleading. He wanted to play golf. He wanted to breathe the refreshing air. Exercise his atrophied muscles. Test out his putter—the golf kind—with the flirtatious Mrs. Schwartzman, before returning to those stultifying chambers, mind-numbing cases, and those mummies wrapped in black robes and propped up on the bench. He knew Sid Schwartzman wouldn't rest his case. He might even be overheard and misinterpreted as prejudicing His Honor's honor. So he leaned low into Sid and softly rendered his verdict: "I understand."

Then sliced—far to the right.

EPILOGUE

Afte failing to win a single state other than Illinois in the Democratic presidential primary, Mayor Michael Rodriguez was elected to the U.S. Senate, where he busily spends most of his days thumping his leg.

Otis Cogsworth is a trustee of the Jack Steele Foundation, which generously funds a variety of not so worthy causes, including Armed Airline Pilots & Passengers Association (AAPPA), Priests Who Pack, and a synagogue firearms education course called Shabbat Shoot-out.

Ralph Kellogg and Bobby Reilly continue to serve time. In Sing Sing Correctional Facility, Ralph was elected president of the inmate council.

Sam Gergala left Asabogue to farm twenty acres of potatoes in Iowa. He plans to leave before the next Iowa presidential caucus.

Sid Schwartzman continues to acquire media properties,

thanks to the invaluable assistance of his daughter, Summer Schwartzman, who was appointed FCC commissioner during President Henry Piper's second term.

Frank Piermont lost his Speakership in a coup led by Whip Fred Stinson. He consoles himself with $150,000 speeches between visits to golf resorts.

Roy Dirkey served two terms in Congress before being elected governor of Arkansas. He's married to Sarah Backfury-Dirkey. They have five children and summer residences in New Hampshire and Iowa.

Lois Liebowitz ran for Congress in what pundits regarded as the most competitive race in America. The outcome was decided by a razor-thin vote. It's all in the sequel.

Sunny McCarthy retired from lobbying to write an exposé on the gun industry. Originally entitled *Confessions of a Gun Lobbyist*, it was renamed *Big Guns*. Sunny continues to write in a beach cottage on eastern Long Island. Near her mother. But not too near.

William Overbay is still in Congress, where not much has changed.